INTRODUCTION

Move a Mountain by Lena Nelson Dooley
Christine Dailey's wedding to the man of her dreams is going according to her schedule. Everything will be perfect. Christopher Davis fears that his fiancée depends too much on her schedules. He hopes she can learn to trust God more than her own planning skills. Christine's plans are sorely tested when the worst snowstorm in over a decade hits the center of Minnesota. Can Christine learn that God can take care of them and get them to the church on time?

Blown Away by Love by Pamela Griffin
Three strikes and you're out—Dale's been warned. But a third attempt at having their wedding brings mayhem for Marie and Dale, when his best man/brother goes on a storm chase for a tornado the morning of the ceremony. Stranded outside city limits, experiencing a host of comic misadventures to get back to his Marie, can Dale find a way to make it to the church on time?

Hurricane Allie by Rachel Hauck
Allie Seton's dream of a Cinderella wedding is finally coming true. But when an August hurricane wreaks havoc over central Florida, Allie's dream swirls into a full-blown nightmare. To make matters worse, her fiancé, Kyle Landon, is stranded in New York City. Allie must learn to lean on God in the midst of chaos, while Kyle hurries to find a way home and make it to the church on time.

Heart's Refuge by Lynette Sowell
Krista and Luke are prepared to wed at beautiful Settler Lake in northern California. As the day approaches, the couple's rocky past looms large. Krista battles with fear while Luke wrestles with old guilt. After lightning ignites a wildfire that threatens the town, Luke helps fight the blaze. On their wedding day, the wind changes and the couple lands in danger. Will they make it to the church on time?

Windswept Weddings

*A grim weather forecast could
create four wedding day disasters*

Lena Nelson Dooley, Pamela Griffin,
Rachel Hauck & Lynnette Sowell

BARBOUR
PUBLISHING

© 2006 *Move a Mountain* by Lena Nelson Dooley
© 2006 *Blown Away by Love* by Pamela Griffin
© 2006 *Hurricane Allie* by Rachel Hauck
© 2006 *Heart's Refuge* by Lynette Sowell

ISBN 1-59789-085-5

Cover image by Getty Images

Published by Barbour Publishing, Inc., P.O. Box 719, Uhrichsville, Ohio 44683, www.barbourbooks.com

Our mission is to publish and distribute inspirational products offering exceptional value and biblical encouragement to the masses.

ecpa Member of the
Evangelical Christian
Publishers Association

Printed in the United States of America.
5 4 3 2 1

Windswept Weddings

Move a Mountain

Lena Nelson Dooley

Dedication

This book is dedicated to my writing friends who have met in my home for several years to critique each other's work—Pamela Griffin, Candice (Candy) Speare, Beth Goddard, Lisa Harris, Jill Moore, Anne Green, Mary Ann Hayhurst, Carol Glindeman, Jeanette DeLoach, Erin Lackey, Linda Godsey, Lory and Joe May, Jamesetta Wyche, Marianne Robards, Ronnie Kendig, Susan Sleeman, Georgeanne Falstrom, Shauna Smith Duty, Dawn Morton Nelson, Rhonda Fields, and Gail Gallagher. We have been together at varying times, but you have all contributed to the author I am today. Donna Gilbert and Kaye Dacus have each visited this group, too.

I'm also dedicating it to the Wordpainters critique group—Candy Speare, Lisa Harris, and Laurie Alice Eakes—and Crit Group 9 at American Christian Fiction Writers—Pamela James, Cheryl Wyatt, Jeanie Smith Cash, Linda Rondeau, and Jenny Carlisle. We are all learning together.

As usual, I dedicate all my books to my wonderful husband, James. We've walked a long path together, often holding each other up in times of stress and sharing times of joy. My journey would be very lonely without you. I love you dearly.

Prologue

Mrs. Oleg Olson
and
Mr. and Mrs. Matthew Davis
request the honor of your presence
at the ceremony uniting
Christine Marie Dailey
and
Christopher Dean Davis
in holy matrimony
on Saturday, February 14
at 4:00 p.m.
in the chapel of
Wayzata Community Church
Dinner reception to follow
in the Fellowship Hall
R.S.V.P.

Chapter 1

The moon above Litchfield, Minnesota, poured liquid silver over Christine Dailey as she cuddled in the back of a horse-drawn carriage with Christopher Davis. The flirty skirt of her red satin dress blew toward her lap, and she pushed it back over her knees, hoping it would stay down. She wouldn't have worn such a short dress if she had known what would follow dinner.

She wondered if he knew that this had been her dream date. The meal at the out-of-the-way elegant restaurant had been a gourmet dream. Even though an autumn breeze nipped the air, this ride through tree-laden areas, where lovely homes with expansive lawns stood the test of time, made her feel like a princess in a fairy tale. Only one thing could make the night even better.

"Are you too cool?" Christopher's breath disturbed her hairdo, but she didn't mind.

"No." Tucked under his muscular arm, she felt anything but cold.

The *clip-clop* of the horses' hooves on the pavement matched the erratic thumping of her accelerated heartbeat. If she spent much more time so close to this man, she just might have a stroke.

Pulling from the comforting cocoon of his arms, Christine glanced up into his dark brown eyes, almost hidden in the shadows. She would never tire of looking at him. Unruly brown curls spilled across his high forehead, and she reached up and gently pushed them back, but to no avail. Christopher took the opportunity to shift her closer. His lips descended toward hers. Her eyes drifted shut waiting for the wonderful sensations his kiss always brought her. Lost in the wonder of their embrace, she barely noticed when the forward movement of the carriage ceased. The jingling harness bells that sounded when the horses shuffled about joined with the bells pealing through her head and heart.

Christopher slowly released her lips, and the love shining from his eyes went all the way through her. He pulled her arms down from around his neck and took her hands in his, rubbing his thumbs across the backs and shooting shocks of sensations up her arms. "I can't get on my knees in this carriage, but I want you to spend the rest of your life with me."

Christine almost forgot to breathe. The moment she had dreamed of since the day she met this wonderful Christian man might be happening tonight. If so, this night would be perfect.

"I love you more than life itself." He paused, and she felt his hands tremble slightly. "Christine, will you marry me?"

She nodded, and her *yes* was swallowed in the soul-deep kiss that followed. Christine wished this moment could go on forever.

Much too soon, he leaned away from her. "I forgot this."

Christopher reached into the front pocket of his slacks to collect the small midnight blue velvet box. When he flipped it open, moonlight glittered off the most beautiful princess-cut diamond she had ever seen. He quickly removed the ring from its resting place and picked up her left hand. When he slid the cool metal onto her finger, it fit perfectly and quickly warmed to her body temperature.

She lifted her hand and turned it in the moonlight, noticing other gems that surrounded the large stone. "It's so beautiful." She glanced up at Christopher's smiling face. "How did you know I like princess-cut stones, and how did you find out my ring size?"

"Oh, I have my ways." Christopher urged her back under his protective arm and signaled the driver to go.

"I can't believe you planned all this." She was sure her smile stretched from ear to ear.

A laugh rumbled through his chest where her cheek rested. "I wanted everything to be perfect for you. I asked the driver to stop where the moonlight was brightest so you could see your engagement ring."

⤟⤠

Monday morning came too soon.

Christine stood behind the counter of her flower shop, halfway between Wayzata and Minneapolis, designing a centerpiece for one of her regular customers when the bell over the front door tinkled announcing the entrance of her best friend and soon-to-be business partner.

"So how was the date last night?" Melissa Clark strode

through the displays and hung her sweater on a hook right inside the back room while she kept talking. "Where did Christopher take you?"

Christine surveyed the almost finished decoration and decided it needed a little more yellow. She took a deep breath to calm her excitement, so Melissa wouldn't guess too soon. "Well, we went to Litchfield. Christopher knew about a new restaurant with good food and romantic ambience." As she stuck the long-stemmed flower into the design, she wiggled her left hand a little so her ring would catch the light.

Melissa came to look at her work. "Is that all you did?"

"No." Christine crossed her arms making sure her left hand was on the outside. She wanted Melissa to notice for herself. It wouldn't be as much fun if Christine had to tell her about the ring. "We also went for a carriage ride."

After picking up a flower and gently rotating it in her fingers, Melissa placed it back with the others. "That sounds like fun."

"It was." Christine used her left hand to push a lock of hair behind her ear. "We stopped in the moonlight." The morning sun cast rainbows of color from her ring across the counter, rivaling the kaleidoscope provided by the flowers scattered in profusion throughout the shop.

"Christine! Is that an engagement ring on your hand?" Melissa's long red corkscrew curls whipped straight out from her head when she swiveled. "Let me see it!"

After Melissa grabbed her hand, Christine gushed, "That's why we stopped in the moonlight. So he could propose. He wanted me to be able to see the ring."

Melissa grabbed Christine and danced around in the limited space behind the counter. "I'm so glad for you. When is the wedding?"

Christine carefully picked up the arrangement and started toward the display cooler. "Will you open the door for me?"

Melissa hurried around her.

After placing the design in the middle of the center shelf, Christine closed the door. "I've always dreamed of a Valentine's wedding. It sounds so romantic pledging your undying love on the day everyone celebrates love."

"But this is Minnesota. It could be snowing." Melissa scanned through the order book then picked up a basket from behind the counter. "How about if I use this one for the Melsons' centerpiece?"

Christine pictured walking down the aisle with scattered, feathery snowflakes drifting to earth outside the windows that lined the sanctuary. Her bridesmaids, dressed in red velvet with white fur trim, preceded her down the aisle, slowly swaying to the time-honored music. "Snow would be a romantic touch— what did you say?"

❦

Nothing like the old man calling him in for a conference to dampen the start of a Monday morning. Chris wondered what had gone wrong. Dad sounded gruff through the phone intercom. When Chris reached the double doors that led to the CEO's office, he took a deep breath and straightened his shoulders. Here he was almost thirty years old, and when he was called into his father's office, he felt like a little boy going to the principal's office. Maybe he would have felt more comfortable around him if his father had been home more while he was growing up. He had to get over this. Maybe he would just get a job somewhere else. He had good credentials. It shouldn't be too hard.

Chris lifted his fist and gave three quick raps on the solid walnut door. It was so sturdy, he wondered if his father even heard. Before he could decide whether to knock again, the door opened. The floor-to-ceiling windows that made up two connecting walls of the executive office outlined his father in warm sunshine.

"Come in, my boy." His father smiled and moved back to allow Chris to pass. Then the older man followed him and took a seat in the navy blue Moroccan leather chair behind the massive mahogany desk. "I have something important to discuss with you."

Chris dropped into the cushioned office chair made of the same materials as the one his father occupied. "Okay, shoot." He steepled his fingers under his chin.

"How are things going with you and Christine?" Matthew Davis sounded more like the CEO asking the question than a father.

"I proposed to her last night." Chris hadn't planned on telling him like this. He had hoped to wait until the whole family was together at their regular Friday night dinner and tell everyone at once. Of course, Chrissy would be with him, too, and the women could exclaim over her ring. Clasping his hands at his waist, he stared straight into the navy blue eyes of his father, waiting for his reaction.

Matthew leaned forward. "Good show. I thought that should be happening soon. So when is the wedding?"

Chris shook his head. Not only at the new phrase his father had evidently picked up from one of his foreign clients, but also at the question. "I'm not sure. We're going to discuss that over dinner tonight. I'm hoping for a short engagement."

A quick laugh burst from his father. "I can see you have a lot to learn about women and weddings."

A pile of work waited on Chris's desk. This personal discussion was taking up valuable time. "Is that what you wanted to talk to me about?"

After placing his palms on the desktop, Matthew pushed to a standing position. "No, but it does concern your future here at Davis Enterprises."

Not wanting to be at a height disadvantage, Chris stood. "My future?"

His father turned and clasped his hands behind his back, looking out at the bright autumn sunlight bathing St. Paul. He stood there for several moments while Chris wondered what was coming.

When his father turned back toward him, a smile covered his face. "I'm going to retire. Your mother and I want to travel before we're too old to enjoy it."

"You're not getting old." Chris couldn't help interrupting.

His father beamed even more. "I know, but we have a lot of places we want to visit." He cleared his throat. "What I'm getting at is that I'm stepping down right away, and you'll be the new CEO. That has been the plan since your grandfather established the company in 1956. I took over in 1986. Now it's your turn."

Chris had to sit down. He didn't know what he expected,

but it wasn't this. He was going to become CEO now, not when he was forty as his father had been. He glanced from the carpet up to his father's familiar face. "I don't know what to say."

His father sat on the desk corner nearest to Chris. "I know it's a lot to think about right now, but being CEO will give you a better salary for raising a family, won't it?" He stood up and clapped Chris on his shoulder. "I've been planning this for a while. That's why you've gradually been given more important assignments. You've earned the title. I think we'll announce it next week in the staff meeting. In the meantime, we can start the transition."

This promotion came much sooner that Chris expected it to, but he knew he could do the job. His father's decision felt like a compliment. Chris smiled all the way back to his office.

⟨◈⟩

Christine looked at her watch for the tenth time since she sat down at the white linen-covered table. The waiter had already brought her a refill of soda. She pulled her purse from the extra chair beside her and started digging through the contents for her cell phone. She couldn't find it until it started ringing, steering her under her empty, zippered bank bag that rested on the bottom of the tote. She glanced at the display.

"Hello, Christopher." Christine tried not to sound peeved. She really hated to wait on anyone for very long.

"Chrissy, I'm sorry. I didn't know the meeting would run so late." He did sound harried. "I'm running to the car, and it should take me less than ten minutes if the traffic isn't bad." Evidently he looked at his watch, because he whistled. "Wow, I didn't know it was this late. So okay, the traffic won't be bad.

See you in a few minutes." Kissing sounds accompanied the slamming of his car door. "Maybe that'll hold you until I get there."

The smacking brought to Christine's mind the kisses they shared last night. She studied the ring on her left hand as she shut her phone and slipped it down the inside of her oversized handbag. Warmth spread through her as she relived every moment of the kiss after he proposed. Even the memory caused her temperature to rise. She knew she couldn't stay mad at him. He was the man of her dreams. And tonight they would plan the wedding of her dreams. The waiter came by to ask if she wanted a refill.

"No, thank you. I'll wait for my fiancé to get here."

Did the man's expression contain pity? Did he think she had been stood up? She hoped not.

When Christine came out of the ladies' room a few minutes later, Christopher sat at their table, talking to the waiter. She hurried toward him, and he stood. When she was close enough he dropped a kiss on her cheek, but the expression in his eyes promised more when they were in a less public place. Shivers of anticipation traveled up and down her spine.

Christopher pulled out her chair, like the gentleman he always was around her. After she slipped into it, he sat down and put his hand over hers and squeezed it. His eyes said *that will have to do for now.* They discussed what they wanted to eat, and he placed the order with the waiter, who now acted more friendly than he had while she waited alone.

"So what took so long today?" Christine really wanted to know.

He leaned back in his chair. "You'll never believe what happened."

"Okay. Tell me." Her eyes traced his features. He looked tired, but maybe a little elated.

Christopher took a deep breath. "It's hard to believe the day I've had. Dad called me into his office first thing this morning. I almost felt as if I were in trouble."

"Why would you feel like that?"

"I don't know. Maybe a flashback from one of my many trips to the principal's office."

Christine reached her hand toward him. He leaned forward and placed his palm against hers, intertwining their fingers.

"Dad is retiring, and I'm going to be the new CEO of Davis Enterprises."

The news astounded Christine. Christopher would be a very young chief executive officer. "Oh that's wonderful! You'll be as good or better than your father. When will it take place?"

"We're going through the transition right now. We'll announce it at next Monday's staff meeting. I'm not sure when Dad will actually leave. But we don't need to worry about that now. We have a wedding to plan. Tell me what you want."

Once more, Christine picked up her purse and dug through it until she found a small notebook. She held it up. "I'm not going to leave anything to chance. I'm writing down everything we decide."

Christopher laughed. She loved the musical sound as it enveloped her.

"So when do you want the wedding?" He scooted his chair closer to the table corner that separated them.

The look in his eyes mesmerized her, making her train of thought derail. She blinked and tried to remember what they were talking about. Oh yes, the date for the wedding. "I've always wanted to get married on Valentine's Day. What do you think?"

"It's all right with me, as long as it's this next one. I wouldn't want to wait for over a year." This time his gaze seared its way to her heart. "You can plan a wedding in four and a half months, can't you?"

After that look, she would do almost anything to please him. She had hoped to have more time.

"Of course I can."

Chapter 2

How was she ever going to get this wedding planned in four and a half months?

Christine couldn't believe she'd agreed. All her life, she looked forward to her wedding. The proposal was all she imagined and more, so she wanted the wedding to equal it. She didn't have time for anything at all to go wrong as it often did. Of course, she and Melissa could take care of the flowers.

The wedding dress would take more time. The nearest large store that carried wedding attire was in Minneapolis. If she took the day off from the shop, maybe she could at least decide on a design. She wondered how much that would cost. Some dresses cost more than she paid for her economy car. Maybe she should talk to Sharon Thornton. Christine's friend from college worked in the marketing department of The Bridal Boutique. The headquarters for the business that supplied many high-end wedding shops across the country was outside Minneapolis. She was sure Sharon mentioned an outlet store there.

"Look what I have." Melissa's statement quickly followed the ringing of the bell above the door to Floral Haven, the shop

Christine opened when Grandmother Dailey died and left her an inheritance.

Melissa hurried across the shop and plopped a stack of bridal magazines on the counter. "You know what I was thinking about?"

"What?"

"You will both be Chris Davis after you're married." She straightened her hair from the mess made by the wind. "That ought to get interesting."

"Don't you dare start calling me Chris! My name is Christine, and I always call him Christopher." *This shouldn't be a problem.* Christine started counting the magazines. "Did you really buy half a dozen?"

Melissa laughed. "More or less. The man from the supplier was there getting ready to pull them and put out the spring issues, so the storekeeper sold them to me for half price. We can look through them and see if you find anything you like."

"I thought we might go see Sharon."

"The one at the bridal factory?"

Christine nodded as she opened the first book. "You're going to be my maid of honor, aren't you?"

When Melissa gasped, Christine looked up at her. Melissa smiled. "I thought you would ask one of your cousins. You have a bunch of them."

"Yeah, fifteen first cousins. But only nine of them are girls."

Melissa giggled. "That's a lot. I can't imagine having so many. Both of mine are guys, and they weren't interested in spending time with a *gurrrl* cousin."

Christine put her elbows on the pages to keep them open

and leaned her chin in her hands. "All of my female cousins lived close to me, and we were all within four years of age. I was in the middle so none of them were more than two years older or younger than me. We had a lot of fun growing up."

"And you've kept in contact as adults, haven't you? I don't even know where those two knuckleheads are." Melissa opened the next magazine in the stack. "What are we looking for?"

While bright sunlight streamed into the shop, painting everything in a golden glow, even the magazine, Christine turned several pages. "I'm not sure what I want in a wedding dress, but I want my bridesmaids to wear red velvet. Maybe with a short cape trimmed in white fur."

"Well, that leaves me out. I'm not going to come down the aisle looking like something on fire. My red curls would be the top of the flames." Melissa shrugged. "Maybe you *should* ask a cousin." A saucy grin accompanied the last statement.

Christine stared at her. "We've been friends since first grade. You are going to be my maid of honor. Besides, we could have you wear the same kind of dress, but in a different color. The cousins can all be bridesmaids. The others might resent it if I choose one of them as maid of honor."

The bell announced the entrance of a couple of customers, and Melissa went to wait on them. Christine leafed through the pages in her magazine, but nothing caught her eye. She had just picked up a different one when the phone rang. She went in the office at the back of the shop so the call wouldn't disturb the customers.

"Floral Haven, Christine Dailey speaking. How may I help you?"

"Chrissy."

"Gram, how are you?" It had been too long since Christine had been to visit her only remaining grandparent. "I'm sorry I haven't been out to the farm in a while."

"I know a lot's going on with your new business." Gram didn't sound like an eighty-year-old woman on the phone. "I called for another reason."

"Do you need something? I could be out there in a few hours. Melissa can watch the shop." Christine picked up a pen and started doodling flowers on the pad by the phone.

"No, dear, I don't need anything. I want to do something for you." Gram giggled like a teenager. "I hear there's going to be a wedding in the family."

Christine dropped the pen. "So Mom already called you?"

"Why didn't you tell me yourself?"

"It only happened night before last. I wanted us to set the wedding date before I called you, and we did that last night. You were on my agenda for this evening. Christopher has a business meeting tonight."

Christine pictured Gram's smiling face and the twinkle in her eyes. "Now you don't have to call me. I'll get right to the point. I'm making your wedding dress."

After taking a deep breath, Christine declined. "I would like nothing better than that, but it would be too much for you."

"Now I don't want to hear anything like that. I made all of the other girls' dresses. Since you're the last to marry, this will be my last wedding dress." Gram sounded wistful. "You must let me do it."

Christine thought about how disappointed Gram would

be if she said no, but she didn't want to take advantage of the older woman. Of course, she didn't look forward to being the only cousin who didn't have a Gram original wedding dress. Christine had looked forward to it for years. She gazed at the calendar above the desk and tried to figure how much time she really had to plan the wedding.

"Christine, did you hear what I said?"

"Yes, Gram. We're getting married at Valentine's. That won't give you much time to make the dress."

"I don't have anything else I have to do, so it won't be a problem. It will be my number-one priority. So when are you coming out to show me what you like?"

If she didn't want to hurt her beloved grandmother, there was nothing else Christine could do. "Melissa and I will be there Sunday afternoon. Bye, Gram." The phone clicked as she rested the earpiece in its cradle. Maybe Christopher wouldn't mind her missing their regular Sunday night date.

"Hey, Christine." Melissa's call alerted Christine that the customers had gone. "Come here and see what I found."

After glancing in the mirror beside her desk to see if she needed lipstick, Christine walked through the doorway. "What did you find?"

Melissa held up one of the books. "These dresses."

A full-color page showed several different colors of a gown that fit the idea in Christine's head. Long flowing dresses with short trains had capes that hit halfway between the shoulder and elbows of the girls modeling them. Something white trimmed the cape and the hem of the skirt, even continuing up the front to meet at a deep vee below the waist. How could anything be more perfect? The jewel colors in the picture ran the whole spectrum from black all the way to white.

"They're the ones." Christine took the book and studied the text. "These are manufactured right here, a product of The Bridal Boutique."

Melissa pulled on her right ear, a habit she'd had since they first met. "Maybe it's time to call Sharon. They could have some in stock, and we might get a good deal on them."

Christine laid the magazine on the counter. "That would be too much to hope for. You know one of my cousins is pregnant and some are tall and some short. They surely wouldn't have the right sizes for all of them without having to order some. I'll call Sharon tonight. Just tell me what color you want to wear. The others don't have a choice."

By the time Sunday arrived, Christine had found the perfect wedding dress. She marked the page in the magazine with a Floral Haven brochure. After going to the early service, she and Melissa would be on their way toward Litchfield. They should arrive in time to eat a late lunch before they drove out to the farm.

❦

After she and Melissa were seated near the back of the sanctuary, Christopher slid into the pew beside Christine. "What are you doing here at this service? We always go to the one at eleven."

"You said last night that you were coming, so I decided to try it." He leaned over and dropped a quick kiss on her cheek. "Besides, I hear the new contemporary service is lively. We might want to start attending this one."

"Not me. Sundays I can sleep later than on other days." She

put her arm through his, and he took her hand.

The service was different, but she liked it. Although the music was more upbeat, it resonated with a strong message of hope, and the sermon was just as powerful as the one she usually heard at the traditional service later in the day. Maybe they would try it again.

Christopher accompanied them to her tiny car. "How about letting me go with you? I love Gram, too."

"No way!" Melissa pushed between them. "Christine might be tempted to let you, but I'm not. You can't know anything about the wedding dress, and you might if you are with us. Go watch a football game or something."

Christopher laughed before kissing Christine good-bye. He did a thorough job of it. More than he had ever kissed her in front of anyone else. By the time he finished, Christine knew her face must be flaming red. It felt hot enough, and the knowing smile from Melissa didn't do anything to help her feel more comfortable.

"You be very careful." Christopher opened her door then dropped another quick kiss on her willing lips. "You're very important to me, you know." He shut the door and stood watching them until the car exited the parking lot.

Christine drove out of Wayzata floating on a cloud. That man did things to her she never had imagined. Her stomach fluttered so much, she didn't know if she would be able to eat when they arrived in Litchfield, and her pulse throbbed so loud she was sure Melissa could hear it.

"That's a becoming shade of red." Melissa's comment sounded casual.

"I'm not wearing red." When Christine turned to glance at her friend, Melissa's smirk stopped her. "Just you wait. You'll fall for someone one of these days. Then it will be my turn."

They arrived at Gram's house without incident. She must have heard them coming down the lane, because she was waiting on the porch to pull them into big hugs. She had always treated Melissa like just one more grandchild.

When they showed her the picture of the dress Christine picked out, she studied it for a few minutes. After asking several questions, she started writing things on a lined pad. Then she took Christine's measurements.

"Gram, you'll have to tell me how much of each kind of fabric to buy." Christine put her arm across Gram's shoulders.

"I'll have to do some figuring before I know." She reached over and kissed Christine's cheek. "You'll be so beautiful in this dress. I'll call you tomorrow or the next day with the information. Now let's go to the kitchen for a snack. I made your favorite macaroon cookies."

Chapter 3

"ow! I can't believe how well things are going for you." Melissa took out a glittery heart garland and handed it to Christine on the ladder. "I was worried when we had to work on the wedding *and* Thanksgiving and Christmas all at the same time."

Christine stretched as far as she could to each side to push in as many of the red tacks as she could without moving the ladder. "You know finding all ten bridesmaid dresses in the colors and sizes we need them is nothing short of miraculous."

Melissa started to bend down toward the box, but quickly stood back up and took hold of the ladder. "Be careful. You don't want it to tip over. Can't have you walking down the aisle on crutches."

Christine carefully stepped down and moved the ladder. "Please hand me the end of that garland. I want to finish this. Christopher and I have a dinner date tonight."

"I'm glad Sharon got those dresses for us at clearance price."

"Me, too." Christine stuck the last tack in the end of the garland. She descended and stepped back.

Melissa walked over to the counter and ran her finger down the calendar page. "What else do you have to do for the wedding?"

"Christopher and I have an appointment on Friday with the caterer to make the final food choices. My cousin Maria bakes special cakes, so she's doing the wedding cakes as her present to us."

"That'll save a bundle." Melissa turned the page on the calendar. "Girlfriend, you are going to have an easy time. You can just coast these last few weeks. You'll be the most rested bride I've ever seen."

⤸⤹

Christopher took Christine back to the restaurant where they went the night he proposed. As the maître d' led them to their secluded table, Christine reveled in the ambience. Low lights in the room allowed the candles to turn the tables into isolated islands in a sea of soft music. The thick carpet swallowed any sound of footsteps as they moved across the floor. After they ordered the very same meal they had eaten the first time they were here, the waiter left them to their privacy.

Christopher reached across the corner of the table and picked up Christine's hand. He lifted it toward his lips and bestowed a quick kiss on her fingertips. Would she ever get over the tingles that shot through her at his slightest touch? She hoped not.

He put his palm against hers and intertwined their fingers, a favorite point of connection between them. "I'm leaving in the morning for Hong Kong."

Christine almost pulled her hand away. "Why?" Before he

could answer that question, she asked another. "When will you be back?"

"It's a business meeting I can't miss." He smiled into her eyes. "I'll be home Thursday evening. In plenty of time for our meeting with the caterer."

Christine heaved a sigh of relief. "I really don't want to go without you being there. It's your wedding as well as mine."

"I'll be there." He glanced around before he leaned toward her to give her a gentle kiss.

When he finished, the waiter materialized beside them with their salads.

"Besides, isn't your final fitting for your tux on Saturday?"

He picked up his fork. "Relax, honey, everything will be all right. We're right on schedule. Remember, God is in control." He took a bite of his salad.

Christine wasn't at all sure Christopher understood the importance of this last month and all they needed to do together. "I guess I'll just miss you."

"That's why I bought us something." He reached into his pocket then held out a cell phone.

"I already have one." She started digging in her purse to find hers.

He placed a hand on hers to still her movements. "Not like this one. It's a satellite cell phone, and I bought me one, too. We can talk while I'm gone, almost anywhere in the world. Like Dad said, being CEO has its perks."

❧

After she took Chris to the airport, Chrissy stayed with him until he had to go through security. He waited as long as he could so they would have more time together. The pucker in her forehead told him that she wasn't happy about him leaving. When he picked up his luggage after it went through the scanner, he turned back to see her standing just outside the security area watching him with a forlorn expression on her face. He blew her a kiss then started toward his gate.

Chrissy's forlorn face haunted Chris's thoughts for the first hour of the flight. If only he could assure her of the peace in his heart every time he thought about the wedding. She was a planner, and it bothered her when anything happened that wasn't on her schedule. Hopefully, the longer they lived together as man and wife, the better she would learn to trust God with everything more than she did now. Oh, she was a Christian, but her plans meant too much to her. He hoped it wouldn't be a problem later on. Chris leaned his head against the headrest of the thickly padded leather seat in first class and closed his eyes. Maybe everyone else would think he was sleeping and leave him alone. He wanted to spend the next several minutes praying for her.

As soon as Chris was through customs, he hailed a cab to take him to his hotel. Since there were so many tourists and international businessmen who frequented Hong Kong, many of the hotels were world class. He had chosen one. After the porter accompanied him up the elevator carrying his bags, Chris tipped the man and closed the door. He walked to the floor-to-ceiling windows and opened the curtains. While looking over the bustling city, he pulled out his cell phone and punched the buttons that automatically dialed Christine's.

"Hello, Christopher." Her voice sounded sweet even through

the electronic gadget. "Are you already there?"

"Yes, in my hotel room."

"Is it nice?"

Was that a wistful note in her voice? He pictured her long blond hair framing the expression. He never tired of running his fingers through those curls. "After we're married, you can come with me when I have these meetings. I think you'll like the hotel. It's a five-star. Really top-notch."

"I'd like that."

He could hear the sigh even over these thousands of miles. Her eyes usually darkened to a forest green when something bothered her. He rubbed the back of his neck with his free hand. It was always sore after such a long flight. "Honey, you know I love you with all my heart."

"Of course, and I love you just as much." Her voice softened on the words they often said to each other.

❧

Melissa came through the door of the shop accompanied by a sharp north wind. She wrestled with the packages she carried, trying to push the door shut against the strong gusts. "Boy, it's really getting cold out there." She plopped the packages and her purse on the counter. "Do you think it'll snow? Most of what fell last week is gone."

"I don't know. Does the wind feel wet?"

"Who can tell? It's really blowing hard."

It was almost time to close the shop for the day. They didn't get much walk-in traffic after six.

Christine opened one of the sacks Melissa had brought in and started toward the back room. "I think I'll turn on the TV back here and listen to the news while I put these away."

After she clicked it on, she turned around and pulled out supplies to store. She wasn't paying much attention until a special announcement came on.

"An unusual tropical storm is headed for the island of Hong Kong."

Christine whirled to look at the pretty Asian woman making a special report for one of the national networks.

"It's too early for the typhoon season, but weather has been unseasonable in this part of the world. The reports are that the storm might reach typhoon strength before making landfall sometime today or tonight."

All Christine could think about was Christopher in Hong Kong. She grabbed her satellite cell and dialed his number, not even waiting to calculate the time difference. The phone rang and rang, then went to his voice mail. She left a message, clicked off her phone, and clutched it so hard her knuckles turned numb. *Oh, God, please protect Christopher. I can't stand that he is so far away, Lord. I want him here with me.* Her grip loosened and blood circulated into her fingers once again. What did the scripture say? Something about God moving mountains. She wished she could believe that He would just miraculously move Christopher from Hong Kong to here in an instant. She dropped into her desk chair and stared at the TV, not even noticing what the local reporter was saying.

Lord, I need Christopher.

It seemed almost as if God was standing in the room talking to her, she heard His answer so strongly in her heart. *Christine, you need to trust Me.*

Chris stepped out of the steamy bathroom with a towel wrapped around his hips and one slung around his neck. He flipped on the TV and started drying his hair with the towel from his shoulders.

"An unusual tropical storm is headed for the island of Hong Kong."

Chris put the towel back around his neck and glanced at the woman giving the news report.

"It's months too early for the typhoon season, but reports are that the storm might reach typhoon strength before making landfall sometime today or tonight."

That really was unusual. He guessed he could cancel the meetings for today and try to get a ticket home on an earlier flight.

A frustrating hour later, he was glad he hadn't canceled the meetings. There wasn't a flight available anywhere. Everything was already overbooked. He wasn't going anywhere before his regularly scheduled flight. He hoped Chrissy hadn't heard the report. It was from a local station. But he couldn't trust that it hadn't made international news. She would be frantic. He picked up his cell and saw that someone had called. After listening to his message, he punched in the numbers for Chrissy.

"Hello." Her answer sounded tentative.

"Chrissy, I love you." Then he heard her sob. "Honey, it's okay. I'm going to be all right." He imagined tears slipping down her soft cheeks. Cheeks he wished he were touching right now. If he could just kiss the drops away and take her in his arms.

"I love you, too." She paused. "Do you think you'll be able to get home tonight?"

"I'm planning on it." When he bought these phones, they sounded like a good idea, but they would never take the place of cuddling her in his arms and holding her near his heart. "Have you penciled in on your schedule to meet me at the airport?"

"I'll be there."

"Honey, just imagine me with you right now. I would kiss you just the way I did when I asked you to marry me."

Her sigh sounded loud through the phone. "I don't want to have to make the decisions without you." He heard her words, but he also understood the underlying worry for his safety she felt but was afraid to mention.

Chapter 4

After the meeting, Chris went back to his room to pack. He called the airport before he ordered a taxi. "Is flight 2991 to San Francisco on schedule?"

"I'm sorry, sir." The man sounded tired, making his singsong English hard to understand. "But because the storm is moving faster than anticipated, the airport is officially closed for now." The harried man hung up before Chris could ask anything else.

Chrissy would be upset. *That is an understatement.* Chris took the global cell out of his pocket. He glanced at it before dialing. The low-battery light blinked back at him. When was the last time he charged it? He should have plugged it in last night as a precaution. Quickly, he punched in Chrissy's numbers.

"Christopher, where are you?" A hint of anxiety laced her tone. "I've been watching CNN, and they've been giving terrible reports from the area of Hong Kong."

He rubbed the sides of his forehead with the thumb and fingers of his empty hand. "Chrissy, I'm in my hotel room."

"When does your plane leave?" Now she sounded a little frantic.

"Not today. They've already closed the airport."

Silence screamed across the line.

"Chrissy, are you still there?"

"Yes." The breathy answer told him that she was trying to control her emotions.

"Now listen really close. My cell phone battery is about to go dead, so I have to talk fast. I love you. I'm going to be all right. I will be home, just not today. And, Chrissy, it wouldn't hurt to pray for me."

As soon as he finished talking, the whisper of an open phone line was gone. Chris dropped to his knees beside the bed, buried his head in his hands, and prayed for Christine while gale force winds howled outside his room.

❧

Exactly a week after he left, Christine waited by the luggage carousel for Christopher to deplane. She had chosen the food for the wedding. One more thing checked off her list. At the time, she didn't care what he wanted to eat, but she knew that wasn't the right attitude. With a thankful heart that he wasn't injured, she had changed his appointment for the final fitting of his tuxedo. He wasn't renting one. As the CEO of a major company, he'd need one fairly often.

Christine dropped her head into her hands and took a deep breath. She wanted him to see a smiling, loving face when he came through from the concourse.

A hand touched her shoulder and shivers of delight raced down her spine just before Christopher pulled her into his arms. "I'm so glad to be home, Chrissy. I missed you so much. Talking on the phone just doesn't take the place of a hug or kiss."

She looked into those chocolate-colored eyes and swam in the depths of the love she saw there. When his lips caught hers in a long-awaited kiss, she didn't even care that they were in the airport with hundreds of people milling around. Only three more weeks until they could show the complete depth of their love.

Christopher pulled back and the expression in his eyes devoured her. "I've missed you so much."

After he picked his one suitcase from the moving carousel, they started toward the company limousine waiting outside the door. Christopher had sent the driver to pick up Christine at the flower shop and bring her to the airport. When they were nestled in the backseat, Christopher kissed her again, with even more fervency than before.

"I just needed to touch you." He snuggled her under his arm. "The week in the lonely hotel room seemed to take forever."

"I missed you, too. So what are we going to do tonight?" She felt him stiffen.

"Since I was gone so long, I may have to work until midnight. There are a lot of things that were left undone because I need to approve them."

"That's okay," she forced through gritted teeth.

"No, it's not, but it can't be helped." Christopher turned her around so he could look into her eyes. "That's why I had Alfred pick you up. I had to see you. After he leaves me at the office, he can take you back to the shop. I'll call you when I have a break."

She reached up and kissed him again. This week might be a lot like last week with them talking on the phone instead of being together, so she wanted to make the most of their time.

Chris returned her soul-stirring kiss. He wanted her to remember it if this week turned out to be like last week. He decided he had to make time for them to see each other face-to-face, even if it was only a few minutes a day.

That last thought must have been prophetic. Things were even more hectic than he anticipated. His schedule was filled with meetings. Executives from different branches of the company came to St. Paul with varying agendas. Chris was sure some of them only wanted to check him out. They'd probably push him as far as they could to see if he would be as in control as his dad had been. The added stress didn't help his frustration at not seeing Chrissy very often. He called her every chance he could, and he started stopping by her apartment for a few minutes before he had to get to bed, so he would be fresh in the next meeting. Those islands of connection kept him from being totally wiped out.

The phone rang, and Christine picked it up. "Floral Haven."

"Chrissy?" Gram's voice pulled Christine's attention from the papers on the desk in front of her.

She leaned back in the desk chair. "Yes."

"Honey, I need you to come for a final fitting of your dress. I only have two weeks to sew all the pearls and sequins on it, and I don't want to do that until everything else is finished. Didn't the dry cleaner say we needed to get it to them a week before the wedding so they could have it pressed and ready?"

Christine loved Gram. She really did, but didn't really want to go right now. She had seen Christopher such a small amount of time this week. She didn't want to miss seeing him even the one night it would take for her to go to Gram's. But she did want a wedding dress.

"Chrissy, are you still there?" Gram sounded worried.

"Yes, I was just thinking." Christine pulled her appointment calendar forward and glanced through the entries. "I'm trying to see when would be the best time to come."

"I hope it can be pretty soon."

Christine made a couple of notes on the already crowded calendar. "I'm coming today. Melissa can take care of things here tomorrow morning. I should be back by noon."

"I'm fixing chicken and dumplings for supper. You always liked them."

Christine laughed. "If you keep feeding me like that, Gram, you might have to let the dress out."

After she hung up from talking to her grandmother, she dialed her direct line into Christopher's office. The call went to voice mail. "Christopher, I'm going to Gram's for the final fitting of my dress. Please call on my cell when you hear this."

The drive to the farm provided a welcome break from the hectic pace of the last week at the shop. She and Melissa had worked on wedding flowers in between filling orders. Why did she ever want a Valentine's wedding? Especially since she opened Floral Haven. It seemed as though every man who lived all the way from Wayzata to St. Paul ordered flowers from Floral Haven for his sweetheart or wife.

Just yesterday, she agreed to hire Melissa's friend to help. Karen did a good job the rest of the afternoon. Christine felt sure the two of them could handle everything while she was gone. After she turned north in Litchfield onto the road that went by Gram's farm, she had to take off her sunglasses. She wore them because even a wintry sun shone bright on snow. But the sky had become overcast. She flipped the radio over to a news station trying to pick up the weather forecast. She had watched the news last night and didn't remember anything about a storm. National news blared from the speakers, and she switched back to her favorite Christian music station. Singing along with the tunes helped the time pass quickly.

By midafternoon she pulled up the gravel road that led to the house, thankful that one of the men who leased Gram's acreage always kept her drive free from snow. She made a mental note to call him while she was here to thank him for that.

Gram didn't let her catch her breath before she had her in the dress. Gram put on her pincushion that looked like a tomato but had a cuff bracelet that fit on her wrist. She stepped back to get a better look of her granddaughter. "Oh, Chrissy, you're even more beautiful than I envisioned."

Christine touched the scrunchie that held her hair in a long ponytail. "I didn't take time to style my hair this morning. I was going to do it before Christopher came over tonight."

Gram pulled the scrunchie, and a riot of curls cascaded down Christine's back. "So, are you going to wear it down or up for the wedding?"

Christine pulled her hair up and turned her head from side to side as she looked in the mirror. "Up looks more elegant." *This gorgeous dress calls for elegance.*

"And it shows off your graceful neck."

"But Christopher likes it down. I want to please him. Besides, it might be pretty cold that day."

Gram smiled. "Good. I have enough tulle to make a nice long veil with a train if you want one to match the dress."

Christine pulled Gram into her arms. "You are so good to me. You've been my rock since Mom and Dad have been gone. What would I have done without you?"

The praise embarrassed Gram, as always. "You'd have done fine. God would have seen to that. I'm just glad I was here to take care of you. Have you found a headpiece you like? I can attach the veil to it and even add some seed pearls and sequins like the ones on your dress."

"Actually, I picked one up yesterday when I went to the fabric store for more netting to use in corsages for the wedding. It's still in the trunk of the car."

After Christine removed her dress and helped Gram replace it on the padded hanger on the back of the bedroom door, she went out to get the package. Dark clouds scudded across the sky, subduing the remaining daylight. Even in her down coat, Christine shivered.

She stomped the snow from her shoes onto the mat on the porch before she went back in. "Gram, have you heard a weather report? Those clouds look like they are carrying snow, and they might drop it at any time."

Chapter 5

After supper, Christine stood at the front window watching snowflakes enter the circle of light on the ground, cast by the lamp on the table beside her. Big fat flakes that slowly drifted back and forth before they settled upon the ones that hadn't melted from the last snowfall. What a pretty picture they made. What treachery they brought to the roadways. Maybe she should try to get home tonight.

Her cell phone rang, and she pulled it from her pocket. *Christopher.* "Hello. So this one night I'm gone, you get away from work early."

"Not really." Papers rustled in the background. "I'm at my desk. I couldn't concentrate on my work. How'd it go today?"

"Fine. Traffic wasn't bad on the way out here." She waited for his next comment.

"Tell me what you look like in your dress. Do you like it?" Christine heard his chair squeak the way it did when he leaned back.

"It's beautiful." She was sure he smiled at that. "I'll look like a fairy-tale princess in it."

"That's all well and good, but I'm marrying a real flesh and blood woman, and I can hardly wait to watch you walking down that aisle toward me." His voice on the line sounded heavy with promise.

Christine glanced out at the flakes that had increased in the short time she had been talking to her fiancé. "I've been thinking maybe I ought to start home tonight. I should be able to get there before midnight."

Christopher's chair squeaked again. "Why would you want to do that? I don't like the idea of you driving so far alone at night. Tomorrow is soon enough."

She pictured him leaning his elbows on his desk. "It's snowing here, and it's coming down harder now."

"That's reason enough to stay. I really don't want you driving home in the snow. Some crazy trucker who doesn't know how to drive in this kind of weather might not be as careful as I know you are when you drive in bad weather."

She paused. Christopher was right. It wouldn't be wise, but what if it snows a lot? "Okay. I'll come first thing in the morning."

❧

Chris reached home at midnight from his exhausting day. His brain felt like mush, and tension had pulled a cramp in his neck. The only bright point had been when he talked to Christine. He knew women really enjoyed all this wedding planning. He would just as soon stand before the pastor with only their families in attendance. They would be just as married without so much commotion. But Chris wanted a happy bride.

He was too keyed up to go directly to bed, so he trudged up

the stairs of the new house he and Chrissy had purchased after he returned from Hong Kong. The furnishings were sparse, but he and Chrissy could take all the time they wanted after the wedding making it into the home where they would be glad to raise their children. At least the master bedroom was completely finished.

After loosening his tie and slipping out of his shoes, he dropped into the cushy recliner in the sitting area. He leaned back and tried to imagine Chrissy in her wedding dress, walking down the aisle toward him. Just thinking about it brought a lump to his throat. Maybe all this wedding stuff would be worth the time and effort. He smiled. *It won't hurt to check the Weather Channel.* He picked up the remote and clicked several times.

"Meteorologists are amazed at the blizzard that is blanketing more than the western half of central Minnesota. Although they had predicted snow, they didn't envision anything like what is going on out there." Footage of the storm scrolled across the screen behind the newscaster. "The highway department has released a bulletin stating that it might take quite awhile before they'll be able to clear some of the farm roads."

Chris sat forward and leaned his elbows on his knees. "Lord, I know Chrissy will be worried. Please keep her and Gram safe. And calm Chrissy's heart. Fill her with Your peace."

The peace Chris prayed about settled inside him. He knew everything would be all right. Quickly, he prepared for bed, knowing that he had to get up early, and he wanted to call Chrissy as soon as he could.

❧

Christine walked down the aisle in cadence with the wedding

march. The silk of her completed wedding gown swished with each step. At the front of the church her groom waited, but he was so far away she couldn't see his face. The longer she walked, the farther away he became. Tears pooled in her eyes. She might have to run to reach him in time.

The ringing of Christine's cell phone woke her. She blinked, glad to see her familiar room at Gram's house, and she grabbed the phone before it went to voice mail. "Hello." Christine glanced at the clock while she answered. It was only six o'clock.

"Hi, honey." Christopher's smooth baritone voice sounded husky. Had he just gotten up or was it emotion? "I'm sorry to wake you so early, but you might not know what's been going on."

She sat up straight in her bed and glanced toward the window. Outside was a blur of white in the waning predawn darkness. "What are you talking about?" The fear of some impending disaster caused her hand that was holding the phone to shake so much it was difficult to keep it close to her ear, so she held it with both hands.

"Last night when I got home, the Weather Channel said this is one of the worst blizzards in years." He paused as if waiting for her reply. When none came, he continued, "You won't be able to come home today."

Tears welled up in her eyes, bringing with them a whisper of a memory. Oh, yes, the dream. Using one hand, she dashed the tears away. "I have to go home. It's only two weeks until the wedding." She finished on a sob.

"Chrissy, it's going to be all right." His heavy breathing filled the silence. "I love you, and I have a peace about everything."

How could he have peace? Who would finish the last-minute details of the wedding?

She must have whispered the question, because he answered her. "Didn't you hire a helper? She and Melissa can take care of the flower shop and the wedding. Don't fret. Promise me."

How could she do that? She had planned a workable schedule for everything. If they got off schedule, she would lose her focus. Feel disconnected. Didn't he understand?

"Chrissy, I know you like to feel in control of your life." Could he read her mind? "Sometimes events are taken out of our hands. It's then we have to trust the most."

Platitudes. She hated platitudes.

"I've got to go to work. Will you be okay?"

"Yes." Her answer sounded weak in her own ears.

"I wish I were there, so I could hold you in my arms. I'll call you later."

It wasn't fair. Christine clicked off her phone, pulled on her warm robe, and walked to the window. She wiped away the film of condensation caused by the heat in the room. Snowflakes filled the air, hiding everything else outside. Why could everyone in the metropolitan area move around in this, and she was stuck out here in Minnesota farmland for who knew how long?

⨎

"Today wasn't so bad, was it?" Gram sat in her rocker before the fireplace and sipped from her mug of hot chocolate.

Christine glanced over from where she snuggled on the couch, one of Gram's knitted afghans pulled over her legs. After she set her mug on the table beside her, she smiled. "Not as bad as I thought it would be. Until you asked me to help you sew the pearls and sequins on the dress, I didn't feel useful."

Gram blew across her cup, trying to cool the liquid. Christine knew she liked hers lukewarm. Gramps had always teased her about it. "You perked up after you talked to Melissa."

Christine nodded. "She and Karen have everything right on schedule. And they're keeping up with all the customers' orders." Christine gazed at the dancing flames. "Melissa even told me she wished she could spend a few days snowed in somewhere. I don't think the storm hit as hard there. Or if it did, the highway department was out on the freeways and streets in force. She didn't have any trouble getting to the shop this morning. You know what the best part of today was, Gram?"

"Why, having you here with me, of course."

Christine laughed. "For me, it was being with you. I loved it when you talked about how you and Gramps courted and about your wedding and honeymoon. I just hope my marriage lasts as long as yours did."

"With God's help, it will. That's the only way we made it."

The melody of Christine's cell phone ringing interrupted the conversation. By the time she extricated her legs from the afghan and reached the instrument, it had gone to voice mail. She waited a couple of minutes, then hit speed dial for Christopher.

⌘

Late afternoon of the third day, Christine stood by the front window talking to her future husband. "You're right. The time with Gram has been wonderful. I'm not sorry we had this quality time together."

"That's good to hear." He paused, and she wondered if he had hung up. "Sorry, I had to put the phone down for a second. You're sounding more peaceful than you have in a long time. I'm glad to hear it."

She noticed movement at the end of the drive. "Something's out there."

"What?" Was that worry she heard in his voice?

"It looks like it might be the snowplow on the road. If that's what it is, Mr. Watson will probably be here before long and clean off Gram's drive. I can come home in the morning."

Christopher gave what sounded like a sigh of relief. "I'm glad. Be sure to call me and let me know when you start out."

Chapter 6

Soon after the snowplow moved down the road, Mr. Watson started working his way up Gram's drive, cleaning off the snow as he came. Christine was glad to see him because she knew she couldn't clean off the long driveway. When he reached the house, she offered to pay him.

"No, Chrissy, I couldn't accept any money from you." He took his hat off and held it in both hands. "I just know I'd want someone to help my mother if she were still alive. It's what neighbors do." He put his hat back on. "Let me be sure that sidewalk is completely cleaned off. Can't have Mrs. Olson falling, now, can we?"

"Well, thank you again." Christine went back inside. "Gram, it looks like I'll be going home in the morning, and none too soon."

"Having you here this long has been a real blessing." Gram smiled. "Come help me get the dress in that garment bag you brought. Didn't the cleaners say they needed it a week before the wedding to guarantee they would have it pressed in time for you to wear it?"

The next morning, Gram insisted on cooking Christine a big breakfast. She didn't have the heart to tell her grandmother that she usually only ate yogurt and a bagel or maybe a toaster waffle before she went to work. Fortified with bacon, scrambled eggs, and biscuits so light and fluffy they almost floated off her plate, Christine started loading her luggage into the trunk of her car. She would bring the wedding dress out last.

"Chrissy," Gram called from the front porch, "I've made you a bag to take with you. Some biscuits with butter and that blueberry jam you like. . .and the rest of the bacon. You might get hungry on the road."

Not much chance of that happening. Christine would be home before noon. But she didn't want to hurt Gram's feelings. She started up the sidewalk toward the farmhouse. Evidently, Gram didn't want to wait for her, because she stepped onto the top step, and her feet flew out from under her.

With horror, Christine watched, as if in slow motion, her beloved grandparent fall, landing on the porch with a thud, the bag flying out of her hand and emptying its contents across the porch and snow-covered lawn.

"Gram!" Christine ran as fast as she could and knelt on the cold floor of the wooden structure, leaning over the fallen woman. Her grandmother was breathing, but her eyes were closed. "Are you all right? Of course not. Gram, can you hear me? Where are you hurt?"

She pulled her cell phone from her pocket. *How do you get emergency help out here?* At home, she would just dial 9-1-1 on her regular phone. Maybe call the operator. She punched the 0 then SEND and pulled the instrument to her ear.

Christine was thankful when a voice answered instead of a computerized answering system. "I don't know how to get help! My grandmother just fell on her porch! She's breathing, but she passed out! I'm afraid to move her, and it's very cold!"

"Just tell me where you are." The controlled voice soothed Christine a little.

After giving the information, Christine took a deep breath, hoping to calm herself some more. Hysteria would upset Gram if she woke up. "Do you think I should move her inside?"

"I wouldn't until the paramedics are there. Can you get blankets or quilts to cover her?"

Christine didn't want to leave Gram long enough to look, but she knew there were lots of afghans right inside. She rushed in, still holding the phone to her ear.

Soon the voice came over the line again. "I've contacted emergency help in Litchfield. One of their workers has an EMT vehicle at his farm, which isn't far from where you are. He keeps it there so he won't have to go to town before he heads out to help victims. Help should arrive in a few minutes."

"Thank you." Christine clicked off the phone and shoved it into her pocket. She grabbed every cover she could find and quickly returned to the porch, piling them on Gram. *Victim. She called Gram a victim. I don't want to think of her that way.*

Gram groaned. Then her eyes slowly blinked several times before she finally opened them, gazing up into Christine's face. No hint of recognition, just a blank stare.

Christine dropped to sit on the porch beside Gram. She noticed the signs of pain that lined her grandmother's face, pain that broke Christine's heart. It was all she could do to keep from sobbing. She blinked back the tears that threatened to overflow and cleared her throat before she spoke.

"Gram, I'm right here, and help is on the way." Christine wasn't sure Gram understood.

Gram wore a confused expression, her eyes roving all around as if trying to figure out where she was. She moved a little, then stopped with a loud moan. Finally her gaze settled on Christine's face.

"Chrissy, is that you?"

Christine leaned closer to Gram, hoping her presence would calm the older woman. "Yes, I'm here."

"I thought you went home this morning." Gram's voice sounded weak, and her eyes drifted closed once again. Her body began to shiver.

Tears made their way down Christine's cheeks. She dashed them away with one hand and held Gram's hand with the other, knowing the connection would comfort Gram. Then she tucked the covers closer around Gram to keep what body warmth she had from escaping.

In the distance, the wail of a siren became apparent, then quickly grew closer. That didn't take long. *Thank You, Lord, for getting them here so soon. Please take care of Gram.*

❧

The morning meeting ran long. Chris didn't get back to his office until twelve thirty. He took his cell phone out of the holder at his waist and looked to see if somehow he had missed Christine's call since he had it on silent mode. He usually felt the vibration. *No, nothing.* He thought she would be home by now. He had hoped to have lunch with her. Punching her speed-dial number, he waited for it to ring. When the phone went immediately to voice mail, he hung up. Maybe she forgot to turn hers on.

He called Floral Haven. "Melissa, has Chrissy arrived yet?"

"Chris! No. I thought maybe this was her calling. This is the first day she's taken so long to call. Maybe the traffic was worse than she expected."

"Thanks." He flipped the phone closed, then buzzed his administrative assistant. "Marta, please have Chef's Touch downstairs send up the daily special."

"Don't you want to know what it is first?"

"No. Whatever they fix is fine. I just need to eat."

"I thought you were going out to lunch, boss."

He smiled at her impertinence. The lovely Chinese woman made an excellent administrative assistant, but she could be a little cheeky. "Christine hasn't gotten back yet."

His cell phone vibrated just as he clicked off the intercom. "Chrissy, I've been wondering about you."

"I knew you would." She sounded tired and something else he couldn't quite identify.

"Is everything all right?"

"I'm not sure." She took a deep breath. "When I was loading the car to leave, Gram fell on the porch steps."

"Oh no! Is she all right?" He quickly changed the phone to his other hand and picked up his pen.

"The doctor thinks so. Nothing is broken. But he wants to keep her overnight for observation."

He pulled his leather-covered memo pad close and flipped the cover open. "Where are you?"

"We're at the hospital in Litchfield. I'm going to stay here tonight, too." She blew out a deep sigh.

"You sound tired."

"I am."

Chris started writing on the pad as he talked. "I have a lighter load this afternoon. I'll be up there in time to eat dinner with you."

"Oh, Christopher." It sounded like a sob. "That would be wonderful."

⟨≈⟩

Although nothing was broken, Gram had many bruises. The doctor assured Christine that her grandmother was in wonderful shape for a woman her age. She would recover. He wanted to send her home as soon as possible. He explained that older patients often did better in familiar surroundings, especially after the sun went down. It concerned him that she lived alone. Gram was asleep probably from some of the medication they had given her.

Christine wandered out to the waiting room. She flipped open her cell phone and called her only cousin who had no children and a flexible job schedule.

"Mona."

"Chrissy, are you as excited as I was this close to my wedding?"

The wedding! Christine hadn't thought about it since Gram's accident. But she couldn't tell Mona that. "Actually, I'm calling about Gram."

"Is she all right?" Mona sounded as concerned as Christine felt.

"She's going to be." Christine walked toward the window. "She fell this morning before I left."

"Where are you?"

"At the hospital with Gram." She rubbed her neck and stretched it, trying to get the kinks out. "They want to send her home in the morning if she is okay. The doctor said she would do better in familiar surroundings, but she shouldn't be alone."

"I can't get there for a few days." Christine could almost hear the wheels turning in Mona's brain. "Is there any chance you can stay a little longer?"

"I'll do whatever I have to for Gram."

<hr />

When Chris arrived at the hospital, he was directed to the waiting area near Gram's room. Walking down the hall, he wondered why hospital walls were always painted that horrible, muddy green. Surely there was a bucket somewhere labeled "Institutional Green." He arrived at the arrangement of couches with floral embossed plastic upholstery to find Christine sitting in one with her feet pulled up under her. An open magazine lay in her lap, and her head rested against the top of the back. A soft snore told Chris just how tired she was. He really didn't want to wake her.

He smiled and sat across from her. Thankfully, no one else shared the room with them. Chris could study her all he wanted to. Her hair was mussed and spread around her on the couch. She probably had makeup on this morning, but none remained. Her natural beauty overwhelmed him. In a week and a half, they would be man and wife. He was eagerly anticipating their wedding night—so much it almost scared him. Chris wanted to make the consummation of their vows wonderful. He had spent many hours in prayer asking the Lord to guide his every move that night.

More than that, he looked forward to spending the rest of their lives together. To grow accustomed to that soft snoring sound. To wake each morning with her sleep-mussed hair spread across the pillow beside his and her face painted with her deep love for him instead of makeup. Just thinking about it increased his breathing rate.

His eyes traced a path up and down, then across and back covering every single inch of her face. The tiny brown dot beside her mouth that they laughingly called her beauty spot. Her perfectly shaped brows. The coal black eyelashes that didn't match her naturally blond hair.

Chrissy must have felt his presence, because her eyes opened. She quickly sat up and smiled, smoothing her rumpled clothing. "Christopher, when did you get here?"

He moved over to sit beside her, pulling her into his arms. "Not long ago."

"Why didn't you wake me up?"

"You were tired." He pulled her even closer and captured her lips, savoring the feel and taste of them.

"I'm so glad you're here. I've missed you so much." This time, she kissed him. He could feel the longing she poured into it.

Only ten more days. Ten long days and nights.

Chapter 7

Morning sunlight slanted across the room, awakening Christine. She wondered why she wasn't stretched out in her bed instead of sleeping sitting up. She opened her eyes slowly so the brightness she could see even through her eyelids wouldn't blind her.

Of course. Christopher sat beside her, his arm holding her close, his head in an awkward position against the back of the couch. She hoped he didn't have a crick in his neck when he woke. She started to get up, trying not to disturb his sleep. His arm quickly tightened around her, pulling her even closer against his comfortable chest.

"Where are you going?" His sleep-deepened voice sounded sexy.

Was this what the rest of her life would be like? Hearing that voice first thing in the morning? Tingles ran up and down her spine. How wonderful!

Christine turned to look up at him. His face was so close with his eyes like melted dark chocolate, her favorite flavor. "I'm going to freshen up before I check on Gram."

"Good idea. I will, too, since she wasn't awake when I arrived last night." He dropped a kiss on her waiting lips. "I'll help you get her home before I head back." That merited another heart-stopping kiss.

❧

Chris washed his hands and face. Rubbing the stubble on his chin, he wished he had brought his electric razor. Of course, Chrissy hadn't seemed to mind. At least he had a razor in his private bathroom at the office.

Last night had been incredible. Yes, they were at a hospital, but spending the time with Chrissy and sharing their responsibilities as well as their love was what life was all about. His anticipation for their marriage increased by the second. Nine more days. Seemed like an eternity.

He quickly dried his hands and went to find his fiancée. Chrissy waited by the nurses' station outside Gram's door. "Can we go in now?"

"Yes, I was just waiting for you."

❧

Christine could hardly believe that the wedding would take place in only five days, actually four since it was so late now. She was glad Mona should arrive at any time. Her cousin called from the airport saying she had rented a car. She wanted to be flexible to meet any of Gram's needs. A horn honked from in front of the house, and Christine made sure Gram was comfortable then rushed to the door.

When she opened it, Mona stood on the porch with a suitcase in each hand and her purse hanging on her shoulder. "Hi, Cuz, how are things?"

Christine stepped back to make room for her to enter. "Do you have anything else in the car?"

"No, I decided to bring everything in one trip." How like Mona. So efficient. No wonder she made good money teaching people time management. She wouldn't have any trouble taking care of Gram.

After all the greetings, the cousins sat near their grandmother in the living room to visit. Mona took the chair closest to the recliner where Gram rested with the veil in her lap. As they talked, she kept sewing on the decorations.

"Gram, are you sure you're okay?" Mona's eyes held concern.

"Of course I am." Gram gave a harrumph of indignation. "Chrissy has been hovering over me like a mother hen. I just have some interesting bruises. They're really colorful now."

"I was only trying to be sure you were all right." Christine was glad Gram didn't have any long-term damage.

Mona turned toward Christine. "You aren't going to try to leave tonight, are you?"

"I really want to, but when I talked to Christopher awhile ago, he insisted I wait until morning. He doesn't like me on the road at night." Christine shrugged. "I guess he's right, and after I talked to Melissa, I'm sure everything with the wedding will be fine. I'm surprised at how well she and Karen are getting along without me. I'm not sure I like it, either."

"Okay, Cuz, I challenge you to a game of Monopoly. No one will play with me in California, because I always win."

Christine smiled. "Oh, you do, do you? Well, not tonight. But before we start playing, I want us to press the wedding dress. Even though I'm going home tomorrow, the cleaners won't be able to guarantee that they'll have it done in time. I think we can do it, don't you?"

Although she had wanted a skirt with yards and yards of fabric in it, after they worked on pressing it for a while, Christine wished she had chosen a sheath wedding dress. She was grateful that Mona was there to help move the dress around so they could press it without making wrinkles somewhere else.

"I can see why people let the cleaners do this." Mona swiped a lock of hair out of her eyes and pulled it behind her ear. "This is hard work."

"Yeah. Thanks for helping me."

"What are families for?"

⁕

When Chris watched the Weather Channel this morning, the forecast was for another day or two without any snow. However, when he switched on the TV when he got home a little before midnight, the forecast was grim. *Why didn't I let Chrissy come home tonight like she wanted to? I thought it would be safer for her to drive in the daytime, and I wanted her to have some time with Mona before she left. Was that a mistake?*

He wondered if Chrissy was still awake. With Mona there, she might be, but if not, he didn't want to wake her. He dropped to his knees beside his bed. The familiar position welcomed him. He poured his heart out to the Lord. Somehow, he knew that Christine's tolerance had been stretched to the limit. He worried how she would take this new development.

When he tried to call Christine on Gram's phone the next morning, the lines were down. So he dialed the cell. Fortunately, it worked.

"Chrissy, how are you this morning?"

"Oh, Christopher, I can't leave. The driveway is already impassable." Her statement ended on a sob.

"Honey, I'm so sorry. I wish I could be there with you. I'd pull you into my arms and kiss all your worries away." He made a soft smacking sound, hoping it would comfort her.

After a long silence, she answered, "I wish you *could* kiss them away."

Trying to take her mind off her troubles, he asked, "What did you and Mona do last night?"

"Would you believe we played Monopoly?"

Chris laughed. "So who won? I know you two are about equal in skill at the game."

"Equal? I don't think so. I beat her, of course."

"Honey, I'm proud of you."

❧

When Christine started to click the button to end the call, her low battery light flashed a warning at her. Why didn't she check last night and plug the phone in for good measure? She would have needed it if she were on the road as planned. After going up to her bedroom on the second floor of the house, she pulled the charger out of her packed suitcase. She attached it to the phone and leaned down to plug it in. Before she reached the wall socket, everything went dim. Only the whiteout from the window allowed her to see her way around the room.

"Chrissy, where are you?" Gram's voice drifted up the stairs.

"I'm in my room." She bumped into the edge of the footboard. The corner really hurt.

Mona shouted from below. "I thought you were going to

help me fix breakfast."

After making her way across the hall, Christine started down the steps, feeling her way along the wall and banister. "I am. I went up to plug in my phone. It needs charging."

When she rounded the corner into the kitchen, her cousin stood hunched over, digging in one of the drawers. "What are you doing?"

Mona stood up. "Gram said the matches are in this drawer. She has lots of candles. She also has a couple of flashlights and three kerosene lamps. We'll have light."

"That's good to know. Where is Gram?"

"In the living room working on your veil."

Christine crossed to the sink to wash her hands, then she remembered that the pump wouldn't work. She turned around and leaned against the sink. "So what are we going to do for water?"

"That's easy," Mona quipped. "We'll melt snow on the stove."

"At least it runs on propane. Do you think the tank is full enough?"

Mona moved to look out the window, as if she could see through all the snow to where the tank stood. "I hope so. I don't want to ask her. If she needs more, she'll feel bad. I plan on only burning a few candles and one kerosene lamp at a time. That way they'll last longer."

What she left unsaid bothered Christine. They might be here until after the date for the wedding—snowed in. "And the furnace needs electricity to run the blower. How will we keep warm?" Christine knew there were a lot of things that could go wrong. A sense of dread dropped over her like an unwelcome cloak. So much had happened. Each time, it took more effort to deal with it. Christine didn't know if she had any resolve left, but she wanted to hide the fact from her grandmother and cousin. They didn't need any more to worry about.

"I've thought of that." Mona leaned closer to the window. "Have you been out on the back porch since you came?"

"No, even though I've been here several days." Christine shook her head for emphasis.

Mona moved to the back door then pulled it open. "There's lots of wood out here. It looks like we can burn the fireplace around the clock for a long time. We might have to sleep downstairs, though. I'm sure the upstairs will be too cool soon enough. It'll be like a slumber party." Her perky voice on that last statement did nothing to lift Christine's spirits.

Christine crossed her arms over her chest. "Well, at least something is going right."

Mona walked close and looked deep into her eyes. "Everything's going to be all right." She pulled Christine into a hug. "You'll see."

Yeah, we'll see. But what Christine saw looming on the horizon would definitely not be all right.

Chapter 8

When Christine went into the living room carrying a lighted lantern, Gram smiled at her. "Good thing I finished your veil last night. It would be hard to see to sew on those tiny seed pearls and sequins in this subdued light."

Christine didn't know what to say. She didn't want to discourage Gram, but she was afraid there wouldn't be a wedding. At least not four days from now. She went over and hugged her grandmother.

"You did a wonderful job on the dress and veil. Thank you." She dropped a kiss on Gram's soft wrinkled forehead. "It's prettier than any wedding gown we saw at the Bridal Boutique when we went to get the bridesmaid dresses." She walked over to the couch and sat down, pulling a knitted afghan over her legs and tucking it in around them.

"Christine, I know why you're so glum. Want to talk about it?"

Gram's quiet inquiry brought tears to Christine's eyes. She didn't want to answer that question. She knew she couldn't do it without sobbing. Her nerves were stretched beyond the limit.

Gram's soothing voice continued, "Even though things seem grim right now, God is still in control."

Before Christine could think of anything to say, Mona came in with her arms full of firewood. Christine jumped up, letting her cover fall back on the couch. "Here, I'll help you. If you try to do it by yourself, you'll drop it all over the place. Don't want any of it hitting Gram."

Mona stood still while Christine took the pieces, two at a time, from her arms and placed them on the grate. While she arranged the split logs to her satisfaction, Mona went back out for kindling wood. Together they stuffed wadded newspaper under the grate, then placed kindling between the newspapers and grate.

"I'm surprised you remember how to build a fire, Mona." Christine liked to tease her cousin. "You don't have many fireplaces in Southern California, do you?"

Mona turned to smile at Gram then reached for the tall box of matches. "Gram taught me well. You remember all the times we spent holidays with her. Some skills you just don't forget."

When the lit match touched the newspapers, they quickly caught, flaring up and igniting the kindling. Before long flames surrounded the larger pieces of wood, providing both warmth and a golden glow to the room.

"So. . ." Mona turned toward the back of the house. "Let's go gather snow for water. We can put it on the back burner of the stove."

Christine felt as if a large stone had lodged in her stomach. Four days from now, she should be getting ready to go to the church for her wedding. Instead, the snowstorm gave no indication of letting up anytime soon. The last time this happened, it took three days after the storm ceased for Gram's drive to be cleared. Three days that Christine didn't have if she wanted to get to the church on time.

A mountain of snow stood between herself and her wedding. She knew the Bible said that if you have as much faith as the size of a tiny mustard seed, she could move a mountain, but she wasn't sure she even had a mustard seed of faith. And this mountain of snow wouldn't be removed before the date for her wedding had passed. A terrible thought dropped into her mind, causing a rift to sink deep into her heart. Can a person have a "heartquake" the way the earth in California had an earthquake? *What if God doesn't want Christopher and me to get married?* Right now, she wasn't very sure. Maybe this was God's way of making her take another long look at everything.

Knowing how Gram could always read her expression, Christine turned toward the kitchen. "I'm going to help Mona." She rushed out before her grandmother said anything. She didn't want to talk to Gram about any of this. Especially about her doubts.

❧

Chris held the phone tight against his ear while his chief accountant went over details of the latest acquisition. Chris couldn't help being proud of the progress he had made with the company in the months since his father left. At first, Chris had worried that he was too young to make the mature decisions needed to keep the company on track. A large number of people depended on this corporation for their livelihood, and he felt the enormous responsibility that entailed. With his rosewood pen, he scratched notes on the pad in front of him while listening to Mr. Jones.

Suddenly, some sort of strange, uncomfortable feeling sliced through him, almost like a stabbing pain. He couldn't hold back an audible gasp.

"Mr. Davis, sir, are you all right?" Herbert Jones had been with the company for more years than Chris knew. It felt funny when he called Chris *sir*.

"Yes. I'm fine, Jones, but I'm afraid we'll have to continue this at another time."

"I'll wait for you to call me back." A loud click signaled the end of the conversation.

An ache spread throughout his chest, centering on his heart. Chris laid his watch on the desk so he could see the second hand. Then he counted his pulse for fifteen seconds. It was in a healthy range and beat strong and steady. Only three months ago he took a physical for the increased life insurance to protect his new family. He went to his own doctor and had Dr. Haddon do a thorough job of it. The doctor pronounced him healthy as the proverbial horse. So where was this ache coming from?

With his hand pressing against his heart, Christ went into the private apartment behind his executive office, which he used when he needed seclusion from the workday world. When Chrissy was at Gram's overnight, he often just bedded down in the apartment instead of going home. Today he wanted privacy.

He dropped into the deeply cushioned leather chair and closed his eyes. *Lord, what is going on here? Is something the matter? What am I missing?* While he waited for an answer, a picture of Chrissy floated into his mind. An expression he had never seen on her face before held hopelessness and pain. "Lord, is it Chrissy?" Speaking the words aloud made God seem even closer, as if He were sitting in the chair across the room from him.

The unspeakable peace from Jesus settled in Chris's heart and the ache subsided some. He closed his eyes and tried to imagine what could have caused her to look like that. *Of course!* So much had happened. Maybe she had all she could take and felt like giving up.

Chris poured his heart out to the Lord, asking Him to touch Chrissy in a way she had never been touched—to somehow let her know that He was still in control of their lives.

⤫

"Chrissy. . ." Mona looked at her with a concerned frown wrinkling her brow. "What's the matter? You look like you've lost your last friend."

Christine couldn't stop the sobs that erupted. Mona pulled her into an embrace and rubbed her back while Christine poured an abundance of tears onto Mona's thick, layered sweaters. All the circumstances that had occurred in the last ten days formed an enormous reservoir of tears, which Christine kept bottled up, hoping they would go away. Instead, this final blow worked as a pump to send them gushing like a never-ending geyser. She cried until her whole body hurt from the effort, but finally the sobs subsided, and she moved back a pace.

"Maybe we should go into the kitchen. As wet as your sweater is, you'll freeze to death out here, even though the porch is enclosed." Christine swiped her cheeks with both hands, knowing that removing the wetness wouldn't erase the traces of all the crying she had done. What would Gram think?

Mona, always the mind reader, said quietly, "Gram knows something is bothering you. You can't hide it from her. Come on in the living room and we'll talk it out."

That was the last thing Christine wanted to do, but she knew there was no way around it. She followed her cousin through the kitchen and across the hall. When she glanced at Gram, the concern that cloaked her face hit Christine like a physical blow. Why couldn't she have been stronger and taken care of this by herself? She didn't want to hurt Gram. Not now, so soon after Gram's fall.

"Mona, why don't you put the kettle on for a pot of tea?" Gram pointed toward the couch. "Chrissy, sit down and tell me what's going on."

Christine glanced toward Mona a moment before her cousin exited the room. How could she not comply with Gram's wishes? So Christine took her place once again on the couch and pulled the afghan up around her shoulders, covering her body completely. Was she hoping it would shield her? It didn't work.

"Are you going to tell me what's going on, or do I have to get it out of you by asking pointed questions?" How like Gram to get right to the heart of the matter.

"You know what today is?"

Gram nodded. "It's four days before your wedding. And it's still snowing. Right?"

Christine shivered. "I can't believe this is happening to me.

71

How could God let it? Everything was going according to plan, then all this—"

"According to whose plan, Chrissy?"

Why did that question hurt so much? Christine didn't want to face what Gram was bringing to the forefront. She had made the plans for her wedding. She really hadn't asked God what He wanted her to do. Except that at one time she felt it was God's will for her and Christopher to marry.

"Didn't God bring the two of you together?" Had Gram taken up Mona's mind reading habits?

"I thought so." Her answer, so soft that no one could hear it, didn't help. "I thought so," she said more forcefully.

"Don't you still believe that?"

Christine reached for a tissue from the box on the table at the end of the couch. Tears once again streamed down her cheeks. "I'm not sure. Look what He's allowed to happen. He could have stopped the storm."

Gram got up from the rocker-recliner and moved to sit beside Christine.

"Shouldn't you stay in your chair?"

"Chrissy, I'm not an invalid. I just have some bruises." Gram settled two colorful throw pillows behind her back. "Now tell me why you aren't trusting God."

Christine sighed. "I'm not sure how to put it into words."

"You're just tired."

Mona came through the door carrying a tray with the teapot, three cups and saucers, and a plate of cookies. She set it on the coffee table in front of the couch. "Talk some sense into her, Gram." Mona began pouring cups of the fragrant, spicy brew.

"Chrissy has to work this out for herself."

When Chris finished praying, he lifted his cell phone. He punched in the speed-dial number for Chrissy. After a few rings, a disembodied voice told him that the phone was not currently in service. He could leave a voice message.

What had happened? He picked up the remote and turned on the large screen TV. The major report on the news station was about the snowstorm. Only a few flakes drifted in the air in St. Paul, but farther west the storm still raged.

"A large number of people in the center of the state have no electricity." The newscaster, wearing a stylish suit and an almost fake smile, droned on. "The National Weather Service thinks the storm will abate later today. If it does, utility companies in other states have pledged to send workers to help restore power as quickly as possible. Maybe they will be able to reach the rural areas sooner than expected. There's even word that a team from Texas will be joining them. Sources believe the Texans probably have never seen the kind of storm that hit central Minnesota this last week. Some people wonder if they'll be prepared enough to really help."

Chris pushed the button to silence the man. *So, the electricity is off.* Evidently Chrissy didn't get to charge her phone before the power went off. He remembered how helpless he was in Hong Kong without being able to contact her. Probably she felt that way and more. Maybe that was why he had the pain. He knew God brought them together. Sometimes Chris knew that their souls were somehow connected. It would help him feel her agony, even at this great distance.

He dropped to his knees on the floor beside the huge chair and leaned his forearms on the cushioned seat, burying his head in his hands. "Father God, Christine needs You more than ever. Lord, show Yourself strong and in control so she can truly believe that she can trust You with anything, even the storm and our wedding."

After the first few spoken words, his prayer continued silently and long.

∞

Mona sat cross-legged on the floor across the table from Gram and Christine. She sipped her tea and stared into the depths of her cup.

At least she wasn't staring at Christine, who didn't want anyone else to see into her soul right now. Something was happening inside her. The heartquake had stopped, and the crevasse didn't feel as wide as it had before.

Gram patted Christine's hand. "I believe God has given me something for you. I'm not sure what it means, but here's what He's saying to tell you. 'If you can't trust God through the storms, how will you learn to hear His still small voice during them?' Does that mean anything to you?"

Christine took a deep breath. Might as well get it all out in the open. "I was wondering if maybe this was God's way of telling me that Christopher and I shouldn't get married. There is no way the wedding will happen as planned."

"So, it will take place when you can get there." Gram's answer sounded emphatic. "It doesn't have to be in four—uh, three and a half days. What you need to do is understand that God is in control. Not you or your plans."

That much was crystal clear. What was it Gram said before? Trust Him through the storm. Christine knew she hadn't trusted Him for much of anything to do with the wedding. She wanted what she wanted—to follow her plans for the wedding of her dreams.

Mona looked up at her with a gleam in her eyes. "I don't think God is saying that it's wrong to plan, but schedules aren't what you trust."

Wow! Christine was getting it from all sides. Most important, it was coming from the inside, too. The Lord's presence in her heart agreed with every word Gram and Mona spoke.

"And remember"—Gram waggled her index finger at Christine—"nothing is impossible with God."

Chapter 9

The morning of the third day before the wedding, Christopher clicked on the TV. The Weather Channel reported that the storm ended late yesterday evening.

"Most of the main roads were cleared by morning, but there is no estimate on when all the farm roads will be re-opened. It could take two or three days. And the electric company personnel can't get to some of the downed lines until the roads are cleared. Many people might not have power for several more days."

After taking his shower, Chris sat in the recliner in the bed-room and picked up his well-worn Bible from the table beside it. "Lord, I need a word from You." Talking out loud kept Chris from feeling so lonely. "I haven't done this very many times, but I'm going to close the Bible and hold it between my hands. When it drops open, Lord, please let it be a passage You want me to read."

When the book lay in his lap, Chris realized that the pages of Isaiah were open before him. What could Isaiah have for him? Chapter 30 started on the first page. He began to read, but nothing spoke to him specifically until he reached verse 21: "Whether you turn to the right or to the left, your ears will hear a voice behind you, saying, 'This is the way; walk in it.'"

"That's what I'm asking for, Lord. I want to hear Your clear voice speaking to me, telling me what to do right now."

A whisper as clear as if someone stood behind his shoulder sounded in Chris's spirit. With bowed head, he listened as the Holy Spirit spoke to his heart giving him direction. With resolve, he thanked the Lord and reached for the phone.

⸎

The morning of the third day before the wedding dawned bright. Christine stood at the front window where she had scraped a hole in the crystal frost that covered the pane. The wintry sun revealed all the diamond sparkles from the snow banked against the house and buildings. Both cars were almost covered.

"What are we going to do today?" Mona came into the living room, stretching and yawning. "I'm sure we won't be able to get out."

"Only if you want to shovel snow." Christine turned and smiled at her cousin. "I don't suppose you've done much of that in California."

"Naw, we let the servants do it."

Christine and Mona laughed at the joke.

"Well, we could play another Monopoly game." Christine leaned down to put more wood on the fire. "That is, if you want to lose again."

Gram started a pot of homemade soup while the girls set up the board. Just as Christine imagined, it lasted almost all day.

They only broke for lunch. By early evening, Mona finally prevailed. At least each one of them won a game while they were here. Soon they sat in front of the fireplace eating more of the delicious soup Gram made.

When she finished, Mona took her bowl to the kitchen and returned with a wrapped package in her hand. "Here. I bought this as a wedding gift, but you might need to use it now." She dropped it in Christine's lap.

Like a child, Christine tore the paper away, revealing a battery operated reading light. The package even contained extra batteries.

"I know how much you like to read in bed, and I didn't want you keeping your executive husband awake." Mona laughed. "Of course, the two of you might be otherwise occupied, and you might not even need this."

Christine felt the blush creep up her neck and cheeks. She hoped something else would keep Christopher occupied at night, but she didn't want to think about it right now. That was for after the wedding.

"Thanks, Mona. I tried to read my Bible after I got ready for bed last night, but it's hard to do by candlelight. I'll get to tonight."

∽∾

Christine pulled her warm plush robe close around her. Under it, she wore her sweats instead of pajamas. Because the floor was too hard, the cousins took turns on the couch. At least Gram's room, next to the living room, was warm enough when they left the door open. After the girls built the fire up, Mona went to sleep. She would have about four hours while Christine kept the fire going. Then Mona would take her turn and let Christine sleep.

Curled up in Gram's big rocker, Christine attached the reading lamp to her Bible, wondering where she should read tonight. She had never done this before, but she prayed that God would open the Bible to the page where He had a message just for her. She ran her thumbs along the gold edge and flipped the book open. It had been a long time since she had read anything from Isaiah. She usually tried to do a chapter of Psalms, Proverbs, or the New Testament. Occasionally, she did one of those read-through-the-Bible-in-a-year things, but not recently.

Her gaze roved over the open pages, and an underlined verse jumped out at her. She wished she had noted when and why she highlighted it, but maybe that was what God wanted her to see again.

"Whether you turn to the right or to the left, your ears will hear a voice behind you, saying, 'This is the way; walk in it.'"

It must have been sometime when she wanted God to speak to her. That's what she needed tonight. *Lord, what are You saying to me?*

In the quietness, the still small voice answered. *Trust Me, child. Just trust Me.*

Christine bowed her head and felt the presence of the Holy Spirit hovering all around her. *I do, Lord.*

Can you trust Me with your wedding?

For a moment, panic seized Christine's heart. But only a moment. With resolution, she took a deep breath. *I trust You with the wedding. I think I always trusted You. I just let things get in the way. Forgive me, Lord. Whatever You want, I'm willing.*

For several minutes the heavy presence of the Lord filled the room in an almost tangible way. Christine basked in that presence, and peace like a soft blanket settled into her heart, covering everything there.

∽∾

Since both of the cousins were tired, they built up the fire one last time near morning and fell asleep. Later, the smell of brewing coffee and sizzling bacon pulled Christine from her slumbers. She sat up and stretched the kinks out of her body.

Mona, who had fallen asleep on the other end of the couch, began stirring. "What time is it?"

"I don't know." Christine stood up and started folding her blanket. "But it smells like Gram beat us up. I could use some coffee."

She walked into the cozy kitchen. "Do I smell biscuits, too, Gram?"

Swaddled in a huge apron, her grandmother turned and smiled at her before taking the last slice of bacon out of the pan and placing it with the others on a paper towel–covered plate. "Yes, breakfast is almost ready, but it's more like brunch time."

Christine couldn't believe how much meat Gram had cooked. "We won't eat that much." She picked up a slice and took a bite.

"I just felt like fixing a big breakfast. Maybe we can have bacon sandwiches for lunch."

"Are we expecting anyone?" Mona's voice called from the other room. "Someone is coming up the drive in a horse-drawn sleigh."

"Must be Mr. Watson. He's probably checking to see if we're all right." Gram poured some of the bacon grease into the old coffee can on the cabinet and started breaking eggs into the skillet. "I'll scramble enough for him, too. He probably ate breakfast early, so he should be hungry by now."

Mona came through the door. "I don't think it's your neighbor. I can't tell for sure, but it looks like a younger man. I'm going to put some clothes on before he comes in."

Christine rushed to the front of the house and pulled the door open a crack. She peered around the door into the brightness. Squinting her eyes against the glare, she shrieked, "It's Chris!"

Mona stopped on the stairs. "Who?"

"Christopher! He's driving the sleigh."

"Did you just call him Chris?" Mona smiled.

"I guess I did." She pulled the door farther open. At least she still was fully clothed beneath her robe.

"Chris!" She stepped out on the porch just as he stopped the sleigh near the front gate. She couldn't believe he guessed so accurately where it was under the snow. He had only been here a few times.

Bundled up in lots of layers, he looked almost Neanderthal, but Christine's heart beat in her throat as she looked at him. She couldn't remember when she had been so glad to see him. He took horse blankets from under the front seat of the sleigh and placed them on the animals. It looked like a really large sleigh.

When he turned, he pulled away the scarves that covered the lower part of his face and gave her a dazzling smile. With halting steps, he made his way through the snow up the completely hidden sidewalk toward her.

Her breathing accelerated. She didn't care what happened, or when. She and Chris were supposed to be together. Just looking at him made her quivery inside.

After he stepped onto the porch, he pulled her into a bear hug. His cold lips descended and covered hers. The heat of their passionate kiss soon warmed them.

"Come into the house," Gram called from the open doorway. "You can warm up before the fire while I finish scrambling the eggs."

They followed her into the house and closed the door. Christine helped Chris start to peel off his layers.

"God told me to fix lots of breakfast. Now we know why." Gram continued toward the kitchen.

❧

Seated across the table from his fiancée, Chris studied her face with amazement. Peace and contentment shone through the smile she gave him. He grinned, remembering the heart-stopping kiss they shared on the porch. Good thing he listened to the Lord.

"Are you girls ready to load up and go away with me?"

"Is that why you came? To take us back?" Chrissy sounded like an excited little girl, but no one looking at her would mistake her for a child.

"An interesting thing happened last night." Chris took the bowl of scrambled eggs Gram passed to him and piled them on his plate beside the biscuits and bacon. "I really wanted a word from the Lord, so I asked Him to open my Bible where

He wanted me to read. It was in Isaiah 30." At Chrissy's gasp, he stopped.

"That's where He took me, too. The verse about the voice speaking from behind you telling you the way to go." She put her fork down and stared into his eyes. "This is so awesome."

Gram seemed to be unaffected by what was happening. After taking a bite and chewing it awhile, she spoke quietly. "I knew God had this all worked out."

Mona nodded and continued eating.

Chris laid his fork down and reached to take Chrissy's hand. "Did something happen day before yesterday? Late in the morning?"

Momentary sadness veiled her face. "It was the most horrible thing in the whole time." She swallowed as if she had a lump in her throat. "I almost decided we weren't supposed to be getting married. It felt like my heart broke in two."

Everything in the room receded as though he and Chrissy were alone. "I felt your pain."

"Felt my pain?"

"I was on the phone with Mr. Jones and something shot through my chest, ending in my heart, making me gasp. I had to hang up." Just the memory was uncomfortable. "I went into my private suite and prayed for you."

With her other hand, Chrissy wiped at the tears on her cheeks. "How could that happen?"

He rubbed the back of her hand with his thumb. "God has tied our hearts and souls together. That's the only way to describe it."

Gram got up to refill the plate of biscuits. "That's when

God gave me something for Chrissy."

Chris glanced at her. "What?"

Chrissy answered for her. "He said, 'If you can't trust Him through the storms, how will you learn to hear His still small voice during them?' It helped me decide to trust Him. After that He was able to speak to me and I heard Him."

Mona got up to take her plate to the sink. "God is awesome, isn't He?"

No one disagreed.

❧

As soon as the dishes were washed and put away, Christine started packing her things. Chris was more than just her fiancé; he was her hero. She wondered how much trouble it had been for him to obtain a sleigh to come get them. Just the fact that he would go to so much trouble touched her heart.

When she went downstairs, Chris came into the house carrying a large, sort of flat box. "I got this from your friend at the wedding dress company. It's for shipping the gowns. There's just room for it under the backseat of the sleigh."

She dropped her overnight bag and took the carton. Soon the dress and veil were safely surrounded by tissue paper in the sealed container.

With Gram and Mona in the back seat and Christine beside Chris in the front, they started across the snow toward Litchfield.

"So what do we do when we get there?" Mona called from the back seat.

"We'll leave the sleigh at the edge of town. I have a car waiting for us there." Chris's breath caused puffs of steam in the cold air. "We'll have you to Chrissy's house before time to go to dinner."

"Dinner!" Chrissy grabbed his arm. "The rehearsal and rehearsal dinner were supposed to be tonight."

"They're still on." He dropped a kiss on her forehead. "Everything is right on schedule."

❧

Right on schedule the next day, Christine started down the aisle clutching her soon-to-be father-in-law's arm with one hand. In the other she carried the beautiful bouquet Melissa and Karen created from her favorite flowers. Lazy white snowflakes drifted outside the windows of the church, but here in the sanctuary, the stained glass windows hid them from sight. Her bridesmaids lined the front in red velvet dresses trimmed with white fur. Melissa, as maid of honor, looked beautiful in a green dress.

Quickly Christine's eyes were drawn to the handsome man across the aisle from her attendants. The man of her dreams. Her hero who didn't move the mountain of snow to get her here. With God's help, he carried her across the mountain to get to this wedding of her dreams. She knew God smiled down from heaven with His blessing.

LENA NELSON DOOLEY

Lena Nelson Dooley made it to the church on time with the love of her life, James. Their wedding almost fory-two years ago started them down the road to a romantic, fulfilling life of following Jesus and raising two daughters. Now with two sons-in-law and four grandchildren, they still enjoy the life they share. They attend Gateway Church in Southlake, Texas, where they are both active in the PrimeTime50+ ministry, a family life group, and Lena is involved in a ladies' life group and volunteers in the church bookstore. She speaks at retreats and women's ministry meetings both in the U.S. and internationally. She and James are interested in missions and have been on many mission trips.

Lena holds a BA in speech and drama and has graduate hours in drama. She has done many things in her working life, but now she is a full-time author and editor. She has had seven novels published by Heartsong Presents. Three of them were voted top ten favorites by readers and she was voted a top ten favorite author. Her first Barbour novella anthology *Scraps of Love* spent several months on the CBD Fiction Bestseller List. She invites you to visit her web site at www. LenaNelsonDooley.com.

Blown Away
by Love

Pamela Griffin

Dedication

To my crit buds, and especially to Mom, a big thank-you for helping me at a moment's notice. To my Lord, my Deliverer, who saved me and my sons from the whirling jaws of a tornado once-upon-a-spring, and proved I could always put my confidence and trust in Him during any storm—natural or emotional—this is for You.

Prologue

The favor of your attendance is requested at the celebration of
marriage between
Dale Michael Endicott
and
Marie Elisabeth Barrett
On the twenty-third day of April, at twelve noon
at Good Shepherd Christian Church in
Sunnydale, Texas
Reception immediately following at Sunnydale Reception Hall
R.S.V.P.
(Three times is the charm.)

Chapter 1

Okay, Marie, correct me if I'm wrong, but you're getting married tomorrow, right? This has been your dream since senior year. So, mind telling me why you're acting as if someone just put itching powder in your bridal bouquet?"

Marie scratched her arm, a nervous habit she'd had since childhood. "You really need to ask, Shalimar?" Her laugh came out a bit high-strung as she eyed her maid of honor, then tossed the silk bouquet to the counter of the recreation hall lobby where the rehearsal dinner was under way. "I just know Dale's going to back out again. I just know it. Why I'm even going through with this is anybody's guess. Do I have some inborn brutal desire for everyone to look at me as the town laughingstock again?"

"No one thought that about you. And Dale didn't back out either of those two times the wedding was postponed. You know that."

"Sometimes I feel as if my entire life is being postponed." Marie shot a brooding glance at the discarded bouquet. "I know that first time couldn't be helped, since he's a doctor's son and a paramedic, and that woman was parked in her van and having a baby. But the second time—"

"Dale's no liar. He missed the flight."

Marie let out a heavy sigh. "I suppose you're right. Sometimes, though, I think he's just hunting up excuses not to marry me."

"Do you love him?"

Marie looked up in surprise that her friend would ask such a thing. "Of course. Would I be here if I didn't?"

"Right. And he loves you. You're both Christians, you share the same interests. Girl—any fool with eyes can see you're crazy about each other. So what gives?"

"Nothing. I'm just being silly. Maybe it's just a bad case of nerves."

Marie attempted a smile, but in the back of her mind lurked her mother's frequent cautions to her during childhood. "If someone really cares, they'll be on time, and they won't make a habit of being late." Mom should know, since Dad had done the same. He'd missed Marie's tenth birthday party, because of putting in overtime, and the fur began to fly between her parents once he'd arrived home that night. When he left for good, Marie had thought for a short time she might have been the reason for the breakup, but the fights between her parents had been continual long before that, part of a daily routine.

"Speaking of our topic of conversation," Shalimar said, "here he comes now."

Marie looked toward the entrance. Her heart gave a little zinging leap at the sight of Dale. With his thick, wheat-colored waves tamed as much as could be from the comb he carried in his back pocket, the sparkle in his hazel-green eyes, and the lopsided grin on his face that never failed to make her smile in return, he was just the person she needed to see right now.

"I wasn't sure you were going to make it," Marie quipped lightly, though a pall of heaviness lay in her tone.

"Ben had to stop and get gas, and then we got to talking to an old friend who dropped by," Dale explained as he came up beside Marie and dropped a kiss near her mouth. "Sorry I'm late. Hi, Shalimar."

Marie's maid of honor nodded with a bright smile that enhanced her exotic African American features. Marie had always thought her friend should have been a model. "I'll let you two talk things out. It's high time you did." With that, Shalimar headed back into the dining room.

Dale's brows drew together in question. "What did she mean by that? Something wrong?"

Marie wished Shalimar hadn't spoken. This didn't seem like the time or place to unload any of her qualms, but then again, maybe it was. She needed to be sure of his motives before they proceeded any further.

"Do you love me, Dale?"

Surprised confusion filled his eyes. "Of course." He dropped a swift kiss to her lips as if to prove it.

"And you really do want to marry me?"

A trace of realization sobered his gaze and made his smile slip. "This is about what happened two months ago, right?"

For some reason his response needled her. "If you mean by that the second time we had to cancel our wedding, yes, it is."

He looked around, and Marie saw that they'd drawn attention from Dale's two young teenage cousins—Donna and Jillian—who'd just left the dinner area chattering and giggling. They gave carefree waves, and he nodded in return, but his smile was masklike. He slipped his arm around her waist, steering her toward the double glass doors.

"Let's talk about this outside."

Marie allowed him to escort her to a bowl-shaped stone fountain, but once they reached it, she broke a short distance away from him. Avoiding his gaze, hands clutching her elbows, she looked inside the fountain. Lack of rain had made the water evaporate a few inches, but the tiny goldfish still had enough of a home to survive. Orange-gold flashes of light darted here and there. Fleeting, rushing around the ring as if bored with where they were swimming. Trapped inside a bowl, never able to get free from it.

"Mind telling me what brought this all up?" Dale asked.

Marie shrugged, blew out a breath, then tore her focus from the fish and swung it sideways to her fiancé. "Twice now there's been an excuse for why you didn't show. I'm just a little leery of what'll happen tomorrow. It's no fun having to address a church full of guests that the wedding's been postponed—again."

"I'll be there." He moved toward her and laid his hands on her shoulders. "I promise."

"That's what you said last time. And, Dale, I mean it. If you stand me up a third time, that's it. There won't be a fourth chance."

She could see she'd stung him, but her emotions ran topsy-turvy. Her mother always told her she wore them on her sleeve for all the world to see. She scratched her arm.

"That's not fair, Marie." He drew back, his brows angled in a frown. "I couldn't help it that a major wreck on the highway made me late to the airport—or that the next flight was booked. At least I did try, and I got a red-eye flight to get back to you as soon as I could."

Marie hung her head, hateful tears clouding her eyes. She despised herself when she acted like this. She knew that second time, months ago, a small family emergency involving his stepgrandfather had necessitated him flying out of town and missing the rehearsal dinner; it really wasn't his fault. She offered to postpone then, but Dale had told her the danger with his grandpa had passed and to go ahead as planned. She didn't want to start another fight with him now. But once again her tongue worked against her, uttering words she'd rather not say, words she'd kept buried for a long time.

"Maybe that's not all it was. Maybe you're just afraid of marriage. I mean, think about it. You never really proposed to me. One day we just found ourselves at that point, talking marriage. But maybe when it all boils down to it, you're trying to find an escape hatch because you don't want to commit. And those two unavoidable incidents became more like golden opportunities."

She scratched her arm harder. He stilled her movements with one hand. "Let's not argue. Not on the night before our wedding." His voice was gentle, putting a lump in her throat. She looked up.

"I know past circumstances can hardly speak for themselves," he continued. "If the shoe were on the other foot, I might feel the same way. But please believe me when I tell you I love you, Marie Barrett. And for me there's no other woman I'd rather marry."

A tremulous smile caught the edges of her mouth. "I want to believe you, Dale. I honestly do. But like my mom always told me, seeing is believing." Why did she keep saying things she didn't want to say? She tried for a more peaceable remark. "Promise me tomorrow will be different. That you *will* be there no matter what. I love you so much and want everything to work out right for us. For once."

"Wild horses galloping through a hailstorm on my front lawn won't keep me away."

With that promise, she allowed Dale to draw her close. The feel of his warm lips lingering on hers made her heart beat and feel whole again. But it didn't erase all the doubt from her mind.

⟡

A hand roughly shook Dale's shoulder, rousing him from sleep. Groggy, he opened his eyes a slit. The image of his brother, Ben, dressed and wearing a windbreaker, didn't connect with the dream he'd just had about chasing wild horses.

"Get up!" Ben threw Dale's shirt onto his bare chest. "We've gotta hurry if we're going to make it on time."

Hurry? The words roused the memory of what this day meant to him, and Dale shot up on Ben's couch, his gaze whizzing to the black deco clock on the wall. "We're not late for the wedding?" No, it was only twelve minutes past eight according to the tall digital numbers. The wedding was scheduled for noon.

With a groan he fell back on the plaid cushions and closed

his eyes, intent on getting more shut-eye. Last night Ben had kidnapped him and brought him to his apartment, where a bunch of Dale's friends had thrown a good-bye-to-bachelorhood party—his third one. He'd endured a lot of ribbing because of that fact, but at least the guys had kept the event clean. They hadn't gotten any sleep until the early hours of morning, though, after the others left, and Dale was tired.

"Come on," Ben urged. "I need your help." Dale's jeans landed with a hard thump against his unprotected stomach.

"What's with you?" Dale growled, knocking the jeans aside and glaring at his big brother. "Can't a guy get some sleep around here?"

"Not with a storm brewing in Millbury, you can't. Alarm went off a few minutes ago. I need your help."

"Go without me," Dale mumbled into the pillow.

How many times in the past five years had he helped his storm-chasing brother by handing him equipment, driving while Ben videotaped, or engaging in whatever other task Ben ordered of him as they approached a funnel or thunderstorm to observe the raging weather and take pictures? Some of which earned Ben spots in newspapers and magazines, since he was a professional photographer. Well, he wouldn't rope Dale into working with him this time, not today. Memory again pushed its way through his foggy mind, and Dale lifted his head from the pillow. "Hey, what about my wedding? You're supposed to take pictures, remember."

"Wedding is hours away." Ben had turned his back and was grabbing boxes of snack foods and a large bag of chips from the kitchen cabinet. "We'll be back in plenty of time since

Millbury isn't far." He held out the potato chips toward Dale. "Breakfast?"

"No thanks." Realizing any notion of additional sleep was only a hopeless delusion, Dale slowly rose to a sitting position, swung his feet to the flat carpet, and looked down. Trying to get his bearings, he rubbed the back of his neck where a crick had started.

"Grayson called this morning and told me about the storm. He's been tracking it for two days."

Grayson—a meteorologist at a local news station who went to school with Ben.

"But why today of all days?" Dale asked.

"Hey, I don't pick when storms happen—they just do. And I want to be in on every one of them, especially a local one like this. You never know when you'll get that perfect shot." He rolled up the paper sack of food, breakfast, Dale assumed. "Like I said, there's a boatload of time before the wedding. I'll get us both to the church in plenty of time for you to take your stand in front of that altar and manacle yourself in marriage. I'm bringing the cameras with me, as well as my tux. You bring yours, too."

"If I wasn't here you'd go by yourself, right?"

"Yeah. So?"

"So can't we just pretend like I'm really not here? I'll find my own way home." He sounded like an idiot, but his mind wasn't clearly functioning yet. Coffee. He needed coffee.

"I was never that great at playacting when we were kids. So I guess it's a good thing for me that you really are here. Some might even call it Providence."

Dale didn't respond, realizing he was getting nowhere fast. He pulled his T-shirt over his head. He could probably call a taxi to take him back to his apartment and his car, because knowing his brother, once he set off on the track of a storm, he wouldn't want to detour. Then again, maybe Ben was right. Millbury was only fifteen minutes away. They should be back in plenty of time before the wedding.

Chapter 2

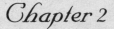

"W"ake up, sleepyhead bride-to-be!" Shalimar's teasing broke through Marie's dreams of Dale riding a white horse, with her pressed up against her fiancé's back, arms circled around his waist. "You've got less than four hours left to prepare for the big day."

A little miffed at being snatched from such a delightful vision, Marie sat up in bed. Her illusionary dream metamorphosed into today's reality—she was getting married this afternoon! Yawning, she stretched her arms high above her head and rubbed the sleep from her eyes. A contented smile took over her lips when she remembered her parting with Dale last night. He'd held her a long time, murmuring reassurances that he would be there before noon, come hell or high water. Their parting kiss on her doorstep erased all lingering worries.

"Mmmmm. I'm hungry. Do I smell muffins—and bacon?"

Shalimar laughed. "Well, it's good to see you feeling better. Lynette made breakfast. All the girls are here and eager to start getting ready for the big event. Nervous?"

Marie shook her head. "I've had a lot of time to get used

to the idea," she said wryly, but in fun. She looked at the alarm clock. "I think I'll call Dale first."

"I wouldn't do that if I were you. I heard the guys gave him a party last night."

"Yeah, I know. He told me it was in Ben's plans. But it's nine o'clock. Surely he'd be up by now, since there's so much to do before the wedding."

"Newsflash—it takes a guy ten minutes to do what it takes a woman two hours to accomplish. Didn't anyone ever tell you about the difference between the sexes?"

Marie ignored Shalimar's teasing and picked up the phone. "Dale won't mind. He's not the type to sleep in late. I've called him in the mornings before."

"Well, it's your funeral." Shalimar struck a melodramatic pose, a far-off look in her eyes. "And the bride wore black, a bouquet of withered crimson roses in her hand."

Laughing, Marie threw her pillow at her maid of honor. "Oh, will you just get out of here?"

"Humph. Fine way to treat a former roommate." Shalimar smiled as she left.

A touch of melancholy trickled through Marie. She and Shalimar had been roommates for three years, but everything must change at some time or other. It was inevitable. At least Lynette was moving in to take Marie's place. All three women had been good friends since their junior year in high school, when Marie moved back to Sunnydale, Texas. That had also been the year she met Dale.

Smiling secretly with pleasure of what their future might bring, she dialed Dale's cell phone number, but got his voice mail instead of a personal greeting. She left a brief message, considered, looked at the clock again, then dialed Ben's.

The phone rang and rang.

❧

"Will you relax already?"

Dale fidgeted in the passenger seat of Ben's black Bronco, tightening his lips over his teeth in a grimace. "I can't help it. I still don't like this." He slugged down the last swallow of coffee, welcoming the heat burning his throat.

"I told you, I'll get you there in plenty of time. Do me a favor and check the videocam battery. It might be low. If it is, there's a new one in that plastic black case on the backseat."

Dale reached behind him to grab the camera from its case and turned it on. "She said that if I'm not there this time, it's over between us. I don't want to risk losing her."

"You won't."

The battery light registered strong, so he shut it off. "It's good to go."

"Great. Just put it down by your feet, in case we need to grab it fast."

Dale did so, then crossed his arms over his chest. He stared out the windshield ahead to the flat gray sky they were approaching.

Ben looked his way and let out a grunt. "Man, you're pathetic. Now you're sulking like a kid? If you're so worried, give her a call. Let her know what's up and that you'll be there."

Dale nodded. "Good idea. About calling her, I mean. Not about telling her what's up." That would only make her nervous, and Dale didn't want to cause Marie any anguish on her big day. *Their* big day.

With a sigh, he reached to the backseat for his jeans jacket. How had he let his brother corral him into this? He blamed his foolishness on lack of sleep. Two and a half hours wasn't enough shut-eye for anyone to engage in rational thinking. His mind had been too fuzzy to really put one and one together, and Ben had herded him to the SUV fast, eager to get on the road for his storm-chasing jaunt. Already the vehicle had been packed with gear, and at the time Dale wondered why Ben had waited until the last minute to wake him. Now that Dale *was* awake, he realized Ben had done so purposely, knowing Dale was never alert enough in the mornings until he'd had a cup of black coffee and at least a twenty-minute start into the day.

Of course, it was too late to backtrack, but Dale regretted his sleepy decision to tag along like an obedient puppy with his master. Ben had always been the leader, since they were kids, but if he didn't get Dale back to Sunnydale in time, Dale would be the one demoted to a life in the doghouse, not Ben.

A search of Dale's pockets produced no cell phone. He twisted around to look on the floorboard and the seat, but his studied observation didn't yield the silver instrument.

He groaned.

"*Now* what's wrong?"

"My phone's gone. It must have fallen on the floor in your apartment. Or maybe it's in the couch." He'd tossed his jacket aside before he'd lain down in the early hours of morning. "Got yours on you?"

Ben shook his head and pulled his cell from his shirt pocket. "Here."

"Thanks." Dale punched in the numbers for Marie's apartment.

"Hello?" Her roommate came on the line.

"Hey, Shalimar. Can I speak to Marie?"

"She's in the shower. Try back in ten minutes."

"Okay." Disappointment twisted his gut. "Could you just tell her I called?"

"Sure. She'll be glad to hear you did. She tried calling you earlier at Ben's but didn't get an answer."

"Yeah." Dale fidgeted at the information. She must have tried calling after they'd already left. Or maybe Ben had turned the ringer off on his phone last night; he was notorious for doing that when he wanted undisturbed sleep. "If I don't call back, could you just let her know I'll see her in a few hours? At the church."

A pause. "Everything okay?"

"Sure, sure. No problems." He forced a laugh.

"So why don't I feel reassured?" Shalimar dropped her voice a notch. "Listen, Dale, just do me a favor. Stay away from any pregnant women or traffic jams. Take the back roads if you have to, but be there. Don't put Marie through a third trial run."

Her take-charge attitude irritated him. "I already told Marie that wild horses wouldn't keep me away, and they won't." He felt the sudden need to end the call before Shalimar unearthed the truth. "Look, I gotta go. Just tell her. And thanks."

Shutting off the phone and slipping it into the console, he looked toward the eerie boiling mass of clouds on the horizon fronting the empty highway. Cumulonimbus clouds—the kind that bred tornadoes. A funnel did appear to be forming, and while that thought reached his mind, the Bronco accelerated in speed as Ben floored it, muttering under his breath about needing to get closer.

Dale clutched the dashboard. He'd thought wild horses weren't anything to worry about—but what about this stampeding Bronco with his brother in charge?

"Will you slow down before you get us pulled over or killed?" Dale muttered.

The red speedometer needle moved a fraction to the left, but not enough, and the car sped farther away from home and closer toward the angry sky.

Dale winced. If he didn't make it back in time, a twister would seem like a mild stirring of dust compared to the maelstrom that lay in store for him.

Chapter 3

"Ben, I'm telling you, this is just another bust," Dale muttered, glancing at his watch one more time. "No tornado's going to hit today. It's time to turn around and head for home." The tail of the funnel they'd seen had been sucked back into the cloud bank before it even formed. Maybe it had all been a shared illusion fostered by lack of sleep.

"You never know what the future holds. If a storm chaser gave up that easy, we'd never get a decent shot." Relentlessly Ben kept his foot on the gas and continued past Millbury to the next town. While he drove he searched the skies ahead, as if to get a bearing on the storm and its movements.

Dale glanced at his watch again. Of the past eight storm chases Ben had gone on, he hadn't spotted a single tornado, though there'd been some great shots he'd taken of a baseball-sized hailstorm while he took shelter under the cover of a metal awning in a park. Tornadoes just weren't all that common. In the five years his brother had been a storm chaser, he'd viewed a sum total of six, often needing to drive for a day or more to reach the location. Some who'd taken up the pastime for as many as ten years had yet to view their first twister. It helped to live in "tornado alley," as one of the locals called their area of Northeast Texas.

On their first sighting of a tornado, Dale had been along for the ride. Neither of them had been looking to chase any storm, and it had caught them unawares. The funnel had been an F-5—a 318 mph monster. Since Ben was a professional photographer, he'd pulled his gear from the back of his SUV. The shots he'd taken of the mammoth twister earned him a spot in the local newspaper, and other photographs he'd sent to a nature magazine. From that day on Ben was bitten by the storm bug.

"Turn the weather radio on," Ben ordered, "and let's find out where this baby's headed."

"You said we were only going through Millbury. Now we're in Canton." As they stopped at a red light Dale looked around him at the buildings of the small town. Ben impatiently thrummed his thumbs on the steering wheel.

"It's only about an hour's drive back."

"An hour's drive?" Dale shook his head. "Ben, I'm getting married in less than three hours."

"Yeah, yeah. I know, I know."

His mind clearly lay elsewhere.

"All right, let me get this straight. You're not giving up this storm chase—again, no more than a bust—and turning the car around to take me back, right?"

"Soon, soon." Ben's eyes searched the dark mass of clouds ahead.

"That's what I thought."

Dale unhooked his seat belt, reached around for his tux laid across the backseat, and opened his car door.

"What the. . .what do you think you're doing?" Ben asked incredulously. "Are you nuts? Get back in here before the light turns green."

"No can do." Dale surveyed his brother. "I'm not about to jeopardize a future with the woman I love just so you can go chase over hill and yon to find a storm."

"I told you, I'll get you back in time."

"There are no guarantees of that, and you've already driven me thirty miles past the point you said we'd go." Dale shot a look behind the Bronco. A beige car had pulled up, though the stoplight remained red. "I better head out. Hopefully, you will remember that you're my best man and be at the church at the right time. If not, I'll get Todd to take your place."

"Have I ever failed you before?" Ben slapped his palm on the steering wheel. "You're being unreasonable. I'll probably be there long before you show. I mean, just how are you planning on getting back home?"

"I'll call someone if I have to, but I *will* be there on time." He slammed the door before Ben could respond. The light turned green, and Dale stepped backward onto the curb. The SUV drove on. Dale noticed Ben shake his head and give him a look in the rearview mirror as if he'd flipped his lid.

Now what?

Studying the nearby buildings, Dale eyed the sleepy little town where he'd made his escape. A rusty white pickup sat in front of a truck stop diner on the side of the street where he stood. Not far from that was a four-pump gas station, the hinged sign offering cut-rate prices in gasoline, creaking as the wind swayed it back and forth.

Trying to decide on the best course of action, Dale inhaled a deep breath. Maybe Ben wasn't far off the mark; maybe Dale had flipped. But he'd made a promise to his sweet Marie, and nothing was going to stop him from seeing it through. Not a tornado, not a crazed brother, nothing.

◆◆◆

"Lynette, that was the best omelet I've had in ages." Marie set her plate on the sink counter and headed back to her chair at the table. "I can't believe I ate so much. I just hope I fit into my dress." She giggled a bit ruefully, eyeing the remnants of food on the platters that she and all four of her bridesmaids and two cousins had devoured. Both cousins possessed angelic voices and were singing a duet before the ceremony.

"Ha, with the way your body seems to absorb the food instead of the fat, I doubt it'll matter much anyway." Stacey, her seventeen-year-old cousin, had been upset about not making progress on her battle of the bulge. Marie noticed she'd just picked at fruit for breakfast and felt sympathetic toward the teenager. Teen years were some of the hardest ones; how well she remembered.

"Has Ricky asked you to the homecoming dance yet?" she prodded gently.

The girl's face flushed but her lips turned up. "He mentioned it."

"Well, good for him!" Marie shared in the girl's triumph. "He's a lot like Dale in that he sometimes needs a push, doesn't he?"

"You can say that again!"

"Oh, speaking of Dale, he called while you were in the shower."

At Shalimar's calm words, Marie whipped around. "How come you didn't tell me then?"

"Guess I forgot." Leaning against the kitchen counter, Shalimar lifted her shoulders in a careless shrug, but her tense expression caused apprehension to puddle in Marie's stomach. Suddenly she wished she hadn't eaten a full plate.

"Something's wrong, isn't it?"

"He didn't say that. He only said to tell you he'd see you at the church."

Still her friend wouldn't look her in the eye and, instead, drained her full glass of pineapple juice.

"Did he say he'd stop by the florist and pick up the boutonnieres and mothers' corsages? He offered to do that since he lives so close." Bogged down with her wedding to-do list, Marie had been grateful for Dale's offer last night. Her own bouquet was silk, something she could cherish for a lifetime, and she'd picked it up last week. Everything had been planned down to the last minor detail. She wanted her wedding to be perfect; anything less wasn't an option.

"Maybe I'd better call the florist and make sure." Shalimar left the kitchen.

Not liking the sound of that, Marie rose from her chair and followed.

Shalimar was already talking to whoever was on the other end of the line, so Marie waited but didn't need to be on the other extension to understand, especially when Shalimar said she'd be there in fifteen minutes. She hung up and turned to see Marie.

Shalimar slapped her hand to her heart. "Girl, you've got to go put shoes on so you can be heard. I had no idea you were behind me."

"He didn't show, did he?"

The fake smile Shalimar gave didn't reassure Marie one bit. "Well, hey, you know he's still got a few hours to go."

"If that's the case, then why did you just tell Dorothy you'd come and pick up the flowers?"

"I just want to be on the safe side. In case he forgets. The man's probably got a lot on his mind."

Marie crossed her arms, determined to act as a human barricade until she got some answers. "Shalimar, what aren't you telling me?"

"It's nothing. Really." She acted even more nervous, as Marie continued to eye her, and fiddled with the belt around her top. "Anyway, I didn't want to upset you, especially since it probably is only nothing."

"So why not tell me and let me be the judge?"

"The flowers—"

"Can wait another few minutes until you spill what you know."

Shalimar expelled a heavy sigh. "Marie, I want your wedding day experience to be a happy one, from start to finish. Why bother giving you information that is probably conjecture in any case, and at the best inconclusive?"

"Okay, that does it. When you start talking like you've already passed the bar, I know something's up. You only sound like a lawyer when you're trying to hide something."

Shalimar rolled her gaze toward the ceiling. "Like I said, it's probably nothing."

"If it's nothing, then it's no big deal. And I want to hear what this 'nothing' is."

The breath that hissed from Shalimar's lips was one of resigned disgust. "Okay, okay. You win. It's just that when Dale phoned it sounded as if he was making the call from inside a car. There's a distinctive sound—like a whirring—that only a car makes."

Marie pulled her brows together. "I don't think we're on the same wavelength. Why should that worry me?"

"Because he's with Ben. And there's a tornado watch thirty miles north of here."

"A tornado. . .I had no idea." Marie closed her eyes, the truth smacking her a shaky blow. Ben, the incurable storm chaser. Ben, who never could take no for an answer when crossed. Ben, who still treated Dale like his little brother, using whatever method was at his disposal to get Dale to come along on one of his jaunts.

Ben, a confirmed bachelor who'd once announced at a dinner party that any man who chose marriage over his freedom was absent a few screws and bolts.

And then there was Dale, who'd missed two weddings already.

Shalimar touched Marie's arm. "Hey, don't look like that. Like I said, it's probably just my overblown imagination at work. I wish now I hadn't said anything, though from the looks of you earlier, you wouldn't have let me out of here until I did."

"You're right about that, and I am glad you told me." Despite her calm words, Marie's thoughts flew in all directions. The next step seemed paramount. "I'm calling Dale. Right now."

Yet once she tried, she got the same response as last time. Ben's phone rang off the wall. Dale's voice mail answered.

Shalimar's grin tried to soothe. "He's probably just running around like a decapitated chicken, busy getting ready for the big event. You need to start getting ready yourself. It's not that much longer till showtime." She picked up a long strand of Marie's newly washed hair. "I can't wait to see what wonders Cynthia will perform with this, especially since she has so much that's good to work with. What I'd give for your curly hair. While she works her miracles I'll make you a cup of hot chamomile mint tea. That should soothe your bridal nerves."

Marie forced a smile. If events were going the way she assumed, it would take a whole lot more than chamomile mint tea to give her any peace of mind.

Chapter 4

Dale wondered again if he was out of his mind for ditching Ben. But what other choice did he have? He still couldn't believe his brother would do something like this to him on the day of his wedding. Then again, maybe he could.

Ben avoided weddings—marriage for that matter. Dale felt he'd owed it to his brother to make him best man since Ben was his only sibling and had helped him a lot in quizzing him on the manuals while he trained to be an EMT. Also Dale suspected that making Ben his best man might be the only way to ensure his brother would even attend the wedding.

The four occupants of the diner regarded Dale as if he were an extraterrestrial—probably because of the black tuxedo slung over his shoulder on its hanger and his otherwise sloppy appearance. Dale directed a smile to the rosy-cheeked older woman behind the counter. The other three men sitting at a table nearby, all who looked like truckers, eyed him suspiciously.

"Mornin'," Dale said. "I was wondering if I could borrow your phone to call a taxi." Mouthwatering aromas of eggs, bacon, and sweetbreads made Dale's stomach pitch from hunger, and he looked at a mammoth platter laden with those items nearest him. As pressed for time as he was, he didn't dare take the opportunity to sit down and enjoy a meal.

The platter's owner, a man with a scruffy beard and plaid shirt, let out a laughing snort. "A taxi? In Canton?" The scrawny young man sitting next to him also got in on the laugh.

"Sorry," the woman said. "No taxi service in town, and I can't let you use the phone for long distance, neither. Only taxi service I know of is in Sunnydale, and that's a different area code." Her eyes were kind, though her news did little to cheer him. "Want breakfast?"

"No time." Dale blew out a long breath. Ironic that the only known cab company was located in the very place he needed to be. He estimated the time from here to there. It had taken Ben over an hour's drive to reach this point. Calling a cab to come all the way from Sunnydale might work, but now that he thought about it, he didn't have much cash on him. Not enough to pay for a taxi at any rate.

"If you could just direct me to the restroom, I'd appreciate it." He felt he should at least put on his tux. Once already the slacks had slid from the hanger and landed on the street. Probably because the material was so silky. At least if he wore the thing, he could try to protect it from getting any dirtier.

She pressed her lips together in a sympathetic gesture. "Restroom's out of order. You can use the one at the gas station next door."

He wondered about that. "Is the area, uh, big enough to change clothes in?"

"You want to change clothes?" She eyed his tux.

"I'm supposed to be at a wedding in a few hours and this thing won't stay on its hanger. I don't want it getting dirty."

"Oh?" she asked, interested. "Who's getting married?"

"I am."

All three men twisted around on their chairs to stare.

"You?" the waitress asked, brows lifting.

"Yeah. And I need to get to Sunnydale before noon. Any chance one of you could give me a lift?" he hopefully asked the table of men.

"Sorry," the bearded guy said. "We're headed in the opposite direction. My boss wouldn't like it if we detoured. I'm on a tight schedule."

"Same goes for me," added the third man, who wore a Rangers baseball cap. "You could check with Jake at the gas station. His nephew is there and might take you where you want to go."

"Okay, thanks." Relief tinged Dale's words and he turned away.

"Wait just a minute," the waitress stalled him. She lifted the plastic cover off a pedestal tray of sweet buns next to the register and, taking a filmy piece of paper, selected one. "For the road. Consider it a wedding present. You look as if you could be hungry." She grinned.

Smiling wide, Dale accepted her generous offer. She was right. Half a bag of salty potato chips and a cup of bitter coffee hadn't done much to stave off his waking hunger. "Thanks, ma'am. I really appreciate it."

"Good luck to you," she called out before the door closed.

In the gas station restroom, he changed into the tuxedo, but left the black dress shoes for later. If he had to do any walking, he preferred his comfortable white sneakers. He got a number of double take glances from two customers and the attendant as he opened the glass door of the main part of the station and approached the register.

"Any chance anyone here could take me into Sunnydale? I'll pay twenty dollars to whoever can. It's all I've got on me."

The attendant, a man wearing grease-stained clothes, eyed his ruffled shirt. "I can't take off work, and my nephew's already left or he could've given ya a lift."

An old man in dungarees and a straw cowboy hat approached from the mini-mart food section of the store. He laid a loaf of bread on the counter, all the while eyeing Dale from head to toe. The man stared at him as if he were wearing a space suit instead of a tuxedo, but Dale decided to give it a try. "Sir, is there any chance you can drive me into Sunnydale? I'd gladly pay for the gas and time lost."

"Only going to Millbury," the man said, pulling out a bill to pay. "Got to take my Myrtle on home."

"Millbury's good." At least it was halfway. "Anything helps. I need to get back for my wedding," Dale explained.

"How's that?" The old man took the sack with his purchase from the attendant. "You say you're getting married?"

"Yes, sir. And I've found myself in a jam, without transportation. My brother took off chasing a tornado."

"That a fact? Well now. . ." He took another long look at Dale. "I reckon you must be tellin' the truth. Cain't see no other reason you'd be all doodaded up like that this early of a mornin'.

116

You'll have to ride in the back with Myrtle, though. I got grease on the seat earlier, and it's sure to ruin them fancy pants o' yours. Upholstery's all tore up, too."

"That's fine, wherever you want me to sit." Dale was just so relieved to find a ride, he wouldn't mind being roped to the roof of the car. "Can I have a sack for my clothes?" he asked the gas station attendant.

The man reached down for one. Dale stuffed his casual everyday wear and nice shoes into the paper sack, then followed the old man outdoors. A green pickup sat near one of the gas pumps.

"Daddy's back, Myrtle." The old man pulled the bread sack from the bag, ripped off the plastic tie, and laid the whole thing in the rear of the pickup. "And I brought you some of that nice white bread you like, for being such a good girl at the vet's."

"Mmaaaaahhhhh!"

In stunned unease, Dale looked past the old man's shoulder and toward the root of the sound. In the back of the pickup stood a live goat.

∽≫≪∽

With two hours and fifteen minutes to go before the wedding, and no sign or word from Dale, Marie constantly battled a whirlwind of conflicting emotions. She'd called Ben's apartment, still getting no answer, then tried Dale's groomsmen. No one had heard from him all morning. One of the guys mentioned that Ben talked about a tornado last night, the words driving home to Marie what she felt must be the truth of the matter.

Dale had gone storm chasing with Ben.

Shalimar and the other bridesmaids tried to reassure her, but Marie wouldn't be comforted. She'd scratched her arms so much that dark pink streaks scaled both of them, and Shalimar gently rebuked her and put cream on them. At least her wedding gown had long lace sleeves so no one could see the damage she'd done.

If there was even going to be a wedding.

"Stop it," Shalimar said, disrupting Marie's black thought. "He'll show."

"How'd you know what I was thinking?"

"Because we've been friends and roommates for years and I know how your mind works. We should get to the church now. There's a lot to do before the big hour hits. Come on."

Marie followed Shalimar to collect her things. She wrapped a bandanna around the soft twist curlers that Cynthia had put in her hair and insisted stay there until the dress was donned once they were at the church. "What if he doesn't show, Shalimar? What if this time is just like the last two times?"

"I don't think that'll be the case."

"But what if it is?"

"Then you'll deal with it as graciously as you did before, with the strength of all your friends to support you." She grabbed her purse off the end table and pulled out the car keys.

Marie pondered Shalimar's words. Yes, she could pretend. Her mother had taught her well how to keep up appearances when the world was falling down. Appearances were always so important to Mother. And Daddy never had met any of Mother's expectations.

"Why borrow trouble, Marie?" Shalimar interrupted her

dismal train of thought. "Instead of wasting elite brain cells worrying about what could happen or might happen, I think you just need to forget all that and concentrate on what's happening right now."

"Wasting elite brain cells?" Marie repeated with an amused quirk of her mouth.

"Yeah. An odd sort of phrase I picked up from my nephew. And I have to tell you, he's excited to play the bass for the reception. His band hasn't had that many gigs."

"The pleasure is all ours. Dale and I liked their sound."

At the memory of that audition, when Dale had stood behind her, his arms wrapped around her middle, his cheek pressed against her hair as they'd swayed from side to side while listening to The Sizzling Cats play their blues/jazzy sound, Marie felt a tear start behind her eye and quickly averted her head. She brushed at her lashes.

"Now then, none of that. Give me your hand."

"Why?" Marie asked, even as she held it out.

Shalimar clasped it in hers. "Because I'm willing to bet you haven't had any kind of spiritual fuel to start your morning. Am I right?"

Ashamed, Marie nodded. She knew better, but from the second she'd woken up, Dale had been uppermost in her thoughts, and time had skied on a downhill course from then on and gotten away from her.

Shalimar bowed her head. "Father, we come to You in the name of our Lord Jesus and thank You for this wonderful day of promise that belongs to Marie and Dale. Please reassure Marie and give her the peace she needs. Help her through this anxious time, and wherever Dale is, help him, too. And please, Lord, just get him to the church on time."

❧

With his eyes closed and the back of his head against the cab of the truck, Dale let his sluggish thoughts slide to Marie, slipping from image to image. Her sunny smile. . .the way the light hit her hair. . .her dark eyes brightening when they focused on him. . .the feel of her in his arms.

A smile on his lips, the mental image of her so vivid, he could almost imagine her warmth now and feel her nuzzling his neck.

Whaaa. . . ?

His eyes flew open. Inches from his, a fuzzy white face loomed, its mouth delicately feasting on one end of his unraveled black tie.

"Ah!" He let out a cry and pushed at the goat, at the same time trying to wrest the black ribbon from its teeth. A struggle followed, but Dale arose the victor. At least he thought he'd triumphed, until he studied the damage done. The wet strip of black was now in shreds.

"Stupid goat," he muttered, giving it a malevolent look.

"Maaaaaaahhhhhhh!" The white bearded lady had the audacity to mock him. And was that a goat smile? It nosed the empty bread sack and began to chew on it.

All through the remainder of the ride, Dale crossed his arms high on his chest and kept his gaze fastened on the goat. He wasn't about to make the mistake of closing his eyes again.

Knowing how important appearances were to Marie, Dale decided he could switch ties with one of his groomsmen. At least the farmer had given him a clean blanket on which to sit, so as not to get his tuxedo dirty. Dale wondered why the blanket couldn't have been used on the passenger seat and guessed the farmer didn't trust a stranger to ride inside. Not that Dale blamed him. It had been a mistake to change clothes, but he was stuck now. If he changed back into his jeans and T-shirt somewhere along the way and folded his tuxedo into the sack, it would get wrinkled. He'd left the slippery metal hanger in the gas station restroom, and it wouldn't do to go to his own wedding looking like a six-foot-one-inch raisin.

Within minutes, Dale saw the sign for Millbury, and the farmer pulled off the road at a crossroads. After exiting his truck, he moved around to Dale.

"This is as far as I can take you." His gaze lowered to the damaged tie as Dale fished for his wallet. "Myrtle do that?"

"Yeah, seems she ran out of bread. I appreciate the lift."

He held out the twenty-dollar bill, but the man shook his head. "Don't seem right to take your money since Myrtle did that." He eyed the goat. "For shame, Myrtle. That wasn't a nice thing to do."

"Maaaahhhhhhh."

The man looked back to Dale. "Shoulda warned you she likes ribbons and shiny things. Let's just call it even. I was goin' this a-way anyways."

"Thanks," Dale muttered as he replaced the bill and crawled from the back of the pickup. As his feet hit the tarmac, he was glad he'd decided to wear his sneakers.

"Good luck with your weddin'. Hope all goes well for ya."

If I ever get there. "I appreciate the well-wishes, sir."

The truck pulled onto a long dirt road opposite the highway. Dale was sure the goat had a gloating expression on its fuzzy face as it turned to look at him and gave one parting, faint, "Maaaaaaahhh!"

"Stupid goat," he muttered before looking both directions down the empty highway. Nothing but grass and trees and sky. At least the sun wasn't blazing down on him, wasn't apparent behind the ash gray clouds at all.

Hoping it wouldn't rain as it had done earlier, Dale puffed his cheeks, blew out a huge breath, and set off on foot for home.

Chapter 5

Marie arrived at the church at the same time her uncle brought her mother, who'd made a special trip from West Texas just for the wedding. Hurrying across the parking lot, Marie approached her mother and the two women hugged.

"I apologize that I couldn't come earlier," her mother said, "but Henry had a business trip and I had to help him prepare for it."

"It's okay. You're here now." No mention of Henry wanting to come, though she doubted her mother's husband would care to see Marie married. He'd made his excuses during the last two failed attempts, also. They'd never gotten along, ever since Marie was fifteen. She'd always hoped Daddy would return to take his rightful place in the family, but after years elapsed she put that childish fantasy behind her. He'd left because he hadn't cared. It still hurt, but she'd come to accept it and the ache was now only a dull memory.

Everyone had left her in one way or another. When she was six, her beloved grandmother was taken suddenly, struck by a car. As a child, she could only reason that Grandma had left her. Then her father left. And later, in a sense her mother left, to marry another man and move them all to another town. Neglecting Marie, her mom doted on her new family. So on her seventeenth birthday, Marie left West Texas and moved back to Sunnydale and in with Shalimar. It had been difficult finishing high school and holding down a job to help pay rent, but she'd done it. Just as she was paying for this wedding, she and Dale both.

"Why the gloomy face?" her mother asked.

Marie forced a smile, not wanting to discuss her fears, knowing Mom would begin to harp on the reason for Dale's tardiness yesterday and apparent absence today as a sign that he didn't care and that Marie was about to be stood up a third time. Instead she aired another thought that had been worrying her. "It looks as if it might storm."

Her mother studied the sky. "I noticed. Not a good sign. Unhappy is the bride whose wedding day is filled with showers."

A superstition Marie didn't need to hear now or at any time. She moved to her uncle and smiled, giving him a quick hug. "Uncle Joe. Thanks for bringing Mom and for taking off work to come today. It means a lot to me."

Red flushed his face when she pulled away, and he averted his gaze. He'd always been so shy. "Aw, weren't nothin' any other red-blooded American boy couldn't do."

Marie smiled at the familiar phrase her grandfather also had used. Of all her family, she wished she could have gotten to know her uncle better.

"Excuse me for interrupting," Shalimar said from behind Marie, "but we need to get you inside and ready for the big event. Hello, Mrs. O'Brien."

"Hello, Shalimar." Marie's mother coolly studied the tall, slim brunette in a disapproving manner.

Wanting to smooth the waters before they roughened further, Marie quickly spoke. "You're right. I wouldn't want anyone to drive by and spot me in my curlers." She tried for a light laugh but it came out tense.

"Why you didn't go to a salon and get it professionally styled is what I can't understand," her mother said. "But I guess working at that computer store you don't make all that much money, do you?"

That stung, though Marie would never admit it. She had never asked her mother's husband for a penny. He'd made it clear years ago that he didn't give handouts. Yes, she and Dale had needed to scrimp in areas while planning their big day, but the results satisfied Marie. And at least they didn't lose anything from the last two failed attempts, except for the deposits.

"Cynthia just graduated from beauty school. She has loads of talent, and I like her style." Marie took Shalimar's arm and hurried up the walk with her. At the moment, she didn't need one of Mom's critical remarks. Not when her mind and heart were in such turmoil over Dale.

She wondered what he was doing right now.

❧

One foot in front of the other. That was the only way he was going to get there. And each step brought him closer to home.

That's what Dale kept telling himself as he continued walking the deserted stretch of highway. Three cows from a field of them to his left stood close to the wire fence and chewed their cuds, watching him as his sneakers thudded across the damp pavement.

Great, an audience.

Feeling their brown eyes never leave him, he turned in irritation. "Don't you have anything else better to do?"

They continued to stare, as if he were some unfortunate creature to be pitied. He shook his head in disbelief. Now he was talking to the cattle, imagining what was going through their heads?

He really did love animals. He and Marie even had discussed getting a dog from the animal shelter. But today the four-footed variety of beast was getting on his nerves. These were no pre-wedding jitters. These jitters were more of the "Will there even be a wedding?" shakes.

If he had to move heaven and earth, sod or roadway, he would get there on time. He wouldn't disappoint Marie again. He looked up at the sky. "I sure could use some help down here," he said. "A private plane landing on the highway maybe?" By the calculations on his wristwatch, he'd need to fly if he was going to get there by noon. "Or how about bringing a race car driver down from the local speedway to give me a lift?"

He let out a self-disgusted laugh, knowing he was to blame for everything. Unwise decisions made for unexpected problems. He'd brought this all on himself and now would have to deal with it. He couldn't expect God to bail him out of his own mess.

It began to sprinkle.

Terrific. That was all he needed.

About the same time that thought slammed across his mind, he heard a faraway motor and the whishing of tires on tarmac. Looking over his shoulder, he caught sight of a blue sedan coming his way and felt a moment's relief.

That is, if the driver stopped.

He understood the dangers of hitchhiking. But desperate times called for desperate measures, so he held out his thumb.

The car whizzed past, then came to an abrupt halt, brakes squealing, about twenty yards ahead. It reversed until it came alongside Dale. The passenger window went down, and Dale found himself face-to-face with a young woman, her hair in a long red ponytail.

"Whatcha doin' all the way out here in the boondocks dressed like that?" she asked in greeting.

"Trying to get to Sunnydale. Can you give me a lift? I'll pay you twenty dollars for your trouble. That's all I have on me."

"Sure, hop on in. I'm going that way, too."

Relieved, Dale did so. Before he could buckle his seat belt, she took off with another squeal of tires.

"I'm Janie, by the way," she offered as an introduction. "So what takes you to Sunnydale?"

"My wedding."

"No joke? You're getting married today?" Her head turned his way as a pink bubble expanded from her mouth. She popped the chewing gum and faced front again. "That's really cool. So, like, what's your name? I guess since I'm giving you a ride, I should at least know that."

"Dale." Now that he sat inside her car, he studied her closer. Not the young woman he'd thought, the remnant of baby fat on her face placed her more at sixteen. Suddenly he wasn't so sure about this arrangement. *He* was safe, of course, but still felt uncomfortable by how the situation would be looked at, not that anyone was around to do any looking. But he was a stranger—a man—riding with a kid.

"Janie, just how old are you?"

She hesitated. "Eighteen."

Eighteen wasn't so bad, he guessed. Dale stared out the windshield and at the spots of rain clouding the glass, then studied the speedometer. "Don't you think you're going a little fast? Speed limit's sixty, and it's started to rain again. You don't want to hydroplane or anything—skid."

"Aw, don't worry. These tires are good. Poppy just put brand-new ones on." She picked up a large paper cup that Dale now noticed sat propped between her jean-clad thighs. Taking a hefty slurp from a straw, she grimaced. "Man, they make these things so thick you can't get anything out of them. Would you take the lid off for me?"

"Sure." He took the cup at the same time she began to search on the dashboard for something.

"You like rock?"

"Not really. I'm more into jazz."

"Jazz, huh?" She didn't sound impressed. "Well, you'll like this. It's sorta got a jazzy, pop, rock sound." She slid a cassette into the tape deck. Out of the speakers boomed raucous sounds of stacatto drums and squealing guitars. Dale jumped back at the sudden onslaught.

"You think you could turn that down some?" he raised his voice to be heard over the noise.

"Sure, whatever." Frowning, she turned the volume about a half decibel lower.

His eyes darted to a bend in the road ahead and then to the speedometer again. "Janie, if you want to make that turn you're going to have to slow down." One hand still on the shake, he slapped his other to the dashboard, "Janie. . ." His grip went white-knuckled. He'd seen too many accidents caused by negligent driving in his years as an EMT. "Slow down!"

"Yeaaaaahhhh!" she squealed like a maniacal speedster as they took the turn too fast. "We're flyin' now!"

Frozen in dread, Dale stared, eyes wide, mouth hanging open. Somehow they made the turn on all four wheels, but half of her chocolate shake spilled over onto his trouser leg.

A siren wailed behind them, red lights flashing. Glancing in the side view mirror, Dale spotted a police car racing after them from its hiding place behind a billboard, where it was probably set up as a speed trap.

Dale felt his stomach bottom out.

⟨⟩

Marie felt literally sick to her stomach with nerves. She loved her mother, but Mom had put on her "critical hat," criticizing the bridesmaid's dresses, the decorations in the church, everything. Worse, Dale still hadn't called. No one had even heard from him. Not the groomsmen, not the florist, not anyone. And failing to get in touch with Dale by phone only upped the level of her anxiety.

From the other side of the room, two of her bridesmaids, Rachel and Lena, avidly watched as Cynthia unrolled the curlers from one side of Marie's head. Marie frowned at her reflection in the mirror. She couldn't help thinking history was repeating itself again. Despite her warning to Dale, he'd obviously stood her up yet again to go chase a storm with his brother. Well, she wouldn't be foolish enough to go through with this wedding fiasco a fourth time! If Dale didn't want to share a life with her, she could take a hint. She wondered if she should call the whole thing off right now. At least if it came from her, it would be less humiliating. Still. . .the thought of canceling the wedding made her heart crack like aged concrete; she just couldn't do such a thing. She loved him too much, insensitive jerk though he was.

Peering into the mirror's reflection of the window, she noticed how the sky had taken on a greenish gray cast. Evidently, no sun would make an appearance, though normally she didn't mind overcast days.

She again looked at her face, her memory tripping back to last year. She'd gone along on one of Ben's and Dale's storm chases, all the way to Dallas, but there'd been no tornado, only a "bust" as Ben had called it. However, later they'd seen a small dust funnel on the side of the road, and Dale asked Ben to pull over. Dale had given her a pair of goggles to protect her eyes, also donning a pair, and the jacket she'd worn protected her arms from getting stung from the miniature whirlwind. Holding hands, they approached the swirling dirt that ended a few feet over their heads and stepped through the dust devil, hair flying every which way. Marie had been amazed to look from inside the funnel at the whirling brown walls, while standing safe inside its center. Just enough room for both of them to stand, face-to-face, in each other's arms. Dale had even kissed her, a slow tender kiss that added to the fantastical moment she'd shared with him.

Would there be other moments like that? The togetherness, the oneness, the sharing of dreams? Her shoulders slumped and she shut her eyes.

Someone knocked at the entrance to the bride's room. "Excuse me. . ." Her uncle again tapped on the door that stood ajar and pushed it open another notch. "Don't mean to bother no one none but, Marie, your purse has been singing quite a tune out here. Sounds like one of them TV show reruns."

Marie stood and approached him as he held out her tote bag. She'd forgotten that she'd dropped it on a chair in the foyer, just outside the bridal room. "My cell phone." Dale had programmed it to play the theme from *Mission Impossible*. What their wedding was proving to be.

Glad the mechanical tune continued to play, she fished in the inside pocket for her phone and flicked it open and on. "Hello?"

"Marie, it's Ben."

Her throat constricted. "What have you done with my fiancé, Ben?" She managed to keep a civil tone, her words coming out both light and ominous.

"You mean he's not there yet? I would have thought he would've gotten there by now. It's him I was hoping to talk to. He left his cell at my apartment, and I couldn't remember the church's number, so I called yours."

The tightening worsened until she could barely breathe. "He's not with you?"

"He was. But he insisted we'd be late if I didn't turn around, so he got out when we were in Canton. I'm heading back now."

"Got out? What do you mean he 'got out'?" She tried to stay calm but he wasn't making sense.

"He said he'd find a way back home. He hoofed it, I guess."

Stunned, she could only stare ahead though she had no idea what she looked at. "You mean he *walked* back?"

"Unless he hitched a ride." When she didn't answer, he added, "Don't worry. He's a big boy and has been in worse situations. I'm sure he's fine."

A hundred thoughts went flying through her head, half of them curt responses she'd like to hurl at Ben right now. The foremost reply in her mind being what she thought of a man who would go storm chase on the day of his brother's wedding.

Closing her eyes, she pressed her fingers to her forehead, rubbing the taut skin there. Somehow she managed to rein in her tongue before she accused him of planning the whole thing to prevent their marriage. Hysterically she wondered if he'd also planned the traffic jam in Missouri two months ago. Or had stationed the pregnant woman in her van off the side of the road last year.

"You still there?"

Hanging by a thread.

"Thanks for letting me know what happened. I have to go now." She flicked off the phone without a good-bye. The man didn't deserve one.

"Trouble?" her uncle asked from the doorway where he still stood.

Marie told him, though she kept her words low since she heard her mother's voice in the next room, talking to someone.

"You want I should go look for him?"

"You'd do that?" Hope flared inside her.

"Sure. It's the least I could do for my favorite niece."

"Thanks, Uncle Joe. I'd really appreciate it." Moved by his kindness, she stepped forward to kiss his cheek, which turned tomato red, as did his whole face. Making a decision, she pulled the straps of her tote over her shoulder. "And I'm coming with you."

His gaze went over her hair, half of it still in curlers, half of it springing around her shoulders. "Uh, you sure you should? You look like you have some more fixin' up to do."

"But you don't know what he looks like, do you? You've only seen him once."

"Can't say I remember him all that well."

"I'll go with him," Cynthia volunteered.

"You have to finish fixing her hair," Lena said suddenly from the other side of the room. "And we're running short on time. I'll go with him."

"Thanks, Lena." Marie felt relieved. "Not a word to Mother, please." She switched her focus to her uncle. "Neither of you."

Her uncle nodded in understanding and left the room with Lena following.

Marie understood the logic about her not going but wished she'd been the one to go with Uncle Joe. Yet she did need all the prep time she could get, or she would be the one arriving late to the altar. And she'd never been late a day in her life. Assuming they would find her absent fiancé in time, and there would even be a wedding, that is.

Oh, Dale. Where are you?

Chapter 6

O ne phone call."

　　Dale nodded at the officer and followed him to a wall with two pay phones, muttering his thanks when he gave Dale the coins needed.

He hesitated before sliding them into the slot and punching buttons. What would he say to Marie? How could he ever face her? More importantly—would she believe him? Three questions that settled what felt like the weight of a two-ton truck on his shoulders.

There was no answer at her place. She must already be at the church. Where he should be. Sighing, he studied his wristwatch. It would take a miracle to get him out of this fix and at the altar in time for his wedding. Maybe it was better Marie hadn't answered. Thinking fast, he called one of his groomsmen.

"Yeah?" A male voice came over the line loud and clear.

"Todd," Dale said in relief. "Listen, I need you to do me a favor. Where are you?"

"At the church, where you should be. Where are you, anyway?"

"It's a long story. Is Marie there?"

"Yeah, she's in the back getting ready with all the other girls. Wanna talk to her?"

"No! I mean, not yet."

"You okay, dude?"

"Yeah, great." Dale released the air through his teeth. "No, not great. I'm in jail."

"Jail! You've gotta be kidding."

"Shh! Don't let anyone hear you."

"No one knows who I'm talking to," Todd's voice came back, and Dale heard the creak of a door opening then closing with a click. "Okay, I'm outside now where no one's listening. How'd you land in jail?"

"I hitched a ride with a wannabe speed racer who not only didn't have her license, but was also underage and shouldn't have been behind the wheel. She was taking her poppy's car out joyriding."

Silence lengthened on the other side.

"You there?" Dale asked impatiently.

"Yeah. Not that I don't think this story sounds like it has great possibilities for one of the most interesting tales I've ever heard in my entire lifetime, but why'd they put you in jail for that? Especially if you weren't the one behind the wheel."

"She had a shotgun in her trunk."

Dale could hear the sound of Todd's breathing.

"For hunting possum. She told the police it was her brother's. Of course the fact that she's the mayor's granddaughter isn't helping *me* much. I think they assume I'm some sort of depraved psycho for jumping in the car with a fifteen-year-old.

Or that we'd hatched plans to become a modern-day Bonnie and Clyde." The last he said sarcastically; his wit came to the forefront at the oddest times.

Todd whistled through his teeth. "Man, when you find trouble, you really know how to dig yourself in deep."

"Yeah, yeah." Dale didn't need this right now. "So can you come get me?"

"Marie's uncle Joe is already heading that way, though I don't suppose he'd know to stop at the jailhouse."

"Marie's uncle is coming here?" Dale softly knocked his head against the wall three times. "Then Marie knows I took off storm chasing with Ben this morning, and that I left him in Canton."

"She knows. Ben called her."

Great. The one thing he'd hoped she would never find out. "Whatever you do, don't tell her I'm in jail. I'll never live it down if you do. Especially if her mother hears."

"You know me better than that, buddy. Hold on a sec. Someone's coming."

Dale waited several seconds then heard a clicking sound, followed by a buzz.

No! He'd been cut off. And he hadn't even told Todd what police station he was in. With no money to make another call, he pulled the receiver away from his ear, stared at it, then hung up and looked toward the sergeant's desk where Janie had been sitting earlier.

The sergeant crooked his finger at Dale, motioning him forward. Dale swallowed hard. At least they weren't escorting him back to that cheerless cell. And the handcuffs were off his wrists now, too.

Abuzz with activity, the station looked small, with few officers present. The sergeant leaned back in his chair and narrowly eyed Dale as if he had all the hours in the day to kill. Dale's eyes flicked over the wanted posters plastered on a nearby bulletin board, and he could almost imagine his mug up there. The sergeant eyed him as if he were the evil Pied Piper, luring children away from the safety of their homes with his pipes.

"Janie tells me you were walking on the highway and she gave you a lift." The officer eyed Dale's tuxedo, with its goat-chewed ribbon, chocolate-splotched pants, and scuffed not-so-white sneakers. "I'm not even going to ask why you're dressed up like that, because what I really want to know"—here he leaned forward—"is what you were doing tagging along with someone who's barely more than a child."

"Hers was the only car that drove by." Dale shifted and muttered the rest, "And I didn't want to be late for my wedding."

"Excuse me?" The officer lifted shaggy brows. "Did you just say your wedding?"

"Yeah. I'm supposed to be married at noon." And with that admission, the whole story came tumbling out, from the start of Ben's storm chase until the police handcuffed him and put him in the back of their car, along with Janie.

The officer's expression lightened considerably during the retelling, and Dale could see his mouth twitch a few times as if he tried to contain a laugh or two.

"Well, now. . ." He thought a moment, staring at his desk blotter before looking up at Dale. "Janie pretty much cleared you, had nothing but good to say about you. And we ran a check on your license. You're clean."

Dale could have told him that, but only nodded.

The officer stood and shrugged into his jacket. "I can't see holding a man in custody on the day of his wedding." He chuckled as if unable to control himself. "Fact is, we've got nothing to hold you here."

"So I'm free to go?" Dale asked, hardly daring to believe it.

"You're free."

"And Janie?" He couldn't help but wonder about the poor kid's fate, even if she had brought it all on herself.

The officer frowned at Dale's interest. "Her grandfather'll take care of her. It's not the first time she's had a brush with the law." He slipped on his cap. "I can take you as far as the city limits if you want a ride."

"That would be great." And more than Dale ever hoped for.

❦

Marie stood by the window, staring out at the stormy landscape. Nearby trees rustled with the wind, the sound of which Marie could hear even inside the building. A couple of boys pedaled past on their bicycles, struggling against the swift current of air. The grass had browned and could use a good rainstorm, but why today of all days? Marie sighed, hoping Dale wasn't fighting the elements like those two boys were. She no longer felt angry about his absence; instead she was fearful for his safety.

She couldn't understand what had compelled him to leave Ben's car and walk back to town. Surely if he had asked, Ben would've taken him home. Marie tilted her head to the glass in thought. Then again, maybe not. Storms were Ben's first love. He and Dale shared similar traits in that they were both stubborn and when they each wanted something, they did all in their power to get it. Remembering the first time she and Dale met, Marie felt her lips turn upward in a wistful smile.

A junior in high school, she'd been waitressing at the local steak house and had approached the table where Dale sat.

"Have you decided what you'd like?" she'd asked him.

"Yes, I have." He'd folded the menu closed and looked her straight in the eye. "You."

"Excuse me?"

"I'd like to take you out on a date. To the movies. Friday night. Seven o'clock."

She gave him an openmouthed stare. The guy was drop-dead gorgeous, with his wheat-blond hair, heart-stopping green eyes, and slim, athletic build. Though she'd seen him in the school halls and noticed him, his delivery wasn't the type to win any awards with her. They'd never been introduced, though she knew his name.

"Sorry, I'm not on the menu." She tried to say it coolly, hoping he didn't notice the catch in her throat or the whispery way her words came out in a rush. "If you'd like something—on the menu—please let me know so I can take your order. Otherwise, I have other tables to wait on if you're not ready yet."

He raised his dark brows in half amusement, half interest, obviously not deterred. Once he made his order, she hurried away, almost asking another girl to switch tables with her. But something had prevented her from doing so. Dale intrigued her, even if his come-on had been a bit on the arrogant side. He hadn't pushed her when she'd brought his steak burger to the table, only asking her if she liked her classes and what teachers she had, but she'd been so nervous she almost let his glass of soda slip from her hand while setting it before him. At school, she'd heard only good comments about him and his family, newly moved to the area. A lot of the girls wanted to date him.

After that first encounter at the restaurant, when Marie later caught sight of Dale, she stared long and hard, intrigued, until he glanced her way. Then she abruptly fixed her gaze elsewhere. The next time he asked her out, after a youth meeting at this very church, she didn't hesitate to accept. And from their first date on, they'd been inseparable.

She had emotionally supported him as he'd trained to be an EMT, and he'd done the same for her when she went to night school to learn computer design. Two years after graduation, their talk evolved into marriage, as if it was the natural course to take. Yet had she pushed him into something he didn't really want since he'd never proposed to her?

"Marie, I just have to tell you again, I love this necklace, though you didn't have to buy us another gift since you gave us the bracelet the first time the wedding was on." Talking all the while, Lynette came through the door and stopped suddenly. "Are you crying?"

Shalimar came in behind her and darted a look at Marie.

Marie swiped at the telltale tear. "Just taking a stroll down memory lane." She looked at Lynette and smiled. "I'm glad you like it. I knew they'd be darling with your lilac dresses, and really, you gals have stood by me through so much and been through this three times now. I wanted you to have something more to show my appreciation." When she'd seen the teardrop pearl necklaces on a spring sale, she'd splurged a little and grabbed four of them up for her three bridesmaids and maid of honor.

Shalimar put a supportive arm around her shoulders. "He'll be here, Marie."

Marie let her eyes close for a second. There was no fooling her best friend. "I want to believe that. . .I need to believe that. But I've been thinking, and maybe I pushed him too hard. Maybe he wasn't ready to commit but didn't want to hurt my feelings."

"A guy who'd leave his brother's car and set out on foot over thirty miles to get back to you sounds ready to me."

Hope flickered. "You think so?"

"Yes. Dale's one of a kind." Her gaze searched Marie's face. "I think the devil's playing mind games with you, and with your history of being hurt by others, you're listening to every lie he's throwing your way."

Shalimar could be right about that. Almost everyone close to her had left in some way—her grandmother through physical death, her father through abandonment, her mother through emotional detachment.

"Let's pray about this. You can never have too much prayer." Shalimar looked over at the other bridesmaids. "Lynette, Rachel, want to come join us?"

"Of course," Rachel said and both girls followed. All of them clasped hands and bowed heads.

"Father, we come to You in the name of our Lord Jesus," Shalimar said. "Please protect Dale, wherever he is, and bring him safely back to Marie. And, Lord, give her the assurance she needs. She's been hurt by so many people in her lifetime. All of those who were close to her have hurt her so much, and she's lost the ability to trust. Help her to grasp just how much Dale really does love her, and heal the hurts of the past so she can go on to fully enjoy the present. Amen."

"Amen," three echoes came.

Her heart already lighter, Marie looked up to thank Shalimar and caught sight of her mother standing in the doorway watching them.

"Mom?"

An expression of hurt on her face, her mother turned and hurried away.

Chapter 7

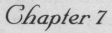

T he sergeant dropped Dale off at a fast-food restaurant near the boundary line of Sunnydale with a parting line of, "Next time be more careful who you catch a ride with."

At his tongue-in-cheek statement, Dale gave a wry nod. "Yeah, you can bet I'll do just that, sir."

"Congratulations on your wedding. Hope you make it home in time."

"Thanks for giving me that chance. I hope so, too."

As the squad car pulled away, the sergeant lifted his hand in a casual wave, which Dale returned. Well, that went better than he'd expected. Now what?

Frustrations of the day had taken a toll on his stomach, creating a gnawing emptiness. He needed a quick bite before he could figure out the next step. He still had his twenty, and decided to buy a hot dog for the road. With the change, maybe he could hunt up a pay phone and call Todd again to come and get him. He wasn't taking any more chances at accepting rides from strangers, that was for sure.

The restaurant was empty of customers, and in no time, he returned outside, cradling his hot dog while bringing it to his mouth and taking a bite as he walked. He loved mustard but didn't want to risk spilling any on his crisp white shirt, so he ate it plain.

A horn honked not ten feet behind him. He almost choked on the bite he'd just swallowed and nearly dropped his soda.

"Hey, Dale—that you?"

Relief whistled through him to turn and see Mac Avery. Dale often took his car to Mac's garage for repairs.

"I can't tell you how good it is to see you." Dale strode toward the driver's side. Mac had just exited the drive-thru and regarded Dale through his rolled down window.

"Pretty spiffy duds you got on there."

"Yeah. Listen, can you give me a ride to my church?"

"Sure thing. I came into Millbury for some parts, but I'm headed back home now."

"Great. Those are some of the best words I've heard all day." Dale hurried around to the passenger side and slid into the car.

"That wind sure is picking up speed," Mac said, popping a french fry into his mouth.

"Yeah." Dale smoothed the hair out of his eyes, glad to be out of the gust, which had picked up velocity in the past ten minutes.

"So what brings you way out here, dressed like that, and why're you on foot?"

Dale couldn't blame Mac for being curious. Once more the story of his morning came out, between his polishing off his hot dog and drink.

"Wheeeeww." Mac let out a long whistle. "Sounds like one of them cornball romance movies my girlfriend likes to watch. The kind where reality takes a loooong vacation," he added with a grin.

Dale couldn't agree more. The day seemed like one never-ending Technicolor nightmare, even if it had been studded with its strange, almost comical moments.

Minutes of relaxed silence passed. Beneath the hood, a sudden *clunkety-clunk* rattled the car.

"Uh-oh." Mac studied the gauges. "I need to pull over."

They had left all buildings far behind, and Dale looked along the deserted stretch of road they were on now. "What's wrong?"

"She just needs a little fixin' up. I spend so much time working on other people's cars, I'm afraid I haven't paid the attention I should to my own."

"You're kidding." Dale couldn't believe this was happening.

"Not to worry. I can fix 'er up so she'll get us home. Carburetor just probably needs a whack or two."

A *whack* or two? This was the man he'd entrusted with his car?

"I plan to spend all Saturday working on her."

Which didn't help matters now; still, if Mac hadn't been in Millbury for parts, Dale wouldn't have gotten this far. That is, if they both didn't end up needing to hoof it.

God, please, please, please. . .I know I said on the road earlier that I made mistakes from the moment I opened my eyes this morning, and I probably deserve this whole miserable day. But Marie doesn't. I love her and don't want her to suffer for my stupidity. Please, God, just get me to the church before it's time for her to walk down the aisle. That's all I ask.

❧

With twenty minutes till curtain time, Marie felt restless. If Dale didn't show, it would be curtains for him. No... She took a deep breath and let it out slowly, ousting the thought with it. Knowing Ben as she did, she doubted Dale was to blame for the present set of circumstances. Though maybe an nth of the blame was his. Still, after Shalimar's prayer, Marie had calmed somewhat and was ready to forgive, even if his actions didn't make sense. Ben, too, though forgiving him would prove harder. What was important was that she knew Dale had tried to reach her, even leaving Ben's vehicle in an attempt to get home.

Her gaze traveled around the parking lot full of cars. Hearing a distant rumble, she looked to the sky and frowned. Deciding she wanted a closer view, even if she was decked out in her wedding gown and veil and someone might see her, she left the window and bypassed her bridesmaids, who were finishing up last-minute preps to hair and face. She headed toward the hallway that led to the rear door.

"Where are you going?" Shalimar asked.

"I just want to check on something."

She sensed her bridesmaids behind her as she opened the door that led to the back parking lot. The hot, sticky air held an electric sort of waiting current, as unusual as the yellow-grayish green cast to the dark clouds.

"Whoa," Rachel said. "I've seen that kind of sky before."

So had Marie. She hadn't heard Sunnydale was supposed to get hit with inclement weather, but then she hadn't listened to the forecast this morning in her rush to get to the church.

"Whose car is that, the one driving into the parking lot?" Rachel asked.

"I don't know, but it sure is a clunker," Shalimar said. "Just listen to the rattling of that engine."

Marie turned her head to look. As the car came closer, her heart jolted to a stop, then beat with a frenzy. "It's Dale!"

Without thinking twice, she grabbed the sides of her skirt and flew down the two steps to meet him as he exited the passenger side of the car and waved thanks to whoever sat inside. The car drove off.

"I'm so glad to see you!" Marie threw herself into Dale's arms, holding him tightly. She buried her face against his coat, then wrinkled her nose and pulled her head away. "You smell like a barnyard." Her words were curious, but she didn't release her hold from around him now that she finally had him there with her.

"Probably because of Myrtle." His own arms tightened around her waist and he dropped a kiss to her lips. "I can't tell you how good it is to be with you again. I never thought I'd make it."

Marie's mind remained stuck on the first track. "Myrtle?"

"The goat I rode with. My first ride." The expression in his eyes softened. "You sure look beautiful."

She blinked at his answer of a goat, dropped her gaze to his tuxedo. Her eyes widened. "What happened to your tie—it's in shreds!"

"Myrtle got hungry. I already plan to get another tie from one of my groomsmen. For me to go without one might not look so good since I'm the groom, but I think it would be okay for Todd." He looked beyond her and nodded. "Hello, Mrs. O'Brien."

Marie barely noticed that her mom now stood in the door-way, she was so busy taking inventory of his appearance. "Your shirt!" She looked agape at what seemed to be a splotch of black grease covering the ruffles on his chest, near the buttons.

"Mac—the guy who brought me here—had car trouble. I helped him so we could get here faster. See, I did make it in time, Marie. I promised you I would, though for a while there I gotta admit I wasn't sure it was gonna happen."

A smile colored his voice, but she had pulled away to look down even farther. Her eyes widened. "And what happened to your slacks?" A huge brown stain covered one pant leg.

He looked down, too. "Oh, that. Janie—my second ride—was speeding and took a turn too fast. Her shake dumped all over me. I guess I should have cleaned up in jail, but they didn't give me a chance."

"Jail!" Dazed, she shook her head. "You were in *jail*?"

"Oops. I wasn't going to admit that one, at least not yet. It's kind of a long story, and I'll tell you the whole thing after the wedding. Promise. It'll be my third time to tell it today." His mouth suddenly dropped open. "My shoes! Oh, man, I left my good shoes and my other clothes in Mac's car." He darted a look toward the church entrance, where Mac had long since driven off, and groaned. His eyes reminded her of a hopeful little boy as he turned back to face her.

"Would you mind too much if I married you in my white sneakers?"

With a slight disbelieving shake of her head, Marie smiled. Once, his question would have made her upset, but now she was just so glad to see him she didn't care if he wore neon orange flip-flops.

Before she could open her mouth to tell him so, a warning siren shrieked through the air, startling them. They both shot a look to a heavy cloud a few miles away, its dark bottom boiling and writhing, and saw a vortex had formed. With an eerie, loud hissing the funnel crooked a gray finger toward the earth in their direction. Standing as if she'd been turned to a statue, Marie could only stare in horror.

Chapter 8

"Take cover—everyone!" Dale called, at the same time grabbing Marie's wrist and running with her. About fifty yards away, the storm shelter entrance stood behind the church, a basement with no windows. They followed the others over the spongy lawn toward it. But Dale could see that with Marie's awkward dress and high heels they weren't going to make it in time. A shallow ditch lay to the side, near the fringe of trees flanking the property. He pulled her along with him, then pushed her down into the ditch at the same time throwing himself on top of her, to protect her as much as he could.

Crazed lightning flashed across the sky like continuous flashbulbs popping. Thunder rumbled and the rain beat down hard. What sounded like a thousand freight trains approaching at full speed invaded his ears. Still he could hear Marie softly cry beneath him, "Please, God. Save us!"

Silently Dale added his own petition, turning his face to her neck and hair, covering the back of her head with his hand and arm as much as he was able. Small sticks and papers flew in a crazy dance all around them. A soda can shot high into the air, lifting, lifting. Something hard struck his leg, bruising it, but he didn't think the injury was major. The wind stung his eyes, and he shut them tight. His ears, however, couldn't be protected from the cacophony. Glass shattered. Metal groaned. Wood creaked and gave. Marie let out a yelp of pain, and Dale assumed the only reason he could hear it was because his ear was so close to her mouth.

Please, God, protect Marie. Don't let any harm come to her. Let us have a chance at a life together. Please. God, she means the world to me. He'd never realized just how true that was until today.

Dale wasn't sure if seconds or minutes passed—all measure of time seemed to be sucked up in the maelstrom—but as suddenly as it started, the wind died down to nothing and calm returned. Opening his eyes, Dale sucked a breath into his lungs then crawled off Marie. The tornado had sped off in a northeasterly course through a cornfield, now miles away from them.

"You okay?" His gaze assessed and took inventory as he helped pull her to a sitting position. A smudge of dirt covered her cheek, and an angry red scratch raced across her neck. Her face was almost white, her eyes huge, like dark smudges, but she moved easily and Dale didn't think he'd done any real damage.

"Just a little bruised, I think," she whispered.

"Sorry for tackling you."

"Are you kidding?" She pressed her fingers against his jaw. "You saved my life."

He helped her climb out of the ditch, and together they surveyed the damage. Torn-up earth to their right showed where the twister had touched down and run a path not fifty feet from where they stood. Cars in the parking lot had been pushed against each other by the force of the mighty wind. About a hundred feet away, a yellow rocking chair stood upright in the middle of the field. A tree was missing, and others had been uprooted and lay on their sides.

With relief, Dale noticed that the church stood like a harbor, rock solid and strong, with only a back window broken. He moved with Marie toward the building. Guests filtered into the parking lot, some acknowledging the wedding couple, all going to check out the damage to their cars and town or observe the retreating tornado, which as Dale watched was suddenly sucked back up into the clouds. *Thank God.*

Marie's mom came hurrying out the storm shelter door, her gaze spinning frantically around. When she saw Marie, she took off at a run toward her and pulled her into her arms.

"Oh, my baby," she softly cried, repeatedly sweeping her hand down Marie's wet veil as though it were her hair. "I was so worried."

"I'm okay, Mom. Really."

Dale heard the surprise in Marie's voice. He knew she'd never thought her mother loved her all that much. Not wanting to spend a moment away from his fiancée's side, but deciding the women needed time alone, he laid his hand upon Marie's shoulder and gently squeezed.

"I'm going to join the others and check out the damage," he said. "There might be some who need my help. I need to find Mom, too. I saw her head for the shelter, so I'm sure she's okay. But I'm not leaving the immediate area without telling you first, just so you know."

Still cradled in her mother's arms, Marie gave him a sideways glance of gratitude, her eyes shining with love for him, her smile trembling, soft.

Dale forced himself to leave her and walked off, then stopped in his tracks. His brother approached from across the street, waving his video camera in his hand. Dale walked faster to close the distance between them.

"You look like you've been through it," Ben said in greeting. "Should have stuck with me. I told you I'd get you back in time."

Dale thought it best not to answer.

"Got some great footage. Who woulda thought I'd capture a tornado practically in my own backyard? An F-2 unless I miss my guess."

"Yeah, who woulda thought? Guess we never would have had to leave Sunnydale after all." Dale's tone came across borderline curt. Catching sight of his petite mom gathered in a circle with some other women, he felt a moment's relief to see she was okay.

Ben hung his head, sheepishly. A character trait that didn't fit his devil-may-care brother at all. "Listen, I'm sorry about this morning. I really didn't think you'd bail on me like you did. You must love her a lot to do something that crazy."

"Yeah, I do." Dale regarded his brother. Ben had never experienced true love with a woman, the heart-bonding kind, so he couldn't understand what Dale felt for Marie. Dedicated to bachelorhood, Ben often told Dale he'd rather go through the years as a hermit than be chained to one woman for eternity. Yet now a wistful sound edged his words, leading

Dale to believe that all was not as it appeared and Ben's former declarations didn't match what he really wanted.

"So, am I still your best man?" Ben spoke the words in jest, but his expression remained serious.

Ben had put him through a lot of misery today, but he was still family. Dale clapped a hand to Ben's far shoulder and gave him a quick one-armed hug. "Sure, but the tornado might make us have to postpone again. I just don't know right now what's what."

"You've had to do that a lot, haven't you? Postpone."

"Yeah. More's the pity."

Ben nodded twice, as if preoccupied, then looked Dale straight in the eye. "Truth is, I thought maybe those other times you got cold feet and were looking for ways out."

"Nothing doing. I don't want a way out." Ben's admission shocked Dale. If his own brother who'd known him a lifetime thought that, then it wasn't so surprising Marie also had doubts concerning Dale's feelings. "I love Marie so much, sometimes it hurts. This may sound corny, but she's what makes my world go round."

"I think I'm actually beginning to envy you." Ben's eyes were dead serious.

"Someday you'll find the right woman. You just have to keep your eyes open. And now and then it's better keeping your mouth shut, too," he added, only half joking.

Ben shrugged and the two men continued to walk across the parking lot strewn with branches and other debris. The tornado siren had quit, only to be replaced by other sirens of emergency vehicles in the distance. They met up with a few wedding guests, and Dale was surprised to see one of the bridesmaids, Rachel, on the opposite side of the street, squatting down to offer aid to a young girl. A thin line of blood marred the girl's pale forehead, against which Rachel blotted a handkerchief. Dale approached, his brother in tow. Rachel looked up, glad to see him.

"Dale! Good. Can you take over?"

"Sure." Dale dropped down on one knee in front of the wounded teen and quickly surmised that she was in emotional shock, evidenced by her dilated pupils, irregular breathing, and the pallor of her face. Her hair dripped with rain; her eyes dripped with tears. She looked no more than fourteen years old.

"I w—was just out riding my bike," the girl said in shuddering monotone, "when I heard the tornado come. I jumped off my bike and h—hid behind that tree. My bike's gone. I coulda been on it." Her voice rose, trembled.

Hiding behind a tree wasn't a good safety measure, but Dale knew it was more important to keep the girl calm rather than give her constructive criticism. "You're okay. Soon I'll have you fixed up and you'll feel even better. This is what I do for a living. Fixing up people. So you're in good hands."

A smidgen of relief touched the girl's eyes and the weak smile she gave him.

"What's your name?" Dale asked.

"M—Monica."

"And are your parents home, Monica?"

"No, they're both at work."

Rachel stood. "Anything more I can do to help?"

"Yeah. Go ask Pastor if he has a first aid kit. And call this in while you're at it. Right now the emergency team will have their hands full meeting the needs of the community, but we should still report this. Also, be sure and tell them an EMT is at the scene but without equipment. Bring back plenty of water and cups. You can pass those out to anyone who needs it."

"Gotcha." Rachel turned to go.

"I'll come with you," Ben offered. "You'll need help carrying all that."

Surprised, Dale glanced at his brother. He couldn't help but notice the spark of interest between the bridesmaid and the bachelor, and smiled, then turned to the wounded teenager, all the while speaking to her in light, reassuring tones as he did his job.

∞

"He's a good man."

Marie turned from studying the damage to the property, knowing she needed to go help, too, but not sure where her efforts could best be used. She stared at her mother in surprise, noting her expression looked both sincere and uneasy.

"I mean it, Marie. Any man who'd go through all Dale did to be here today deserves an award. You're blessed to have him." She lowered her gaze to her polished nails, running her thumb along their edges. "I wasn't always a perfect mother. I'm not sure I was even a good one. I'm often hyper-critical of people and the way they do things."

Flabbergasted by her mom's confession, Marie scrunched her brow in uncertainty. "Why are you saying all this?"

"I heard that prayer Shalimar prayed over you, and I know

your friends must feel the same way you do."

"Mom—"

"No, let me finish." Her stance grew more fixed, bolder. "When your father walked out on us, I was hurt, barely able to cope. But I was wrong to speak of him the way I did—and in front of you. After hearing Shalimar's prayer, I realize now the mistakes I made."

"I'm not sure I understand."

"Honey." Her mother took gentle hold of her upper arms then dropped her hands back to her sides as if unsure. "Trust is earned, and Dale has more than done that by his actions today. But people still make mistakes—he'll make mistakes. I'll make mistakes. You'll make mistakes. No one's perfect. You can't judge others' love for you by one failure, or even two. I guess you're not really supposed to judge them at all." She gave a careless little sniffle, blowing air through her nose. "I'll admit, I was hurt when I heard Shalimar and your friends talk about how all those closest to you have hurt you. I suppose I never cared for Shalimar because you left home to move in with her, despite my objections. And I've made no bones about that. But I can see she's a good friend for you. I'm glad you have her."

"Thanks, that means a lot to me." Marie had never heard her mother unload like this.

"I'm just sorry that you don't feel you can trust me now, that you're afraid I'll pounce on you or put Dale down. Otherwise you wouldn't have felt the need to withhold from me the information about Dale's problems in getting here today." At Marie's gasp of surprise, her mom explained. "I overheard two girls talking in the restroom about your uncle going to look for

Dale, and one warned the other not to let me know. When I really thought about what they'd said, I saw Shalimar was right. In my own pain, I wounded you and made you an enemy. And for that I'm sorry."

"Never an enemy, Mom." Not sure how else to respond, Marie gave a helpless shrug. "But it's okay. I know you had a hard time of it in those days."

"No, it's not okay, and I shouldn't have excluded you after I married Henry, either. I never meant to; it was just such a new life, being a lawyer's wife, with new responsibilities, everything had to be so perfect, entertaining his friends, throwing parties, and I didn't have the time I used to have—"

"Mom, it's okay. Really." Marie wasn't sure how much more she could handle before she collapsed into a pool of tears filled by hurts of the past.

"You're right." Mom sighed. "Today's your wedding day. I shouldn't be dumping all this on you."

"I sincerely doubt the wedding's still on." Marie wondered how her mom could even think such a thing, in the wake of what just happened.

Her mother looked around as if just noticing the area had been hit by a tornado approximately ten minutes ago. "Oh, right. I guess this does put a damper on things. Maybe tomorrow will work out better for you."

Marie couldn't help but smile. Mom might be overcritical at times and somewhat unrealistic, but she did have a good heart. Moving forward, Marie gave her a quick hug.

"What was that for?" Astonishment widened her mom's eyes.

"Just because." Her smile matched her mom's. "I'm really glad you're my mother." She sobered. "But now I guess I should pitch in and see what I can do to help. I'll need to change clothes first. Can you help me out of this dress?"

"Of course." Her mom looked pleased that Marie had asked, and Marie felt a twinge of remorse for excluding her from helping to plan the wedding. At the time, Marie had thought her mom wouldn't be interested.

In the bridal room, Marie went through the cumbersome task of removing all her finery, soaked and heavy from the rain, then dried off and donned her casual clothes. Five minutes later, as her mom hung up the wedding gown, Marie headed to the door. A tap sounded on the outside before she reached it.

"Marie? You in there?"

At the sound of Dale's voice, she opened the door, a smile rising to her lips. Even with his tuxedo grimy, his tie a tattered mess, and his whole appearance more rumpled than when he'd arrived at the church, he was candy to her eyes.

"Can I talk to you alone for a minute?" He pointedly looked at her mom, smiled.

She returned it. "You two go on. I just want to hang these things up so they don't wrinkle any more than they already are. And I'd like to try to see what I can do about getting those dirt stains out. You both have a lot to discuss, I'm sure."

Marie silently agreed. Today's entire experience had taught her a hard lesson. She needed to say what had been running through her mind while she'd changed clothes, no matter how difficult it was for her. For Dale, she must do what was right.

Chapter 9

As they walked to the rear door, Dale looked at Marie. "We do have a lot to discuss, don't we?" They stepped outside. The sun made a weak entrance through the gray clouds, as if struggling to regain its throne. The faint shimmering rays felt welcome.

"Yes. I'm so grateful for the man you are and for your love. I love you so much, Dale."

His brows arched. "Then you're not mad about earlier? About all this?" He waved a hand around the area.

"Well, of course I'm not happy we got hit with a tornado, but it's helped me to see things a lot more clearly. Blew away some of the cobwebs, so to speak."

"Oh? How's that?"

She faced him and took hold of both his hands. "I realize now that sometimes I've blown things out of proportion and been too structured, believing everything has to go a certain way for it to succeed or hold any special meaning. I've learned today that outside influences can and do interfere, and anything less than my expectations doesn't necessarily mean a person is unworthy of my trust. Or my love."

"Wow. You learned all that through a twister?"

She laughed. "You bet." Despite the circumstances, she felt strangely lighthearted, as if removed from what was happening around her. For the first time she understood the term about being at peace even in the midst of a storm, or in this case, the aftermath of one.

"Know what I learned?"

She lifted her brows expectantly.

"Never wear a tuxedo till you get to the church. Never ride with hungry farm animals, and never, under any circumstances, get in a car that has speedway racing stickers plastered all over the back bumper."

She chuckled. "I can't wait to hear about your morning, and I know we need to talk, but shouldn't we go help the others?" Marie wanted to avoid what she had to say as long as possible.

"No need to. Except for that girl I just bandaged up, no one else was hurt in the area. Damage is minimal—not counting that big field over there, which apparently is the main path the twister took. Only a farmhouse and barn got smashed, a few roofs got ripped off, but from what we and others have learned, all other buildings are standing and there are no fatalities."

"Oh, Dale, that's wonderful. Praise the Lord for that!"

"I also talked to Pastor Carmichael. He's eager to go ahead with the ceremony. Truth is, now that he's finally got us here, I don't think he wants to let the opportunity slip by again, tornado or no tornado." One side of Dale's mouth crooked upward. "Since the church is still standing, and the guests for the most part have stayed, I second the motion. Let's get married."

She blinked, stared. "You're kidding, right?"

"I've never been more serious in my life."

"But our clothes!" She thought about the dirt and grass staining her skirt. Her veil was also torn. Cynthia did have a blow dryer, which could dry the material as well as her ruined hairstyle, but surely Dale was joking.

"We can get cleaned up, and what we can't clean we'll ignore. I'll trade ties with Todd. Or we can switch to our street clothes. I really don't care what we wear, so long as I get to spend the rest of my days with you. When I thought I wouldn't be here in time, I felt sick inside, since you'd told me this was my final chance at tying the knot."

His words made her prickle with guilt and reminded her of what needed to be said. "Dale, about that. I'm sorry. I was just upset. I didn't mean it. I'll wait, as long as you need me to. I was wrong to give you an ultimatum, and I feel we should postpone the wedding to a day when you're ready, too. The last thing I want is to make you feel pushed into doing this."

"But I am ready, and I don't want to wait." His eyes twinkled, and Marie's heart gave a little lurch. Whenever he got that look she knew to prepare herself for a shock.

He took hold of her left hand—and dropped to one knee, staring up at her.

"Dale, what are you doing?" She tried to pull her hand from his, but he tightened his hold. She looked around self-consciously, glad to see everyone was too busy to pay attention to them.

"Something I should've done long ago, and you reminded me I never did do." With his other hand, he gently covered hers that he clasped. "Marie, you're the wind beneath me and what keeps me going when I want to give up and quit. You're the reason I get up in the morning, hoping to spend time with you, to see your face. I've loved you ever since high school, and I'll go on loving you until all our hair goes gray or falls out or both."

Shyness gone, she bit back a smile. His poetic words touched her, and his inborn, inadvertent humor drew her to him all the more.

He shook his head slightly. "You know what I mean. Marie, if I have to go through another day like this without you, I'll go nuts. But with you beside me, as a part of me, I can tackle anything. Say you'll marry me. Today. Now."

She studied the sincere hopefulness shining from his clear eyes, the slackness of his expression as he waited, his faint smile. His wasn't the most eloquent of proposals, but it was all she desired, and a symphony to her ears. Time schedules, a myriad of details to be met, flawless attire—none of that seemed to matter anymore. She, like most other women, had always longed for the perfect wedding, but how better to describe perfection than it being all about true love? The joining of two hearts and souls as one, in and through Christ Jesus—that was all that truly mattered. The rest were just little extras, here one day, gone the next. But their love was big and would last a lifetime. She no longer had any doubts about that.

"Yes," Marie whispered. "I'll marry you whenever you'd like."

Dale quickly stood to his feet and enfolded her in his arms. From behind, they heard Dale's twelve-year-old cousin say to someone, "Um, am I missing something here? Isn't that why we came today, 'cause they're gettin' married?"

Dale laughed, Marie with him, and both turned to look at his two young cousins who'd come up behind them. "Right you are, Donna," Dale enthusiastically agreed. "And thank God He got me to the church on time!"

⌾

Reception in full swing, Marie heard Dale groan when Ben approached the microphone. He aimed a few jokes about the "three-times-is-a-charm wedding" at his younger brother, who took them well. He then spoke of what a great guy Dale was and how blessed he was to have Marie, wishing both of them a good life. Before Marie had a chance to recover from that shock, Ben dedicated the next song to his "newly wed but never thought we'd get there brother," a look of mischief on his face. The musicians grinned the wedding couple's way, and began playing the rousing old show tune from *My Fair Lady*, "Get Me to the Church on Time."

"Why are you smiling like that?" Dale asked Marie, his smile just as wide.

"Am I smiling?" She slid a forkful of bridal cake between his lips and chuckled when the white and lilac frosting smeared the corner of his mouth. With her cake napkin she brushed it away. "Your brother really isn't such a bad guy. I noticed Rachel seems to think so, too." She glanced to where the couple was dancing in a comical way. Ben was no dancer like Rachel, who'd taken both tap and ballet, but she was laughing at his antics, going along with all the awkward spins and fast twirls he led her into.

"Yeah, pretty amazing how fast they honed in on one another."

165

Marie studied Dale. "But to answer your question, I've been replaying those words we spoke: 'to love and to honor, in sickness and health, forsaking all others as long as we both shall live.' "

"I do."

"So do I." She didn't think she could be any happier than right at that moment. A third of the guests had needed to leave, to check on their homes and family, but those out-of-towners who hadn't been personally affected by the tornado had stayed. As well as those who'd called their homes and neighbors to learn all was well. And all was well.

Despite the storms that blew their way, she had finally married the man of her dreams. The third time really was the charm. And so much more had happened in these past hours, as if God was mending the tears in Marie's life, just as the people would soon clear away the debris and put their town in order again.

Before the ceremony, which had taken place a little less than an hour ago, her mom fixed Marie's torn veil with her handy travel sewing kit. As she'd sewn the gauzy strips back together, both women talked as if they were old friends. In those twenty minutes, Marie felt closer to her mom than ever before. Even Henry called on her mom's cell to wish her a happy wedding, a gesture that stunned Marie. And strangely enough, though the women were different in personality, Dale's mom and Marie's mom were getting along as if they'd been best friends for life. Marie looked over the reception hall to the far table where they, along with another interested guest, pored over childhood photographs of the bride and groom from the albums they'd each brought from home.

"I cringe to think what pictures Mom might have put in there," Dale said, following Marie's gaze. "I guess I should've checked to see if they passed inspection first."

"You were a beautiful baby," she soothed. "I loved the picture of you all muddy from the creek with only your Snoopy boxers on."

Dale groaned. "She put that in there?" He looked at his tux, which he'd cleaned up as best he could but which still bore faint traces of grease on the shirt. "Guess I haven't changed all that much," he said wryly. "I'm still a mess."

Marie thought him the most handsome man at the reception. "To tell the truth, I hardly noticed."

They stared deeply into one another's eyes, a message that couldn't be vocalized linking them, heart to heart. The band switched to a slower song, and Marie smiled. "They're playing what they did when we first auditioned them."

"So, beautiful, you wanna dance?"

"With my favorite guy in the whole world? I'd love to."

On the ballroom floor, Marie linked her arms around Dale's neck while he did the same to her waist. Slowly they swayed as one and stared at one another, nearly oblivious of the other couples dancing around them.

"I still can't believe you went through so much to get back here today," Marie said softly. "What made you keep it up and not quit, Dale? Even if it was just about what I said last night, that was a lot for one person to go through. I probably would've given up after the goat ate my tie."

"I almost did give up, in jail, but I just couldn't do it. This was too important. You're too important." He snuggled her closer, pressing his forehead to hers. "You never pushed me into marriage, Marie. I went into it with my eyes wide open." He grinned. "I guess you could say I was blown away by love."

His words made her feel alive yet at the same time cosseted in dreamlike softness, and she looked up at him in adoration.

The sudden sound of the guests' spoons clinking against crystal glasses in unison made Marie's face warm as she realized what this particular wedding custom meant. The ringing continued, other spoons joining in the clinking, as everyone there eyed them in expectation.

Dale smiled. "They're asking us to do something."

"Yes."

Anticipating the moment, Marie turned her face upward as Dale lowered his mouth to hers in a warm, tender kiss. The guests applauded and a few whistled through their teeth. Yet, lost in each other, neither Marie nor Dale paid the slightest bit of attention to them.

PAMELA GRIFFIN

Award-winning author Pamela Griffin makes her home in Texas, where, thankfully, she's only viewed tornadoes from a distance. Multi-published, with approximately thirty novels/ novellas, she loves to spin Christian tales of romance and gives God the glory for every amazing thing He's done in her writing career. She invites you to drop by and visit her Web site at: Pamela-Griffin.com.

Hurricane Allie

Rachel Hauck

Dedication

Thanks to Christine Lynxwiler for friendship, late-night chats, and honest critique of this story.

To my mom, Sharon Hayes, who taught me to wake up singing.

Prologue

Believing God has brought them together
Allie Jane Seton
and
Kyle Montgomery Landon
Invite you to agree with them
As they covenant with God and each other
In holy matrimony
Saturday, August Twelfth
Five o'clock in the evening
New Life Church
Vero Beach, Florida
Black Tie Requested

Chapter 1

Vero Beach, Florida, July 29—Saturday, 6:00 p.m.

Allie Seton was getting married. The thought shot an icy tingle over her scalp and made her toes curl into the worn places of her favorite flip-flops.

In less than two weeks, she would be Mrs. Kyle Landon, the Princess Bride.

But right now she sat on the deck of her beachfront home, watching the white-capped waves lap against the shore. Next to her, sipping a fruity drink, was her best friend from junior high, Kendall Smith.

"So, how's it feel?" Kendall asked, using her straw to spear a piece of pineapple.

Allie wrinkled her nose with a smile. "Amazing."

"Remember how we used to make believe we were getting married? We'd dress up in your aunt's old bridesmaid dresses and hum the wedding march. We were what? Twelve? Thirteen?" Kendall squinted at Allie, the afternoon sun shining in her eyes.

Allie laughed. "Twelve. And we air kissed our pretend grooms." She pulled her sunglasses from her eyes. "Here, you could use these more than me."

Kendall slipped on the shades with a thank-you and a giggle, sounding like she was twelve again. "We were such dreamers."

Allie reclined against the back of her beach chair. "I suppose I still am."

With a sigh, Kendall agreed, "Me, too." She speared another piece of fruit from her glass. "I thought you were nuts when you stopped dating in high school."

"You and the rest of Vero Beach High," Allie said with a grin. "But after the fiasco with Jeff Grant in tenth grade, deciding not to date was easy. I nearly flunked all my finals. One day I looked myself in the mirror and said, 'Allie Seton, you should respect yourself more.'"

Kendall's lips twisted with a smirk. "I should've listened to you and done the same thing."

"I've never regretted it. Dating wasn't worth the emotional hassle and in a way I preserved my dreams. I still believed there were a lot of good men out there."

"Then along came Kyle. Can we clone him?"

Allie shook her head. "No, he's uniquely mine. But you could up your standards a little, Kendall."

"What's that supposed to mean?" Kendall made a wry face.

"You don't have such a great track record with men," Allie said.

Kendall pinched Allie's arm.

"Ouch." Allie laughed and jerked her arm away. She pointed at her friend. "You know I'm right. Remember that rogue guy you followed around our freshman year at FSU?"

"Oh, please, you know I was temporarily insane."

Allie hooted. "I'm not sure you've recovered."

"Speaking of 'remember that guy?'" Kendall sat forward with a sudden laugh. "Remember that guy who kissed you in the middle of the FSU-Miami football game our senior year?" She slapped her leg with a hoot.

Allie moaned. "Yes, I do. There I am, on a beautiful football Saturday, enjoying the game and the crowd, and I look down and there's this guy, staring at me with this—this—grin on his face."

"You flirted with him."

"I did not."

"You waved," Kendall accused.

"Well, he waved at me." Allie adjusted the straps of her sundress with an exaggerated huff.

"He must have crawled up twenty rows of fans just to taste your lips." Kendall was still laughing. "Your expression was priceless."

Allie grinned at the memory. From time to time, she wondered about the man who'd kissed her and followed her out of the stadium, begging her for a date.

She never saw him after that, well, at least not that she knew of, anyway. The sound of his voice, the contours of his face, and the color of his hair were all locked away as unmarked memories.

"I guess he was really sorta sweet under that obnoxious exterior and long hair," Kendall said.

"I don't even remember what he looked like," Allie said.

Kendall set her empty glass down on the deck beside her chair. "So, Kyle's everything you dreamed of when you left the dating game to wait for the newlywed game?"

"Yes, he is, flaws and all." Allie couldn't stop her wide grin. "I can't imagine marrying anyone but him."

Kendall tipped her head toward the sun. "I'm so jealous I can't stand it. But I love you, so I'm more happy for you than jealous for myself. Oh, hey. Let me see your ring." Kendall sat up and held out her hand.

Allie's heart skipped a beat and she tucked her left hand under her leg. *Just say it, Allie.* She hesitated then said, "I don't have a ring."

Kendall whipped off her sunglasses. "What? No ring?" She sounded incredulous.

"He couldn't afford one, but we—"

"No ring?" Kendall echoed. "How could you say yes without a ring?"

Allie fidgeted, squeezing her leg with her left hand. "I love him. It was the right thing to do."

"Ha! What kind of man asks a girl to marry him without a ring?"

"Kendall," Allie said in protest, giving her friend a steely gaze. But Kendall's soft smirk told Allie she was only joking. Allie swatted at her. "You sound so convincing."

Kendall fell against the lounge chair with a sigh. "You know," she said, "if a guy like Kyle comes into my life, I'll buy *him* an engagement ring."

Allie laughed. "Oh, right. You would not. I know you too well."

They bantered back and forth on the subject of engagement rings until Allie's older sister, Jewel, stepped through the dining room's French doors. "Kendall, come help me do this."

Kendall straddled her lounge chair and stood. The ocean's breeze lifted and twisted her curly dark hair. "It's shrimp, Jewel, just drop them in the water and let 'em boil."

Jewel made a face. "That's exactly what I want you to do."

"Girl, I never knew you to be so helpless."

Allie grinned as her sister and friend went inside, arguing about boiling shrimp. When they were gone and the deck was quiet, Allie's thoughts drifted to Kyle.

He'd captured her heart the moment she saw him, standing at the head of the DeLeo & Landon conference table. Her business partner, Eva Drysdale, had bumped into Allie when she'd stopped suddenly to stare.

A few minutes later, Jewel poked her head out the door. "We're ready to eat."

Allie sat up and looked over her shoulder, tucking away her private thoughts of Kyle. "That didn't take long," she said, standing.

"No, about three minutes and *ta-da*, boiled shrimp, ready to eat."

"Good, I'm starved." Allie smiled at Jewel and followed her inside. The air conditioning cooled her warm skin, causing goose bumps to run down her arms.

"Here you go, guest of honor," Jewel said, ushering Allie to a chair decorated with gold and silver balloons.

"This is beautiful," Allie said, glancing at the china-laid

table and women who sat around it. Their eyes reflected familiar souls.

On her right were Mom, Louise Seton, then Grandma Alice, Aunt Rebekah, and two of Mom's longtime friends, Gracie Gunter and Frannie James.

On Allie's left was her matron of honor and cherished sister, Jewel Ingalls. Next were Allie's bridesmaids, Laura and Reneé. Then there was Eva, the tiger woman of their interior design firm. And last but not least, Kendall, her maid of honor.

Allie felt warmed by their presence. Their love was her silk blanket.

Jewel tapped the side of her crystal glass with her salad fork. "We're here to celebrate my little sister's last days of being a singleton."

Everyone laughed and Jewel paused to smile at Allie. "We are so happy for you and honored to celebrate your wedding with you."

"Thank you for being a part of Kyle's and my day." Allie dabbed under her eyes with her fingertips. "It wouldn't be the same without you."

"Don't go weepy on us," Gracie admonished with a raspy laugh, reaching for her napkin. "We have all this food to eat."

"Okay, okay," Allie said, smiling and clasping her hands. "We can eat, but first I want to say thanks to Kendall for coming. She was in Orlando on business and changed her flight home to Lexington so she could surprise me." Allie tipped her head toward Jewel. "Thank you, dear sister, for helping Kendall find her way here."

Jewel tipped her head toward Allie in response. "It's the

least I can do since I used to torment both of you."

Laughter floated above the mahogany table and Gracie slapped her palm on the table. "Let's pray and eat."

❧

An hour later, Allie had eaten all the shrimp and salmon she could hold. She felt content and satisfied, not merely with food, but with life. She loved the voices mingled with laughter around her table. She loved that her wedding was two weeks away. The notion made her stomach turn cartwheels.

Jewel clapped her hands lightly. "Attention, everyone," she said, turning to Allie. "I know you've had two bridal showers already, but we wanted to do something small and intimate, just for you."

Laura and Reneé appeared at her side with silver-wrapped presents and golden gift bags dangling from their fingers.

"You spoil me," Allie said, feeling overwhelmed. For the next ten minutes, she opened gifts of perfumes and lotions, everything to make a bride feel beautiful. She hugged and kissed Mom for her gift of a day at Essence Spa the Friday before the wedding.

"It's perfect," Allie said.

"Kyle won't know what to do with such a beautiful bride," Laura sighed.

Allie's mother winked at the ladies. "Oh, I think he will."

The women chortled while Allie's cheeks burned. "Okay, you all are embarrassing me."

"And now, your final gift." Jewel passed Allie a small box wrapped in gold paper.

Allie furrowed her brow. "Is it from you, Jewel?"

"Open it and see."

Allie gently tore away the wrapping and found a note inside a small velvet-covered jewelry box.

Meet me at the Blue Heron Pavilion, eight o'clock. I love you, Kyle.

⟨∞⟩

Kyle Landon waited for Allie at the edge of the pavilion, squinting to see beyond the flock of seagulls gliding just above the shoreline, waiting for her petite form to appear from the evening shadows. The wind tugged at the open collar of his navy oxford shirt and pressed his beige khakis against his legs.

He'd walked this stretch of beach with Allie from her bungalow to the pavilion a hundred times. The scent of her perfume always floated between them on the breeze, and if he lived to be ninety, Kyle would never forget she smelled of roses and sage.

Their first date had been last January, two days after she walked into the DeLeo & Landon conference room. They had dinner at The Ocean Grill, and afterward she'd invited him to her home for coffee and crumb cake.

"How'd you know crumb cake was my favorite?" he had asked, holding open the passenger side door of his car, allowing her to slip in.

She'd winked at him, a spark of merriment in her green eyes. "You had three pieces during the Hayes complex meeting the other day."

The memory made him laugh out loud. So, she had noticed him. In detail, it seemed. He'd certainly noticed her. In fact, she nearly caused his heart to stopped beating.

From the beach, Allie called to him as she approached, her long, straight hair streaming behind her like mahogany ribbons.

Kyle grinned and jumped the pavilion steps. Sand spilled into his deck shoes and bit at his toes. When he reached Allie, she fell into his arms.

"Did you have a fun evening?" he asked, kissing the top of her hair.

"Yes, I did. Then my sister passed me your note," she said with a laugh, looking up into his eyes. "Are we in sixth grade?"

He grinned and brushed her hair away from her shoulders, running his fingers through the soft strands. "Close your eyes."

"Why?" She squared her shoulders and tipped her head to one side, squinting with suspicion. "What are you up to?"

"Just do it, please," he said, gently pressing his fingers against her eyelids.

She cocked her hip and closed her eyes. "Can I peek?"

"No, but I'll tell you what," Kyle said, pulling a remote from his back pocket. "Let's just get things started." He pointed the controls toward the pavilion. The brassy, mellow sound of Glen Miller's "Moonlight Serenade" filled the air.

Allie snapped upright, inclining her ear. "Are you doing something romantic?" She patted her hand over her heart. "Be still my heart."

"Funny," Kyle retorted. "Very funny." He took her hand. "Walk with me, but no peeking."

"Okay," she muttered, a timbre of emotion in her voice.

Kyle led her by the hand up the pavilion steps, anticipating her reaction to his surprise. He patted the wooden seat that ran around the perimeter of the pavilion. "Sit here," he said.

"Can I look now?" Allie ran her hand along the seat's edge, then sat slowly.

"No," Kyle called over his shoulder as he plugged in the strand of Christmas lights he'd borrowed from his business partner, Jamis DeLeo.

Next, he picked up a box of rose petals and scattered them over the worn wooden floor, then situated two dozen roses on the short picnic table, right in Allie's line of sight.

"Kyle, babe, what are you doing?"

"Hold on." Kyle took one last look around. *Looks good. Show's on, Landon.*

He moved over to Allie and pulled her to her feet. Stepping behind her, he encircled her in his arms and brushed her left ear with his lips. "Okay, now."

Allie opened her eyes. "Oh, Kyle. It's beautiful. . . ." She stopped, covering her mouth with her hand. "Roses. . ."

Kyle rested his cheek against hers. "I wanted tonight to be special."

Allie turned in his arms and touched her hand to his cheek. Her warm touch launched rockets of emotion from his heart.

"What's so special about tonight?"

With a deep exhale, Kyle kissed her, lingering in a moment of love and trust. "I'd better do what I came here to do."

She stepped away, clearing her throat and smoothing the flyaway ends of her hair. "Right."

Kyle slipped his hand into his front pocket and slowly bent

to one knee. "I'm sorry I wasn't able to do this five months ago, but. . ." The melody of "Moonlight Serenade" arched over them as Kyle slipped a sparkling diamond solitaire onto Allie's finger.

Chapter 2

Monday, July 31

Monday morning Jamis DeLeo met Kyle in his office. "Art Chambers called last night."

Kyle set his laptop case on his dark oak desk. It was barely seven a.m. and he needed a cup of coffee—especially if Jamis had bad news. "And?"

If he had a dollar for every hour he'd spent designing condominiums for Art Chambers and the Eventide Development Corp., he could've given Allie an engagement ring in March when he'd asked her to marry him.

Jamis smirked, his arms akimbo. "They loved your ideas and are ready to do business with us."

The news jolted Kyle awake and he smiled a slow smile. "Their condo projects alone will keep us busy for five years."

"Yes, and with the projects we're already working, DeLeo & Landon, Architects, will finally be in the black." Jamis sat in the walnut-colored leather chair opposite Kyle's desk, looking very pleased with himself.

Kyle made a subtle "yes" motion with his fist. "I've been praying for two years for God to bless the business."

Jamis leaned forward, arms propped on his knees. "Well, He has. Now, the hard work begins. Art wants us to meet with his partners."

Kyle unzipped his laptop case and pulled out his palm computer. "I'm game. Allie and I return from our honeymoon on the nineteenth. How about a meeting here on the twenty-first?"

Jamis laughed. "Love has warped your brain, my man."

Kyle eyed his partner. "Your brain could use a little warping."

"No, no, not me," Jamis said, waving his hands. "I'm a certified member of the confirmed bachelor's club."

Kyle started to say something, then changed his mind. It didn't do any good to bring up Lila and the past. He hated to see his friend's heart still bound from a ten-year-old wound. But at thirty-five, Jamis DeLeo seemed content to spend his life working, not loving.

"They want us in New York the week of the seventh," Jamis said point-blank.

Kyle stopped making notes. "The week?"

"We leave Monday, come home Thursday," Jamis said. "Esther's already arranged our flights. You'll be home in plenty of time to walk down the aisle." Jamis stood and leaned on Kyle's desk. "With a signed contract and a huge check."

Kyle shook his head. "I'm getting married that week, Jamis. I can't leave. Allie will kill me."

Jamis walked toward the door with a smirk. "That one-karat

diamond you gave her last night ought to be worth one get-out-of-jail-free."

❧

A little after three Monday afternoon, Allie knocked on Eva's office door. "I'm going for my final dress fitting," she said, peering into her partner's bright office. Large windows faced east and south, letting in the afternoon light.

Eva removed her reading glasses from her nose. "You are going to be the most beautiful bride in Bridedom."

Allie laughed. "Well, as long as Kyle thinks so. But I gotta tell you, Eva, after two months of nothing but salads for lunch, I plan to be gorgeous."

"Nothing but salads, huh? No wonder you're starting to look like Laura Carrot."

"Thank you for *that*," Allie said with a wry twist of her lips. She turned to leave, but stopped. "Oh, by the way, Mom, Dad, Kyle, and I are meeting my wedding planner, Ruby, at the Vandercliff Mansion to sample dinner plates. Would you care to join us?"

Eva pointed at her computer screen. "I'd love to, but I've got to finish these proposals."

"Come on, Tiger Lady, you've been working like crazy on bids all week. Have some fun."

Eva fiddled with her reading specs, scanning the work on her desk. She looked up at Allie. "I guess all this can wait."

Allie smiled. "Good! I'll call you when I'm on my way over." She stared at Eva, then suddenly stomped her heels with excitement. "I'm getting married, Eva. Me!"

Eva rocked back in her desk chair. "I remember that feeling

when I married Spenser ten years ago."

Allie reined in her excitement and leaned against the door frame. "I'm sorry, Eva, I'm being insensitive."

"What? Pish." Eva got up and walked over to the eastern window. "We've been divorced over three years." She glanced back at Allie. "Things will work out better for you than they did for me."

Allie noted that the sadness in Eva's voice lessened a little every time they talked about the end of her marriage. She was healing, piecing her life back together by letting Jesus love her and by pouring her passions into their young company.

"I guess we never think true love ends, do we?" Allie said softly.

Eva pursed her lips and shook her head. "No, but I knew he wasn't right for me. I just didn't want to admit it."

"I guess we can never be one hundred percent sure." Allie looked down at her left hand and ran her finger over the smooth diamond.

Eva shifted her gaze to Allie. "You and Kyle are nothing like Spenser and me. And you have little miracles to confirm your relationship, like the Vandercliff having a last-minute cancellation."

"That was amazing," Allie said. "I've dreamed of holding my wedding reception there since I was a junior bridesmaid in my aunt Rebekah's wedding."

Eva held up her wrist and tapped the wide face of her watch. "You're late."

Allie jumped forward. "Ooh, I am. See you in an hour or so."

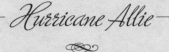

The smell of summer rain scented the hot August day as Allie dashed inside Gigi's Bridal Boutique.

"Darling, you're here." Gigi Bellamont floated from behind the front desk, her long, slender arm extended toward Allie, bent at the wrist as if waiting for Allie's kiss.

"Yes, Gigi, here I am," Allie said, grasping Gigi's fingers and giving them a slight shake.

Gigi called to the back of the room in a sing-song, "Oh, Debby. Bring Allie's dress, please."

Tall, regal Debby stepped from the back. "Hi, Allie," she said, holding up Allie's gown. "Here it is."

Allie gasped with a grin and pressed her hands over her fluttering stomach. "Don't you just love this dress?" She glanced at Debby while lightly brushing the silky white satin.

"The dress is lovely, and the lace cap sleeves are perfect for you, Allie. You have great shoulders," Debby said.

Allie laughed. "First time I've heard that, but thank you." Yes, the dress was perfect. It made her feel beautiful.

Gigi flitted her long fingers over her head. "Darling, you are going to look fabulous, I just know. I have a sixth sense about these things."

Allie stifled a smile at Debby. "Thank you, Gigi."

"Try it on," Debby said. "I want to make sure the alterations are right."

Allie took the dress into the fitting room, feeling as if her whole body was smiling. "Oh, it fits perfect," she said loud enough for Debby to hear.

"Come out and let me see," Debby said.

When Allie stepped out into the main room, Debby sighed. "Allie, you're a princess." She walked around the dress, checking her alterations.

"I've been dreaming of this day since I was a girl." Allie arched around to see the back of the dress in a full-length mirror. I can't wait for my wedding day to get here."

Debby stooped to pick up the edge of the cathedral train and billowed it behind Allie. "You'll be princess bride for the day. Then the real fun starts, your married life."

Allie peered over her shoulder at Debby. She'd been so focused on the wedding, she hadn't thought much about the marriage since their counseling with Pastor Tim had ended in June.

Plenty of time to think about that later. . . .

"Darling, here, try this veil." Gigi strode over with a veil in her hand.

Allie fingered the hem of the lacy veil. "Gigi, this is not the one I ordered."

"But it goes so well with the cathedral train, darling," Gigi lifted her arm to fit the veil on Allie's head.

"Gigi." Allie grunted as the shop owner shoved the veil's comb into her scalp. "I really like the elbow-length veil. This one is too long."

"But this is so perfect, darling." Gigi fluffed the edge of the veil.

Allie glanced at Debby. *Help. Please.*

"Gigi, I think we have something that Allie would like in the back room," Debby said, then leaned close to Allie and whispered, "I can make a veil to match the one you ordered."

"Thank you," Allie mouthed. She slipped off Gigi's veil and rubbed the sore spot on her head. "I'll pay you."

Debby scoffed. "The invitation to your wedding is payment enough. I've been looking forward to your wedding since I met you five months ago. And I love the Vandercliff." Her warm smile comforted Allie.

"That place is fabulous."

"Yes, but girl, you are even more fabulous in this dress." Debby pinched the waistline tighter. "I think you've lost more weight. Let me take it in a little on each side, and make sure those pearl buttons are secure."

Allie touched Debby's arm. "What would I do without you?"

"Strangle Gigi," Debby said with a light laugh. "You can take the dress off now. It'll be ready next week."

Allie headed back to the dressing room, pausing at the door. "Next week. . . I'm getting married!"

Gigi walked over with her tapered hands resting on her narrow waist. "Yes, and don't let that pesky hurricane bother you, darling. They are so unpredictable."

Allie gripped the edge of the dressing room door. "Hurricane? What pesky hurricane?"

❧

Monday evening

Kyle pulled his Mustang into Allie's driveway and parked in the shade of the scrub oaks behind her drop-top Mini Cooper. They'd spent more than an hour sampling entrées at the Vandercliff Mansion, and while the food tasted wonderful, Kyle had been distracted, concentrating more on how he should tell Allie about his trip to New York with Jamis than whether their guests would prefer filet mignon or chicken cordon bleu.

Allie watched him from the wide brick porch of her bungalow, her whole face squinting in the sun's setting light. "Why the frown, Landon?"

He jogged up the steps. "Just thinking." He pulled Allie to him and kissed her.

"You don't like the reception menu, do you?" Allie asked when he released her. "You were so quiet the whole time we were deciding."

"No, no, it's fine. Filet mignon and chicken cordon bleu—a guy can't argue with those choices."

"Okay, if you're sure." She headed inside. "Do you want a soda or something? Coffee?" She kicked off her shoes, then regarded him with her hands on her waist. "Why are you looking at me like that?"

Kyle walked over to her and slipped his arms around her, nuzzling her neck. "I can't believe I found you."

"Found me? Was I lost?"

"No, I was." He took her by the hand to her couch, a deep red color that only Allie could make work in a room.

He gazed at her for a moment, awed that a guy like him was marrying a girl like her. And not just any wonderful girl. But *her*. The girl from the game, the girl with the sublime almond-shaped eyes who smelled like spring roses.

When she walked into the DeLeo & Landon offices eight months ago, Kyle felt as if a missing link to his past had finally surfaced in his present.

Allie smoothed her hand over his chest. "Is everything all right?"

"Yes, fine." He smiled at her. "I have a lot on my mind."

The expression in her eyes grew dark. "You heard about the hurricane, didn't you? I heard at Gigi's."

Kyle nodded. "Yeah, I heard. Hurricane alley might be hit with Hurricane Allie. Funny, isn't it."

"Hurricane Allie?" Allie fell against the back of the couch. "This storm is named Allie?"

Kyle settled against the red cushions. "Yes, first named storm this year."

"Well, it's not funny." Allie jumped up and paced the length of the living room. The fifty-year-old wood floor creaked when she passed by the TV.

Kyle made a mental note to fix that after they were married. "Babe, sit down, I need to talk to you."

Allie joined him on the sofa. "You don't think we're going to have a hurricane, do you?" She gripped his hands. "It would ruin everything."

Kyle peered into her green eyes. "First of all, the hurricane is too far out to predict where it's going to hit. The path projection I saw had it going anywhere from Cuba to Jacksonville."

Allie exhaled. "That's good to know."

"Second," Kyle continued, "we're getting married, hurricane or not."

"Good, because I just spent five months planning the perfect wedding."

"I know," he muttered. That comment didn't help his situation any. While she may be appeased about the threat of a hurricane, she wouldn't be easily appeased when she got the news about his trip. Maybe he should just tell Jamis to go to New York without him. There would be other deals.

"Can you imagine? Wherever that hurricane hits, somebody's wedding will be ruined." Allie lifted her hands to the ceiling. "Lord, please, send it out over the Atlantic."

"Babe, we got the Eventide deal," Kyle blurted his news.

Allie slowly lowered her arms. "What?"

"Jamis and I got the Eventide account," Kyle said, sitting forward, braced for her response.

"Kyle, that's fantastic," Allie said, brushing his cheek with a kiss. "Good for DeLeo & Landon."

Kyle relaxed a little. "This will solidify our business." He paused, adjusting the band of his watch. "But. . .part of the deal is a trip to New York next week."

Allie's smiled faded. "Next week? You can't leave next week. We have wedding stuff to do. Can't Jamis go without you?"

"Babe, I have to go. I'm the architect. Besides, this is our first major account."

"Kyle," Allie started, "certainly they understand you're getting married the next Saturday."

Kyle stood. "I'm not going to plead wedding duty to a bunch of New York investors, Al. This is my career, *our* livelihood, *our* future."

Anger colored Allie's expression. "How long will you be gone? We have dinner with our families and out-of-town guests Wednesday night at The Blackbird. A dinner your parents are paying for."

"I'll just have to miss it."

"Miss it? I can't believe what I'm hearing." Allie rose from the couch. "You're going to just run out on our wedding plans."

Kyle expected her to be upset, but not angry. How could he make her see that building his business was part of building a successful marriage?

"Allie, missing one dinner is not running out on our wedding plans."

"Okay, then tell me who's going to pick up our rings on Tuesday and your groomsmen from the airport on Wednesday?" She jammed her hands onto her hips and leaned toward him. "All of the groomsmen are scheduled for tux fittings on Thursday."

Kyle gawked at her. Normally details swirled around Allie like New Year's Day confetti. "Wow, what happened to my Allie who thought a date book was a prison and a palm computer *stifling?*"

Allie made a face. "This is my wedding, not a dinner date with friends."

Kyle could tell she was about to cry. "I'm sorry, babe, that was rude." He pulled her into him.

She dropped her face against his chest. "I just want you to be here."

"I'll be back before you know it. I'll ask Josh or Wade to pick up Eric and Max from the airport and take them to get their tux fittings."

Allie looked up at him. "What about your tux? The rings? The hurricane?"

"I'll call to get my tux fitted this week, and Josh can pick up the rings. And I'll call the hurricane center and demand they send the storm out to sea."

"I'm serious. You've been through hurricanes before, Kyle. You know they wreak havoc for weeks afterward."

He kissed her forehead. "This early in the season, the storm will probably go north. And I'll be home for our wedding. Don't worry."

"Oh yeah," Allie said with a twinge of sarcasm, "and if not, do you prefer Josh or Wade be your substitute groom?"

Chapter 3

Vero Beach, Friday, August 4

Channel 12 Eyewitness News was on with "The Morning Crew."

Anchor Laura Lindberg said, smiling at the camera: "Well, Tom, what's the latest on our first hurricane of the season?"

Tom Delaney, standing in the weather center, answered: "Looks like Hurricane Allie is gaining strength. Right now, it's still a category one, but the National Hurricane Center is predicting Allie will be a category two next week."

Allie stood in front of the TV with a cementing sensation of dread as Tom Delaney described a satellite view of the Atlantic. *Please, Lord. . .*

Computer-generated images moved the hurricane toward southeast Florida. *Oh, Lord, not here.*

Now at the anchor desk, Tom Delaney advised: "Stay tuned to Channel 12 for an up-to-date severe weather forecast."

Pointing the remote at the TV, Allie pushed OFF. Tom and Lauren were a little too cheery for her as they asked their loyal viewers to stay tuned.

Lord, what will I do if there's a hurricane? She meditated on the situation, walking into the kitchen for breakfast.

When the phone rang, Allie knew it was Kyle. They'd argued again about his New York trip Thursday evening. He went home around midnight, tired and frustrated, and without a resolution.

"Hi," she answered softly.

"Hi," he echoed. "How are you this morning?"

"Fine. Did you see the news?"

"I'm watching as we speak," Kyle answered.

Allie dropped two pieces of bread into the toaster. "It's too early to tell. Chances are Allie won't strike Vero Beach."

"That's what I'm thinking," Kyle said.

"Okay, so forget hurricanes. You're still going to New York the week of our wedding, aren't you?" She pulled a knife from the silverware drawer. The Christofle flatware was an early wedding present from Grandpa and Grandma Seton.

"Babe, please don't start this—"

"Is this how our married life is going to be? Work first, Allie second?"

"That's not fair."

Allie winced, knowing it wasn't, but she was caught in her emotions. "No, I guess it's not."

"I'm doing this for us, Allie. I have to put some time and energy into building a business our family can depend on," he said.

"I understand that, Kyle. I run a business, too, you know."

"I know," he said softly.

"It's just you picked the week of our wedding to strike it rich." She smiled at her own words, knowing Eventide set the dates. Not Kyle.

He laughed low. "Right, I told Art Chambers, pick the week of the seventh. I need to get away from my crazy fiancée," Kyle said with a teasing lilt.

"Aren't you the funny man this morning," Allie said, peering into the toaster. It was old and sometimes burned the bread if she didn't watch it.

"You have so much to learn about morning-Kyle," he said.

His intimate tone sent a warm rush through her. "Oh, there's a morning-Kyle?" Her toast jumped up, perfectly crispy and brown.

"Yes, and he's very entertaining."

"Good to know." Allie dropped her toast on a plate and sliced off a pat of butter. She thought for a moment. "Kyle, don't you think it's slightly odd that the season's first hurricane coincides with the week of our wedding?"

"No, do you?" His words were compact and forced.

"I don't know. . . Do you think it's some sort of sign? It makes me wonder if—"

"We should get married?"

"Doesn't it make you wonder a little?" Allie held the butter knife over her toast and a melted glob dropped onto a crumbly corner.

"No. A hurricane isn't a sign we shouldn't get married. Let's not lose sight of the big picture, Allie. Marriage is about more than the wedding ceremony. It's about you and me building a life together."

Allie bristled. "Don't lecture me. This is my only wedding, Kyle. I can never get it back. If it's ruined, it's ruined for the rest of my life."

"Sweetie, I understand. But the bottom line is we love each other. Next Saturday is one day. We're going to have thousands of days together."

"If there's a hurricane, our friends won't be able to come, roads will be closed, and we'll lose power and phone service. The church and the Vandercliff might be damaged."

"Allie," Kyle said, in a low, serious tone. "Do you want to marry me?"

Allie carried her breakfast to the table by the bay window. A pelican flew into view and glided over the water's surface. "What kind of—"

"Do you want to marry me?"

Allie pictured the church sanctuary, bathed in candlelight, and imagined herself walking down the aisle on her father's arm while two hundred black-tie guests looked on. She could almost hear Pachelbel's Canon playing. "Yes, I want to get married."

❧

Tuesday, August 8, 10:00 a.m.

The sign taped to the outside of the door was crooked. Allie tipped her head slightly to read Gigi's loopy handwriting.

Closed for Hurricane Allie
Sorry, darlings. I'll return soon.
Gigi Bellamont.

200

Allie tapped her fist against the glass door. "Gigi! They don't even know where the hurricane is going to hit yet—and I haven't picked up my dress."

She wanted to cry. But what good would that do? Gigi was gone and tears wouldn't magically open the door.

"She's done gone," a man's voice called from behind her.

Allie turned to see a lanky, leathery man walking her way, hitching up his jeans and sporting a crooked grin.

She pointed to the sign. "Yes, I see."

"She's as fidgety as they come. She tol' me, 'Gigi's terrified of hurricanes, darling.' " He tried to imitate the French woman's lilting accent, but Allie thought he still sounded like a Fellsmere redneck. He jerked his thumb over his shoulder toward the curb and his beat-up old work truck. "I wanted to cover her windows and doors, just in case."

Maybe he... Allie squared her shoulders with hope. "You wouldn't happen to have the key to her shop, would you? Oh, please... My wedding dress is inside and I need to pick it up!"

He chuckled. "Nope. Don't have no key." He sauntered back to his truck.

She scurried after him. "Please, I'm desperate."

The man shook his head and snapped open the truck's tailgate, his expression fading from merriment to sympathy. "Wish I did, fer yer sake."

He slid a piece of sheet metal from the bed and walked over to the shop. A Pigpen-like cloud seemed to surround him. "Maybe Gigi's instincts were right for once."

Allie wrinkled her nose against the odor as she fumbled in her purse for a business card. "If you find you do have a key, call me. Please. I could pay you for your time." She held out her purple card.

He waved it away. "Done told you, I don't got no key. Wouldn't want one if she offered it to me. I've seen her attack folks like a hungry dog. No siree. No key for me."

Allie kept her hand with the card extended until he walked past her for the third time without glancing her way. She tucked the card inside her purse and said, "Thank you, I appreciate your time."

⁤⁤⁤⁤⁤⁤∽

New York City, 8:00 p.m.

Kyle buttoned his starched white shirt while watching the city from the window of his midtown Manhattan hotel. Twenty stories below, New York bloomed under the evening lights.

He never imagined a city could be so enchanting. Allie would love it here. Art Chambers promised him the decorated Christmas tree in Rockefeller Center was unmatched by any in the world. He made a note to check with the hotel for holiday reservations.

Allie loved Christmas. Kyle chuckled, remembering when she *informed* him that the Christmas tree must go up the day after Thanksgiving. And surely he wouldn't mind stringing a few outdoor lights in the weekend sun, would he?

With his shirt buttoned and tucked in, Kyle reached for his tie. Allie's holiday spirit paled in comparison to her wedding fervor. If he was honest with himself, he thought her enthusiasm over the wedding itself overshadowed her enthusiasm for him occasionally.

Her answer to his question "Do you want to marry me?" rattled around in his soul.

"Yes," she had said. "I want to get married." Kyle hoped he understood her meaning, but it bothered him that she didn't say she wanted to marry him. He thought about talking to her several times over the weekend, but they were so busy, the timing always seemed off.

He pictured her walking down the beach the night he gave her the engagement ring—barefoot with her flip-flops dangling from her fingers and her skirt blowing against her legs. If he could, he'd give Allie the world on a silver platter.

Besides her awkward answer, Kyle felt uneasy over the conflict between Allie and his job. He'd worked hard on the Eventide account and he wanted the reward of signing the contract with Jamis. Building DeLeo & Landon was for Allie, for their future. It seemed straightforward to him, but to Allie, complicated, with odd angles.

A light knock resounded on the hotel room door. "You ready?" Jamis called.

Kyle let Jamis in and slipped into his suit jacket. "Let me check the weather first."

"No, we're late." Jamis clapped his hands, loud and rapid. "I got a cab waiting downstairs."

❧

Vero Beach

A reprieve. Allie smiled, sitting in her parents' living room, watching the weather station's Michele Burg report from Vero Beach with an evening update.

"Right now, category one Hurricane Allie is stalled about seventy miles south of Nassau Island in the Bahamas."

"The hurricane has stalled," Allie said to her mom as she entered the room with a large bowl of popcorn, as if watching a weather report was like curling up to watch a classic movie.

Mom plopped down next to Allie on the sofa. "Well, that's good for us. Not so good for the Bahamas. Isn't Michelle standing near your house, Allie? Isn't that the Blue Heron pavilion?"

Allie squinted at the television. "Can't tell, but. . ." She smiled at her mom. "The wedding will happen as planned. Now, for Gigi to come home, open the shop, and let me get my dress. . ."

Dad came into the living room, mopping sweat from his brow with an old rag. "I cut a few new pieces of plywood to replace those warped ones of yours, Allie. We'd better get your house boarded up by tomorrow night."

"No need, Pop," she said, hopping off the sofa with a big gesture at the television. "The hurricane is stalled. Who knows where it will go?"

Woodward Seton peered around to see the screen. "It's a wobble, Allie."

She frowned. "A wobble? Michelle Burg isn't calling it a wobble."

Dad exited to the kitchen. "It's a wobble," he called over his shoulder. "Does Kyle have someone to lower his hurricane shutters?"

Allie frowned. "I have a key if we need to go over there, but we aren't going to need it."

Dad reappeared swigging from a glass of water. "I think we are going to need it."

Chapter 4

New York City, 10:30 p.m.

Kyle endured the after dinner conversation with a frozen smile on his face, wishing Jamis and Art would abandon their dreary debate about graphite versus metal golf clubs.

He'd tuned them out over an hour ago. Allie's statement nagged at him. "I want to get married," she had said. *But, does she want to marry me?* The thin difference in phrasing mattered to him.

Across the table, Art's colleague, William Lutz, snorted as his head bobbed forward. Kyle shifted in his seat and covered his laugh with a cough.

"What do you think? Graphite or metal?" Jamis tapped him on the arm with an expectant expression.

Kyle stood. "I think I'll catch a cab to the hotel." He shook William gently. "Time to go home."

Near eleven o'clock, Kyle hung up his shirt and suit then

took a long, hot shower. Afterward, he surfed the cable channels until he found the Weather Station. Hurricane Allie, he saw, was stalled over the Bahamas.

Kyle tossed a few almonds from the minibar into his mouth and reached for his cell. He started to dial, but after thinking for a moment, he hit END. He wanted clarification on Allie's cloaked marriage comment, yet he didn't want to start *that* conversation when he was bone tired.

Instead, he hooked up to the hotel's Internet access and sent a dozen roses to Allie's office with a simple note: *"Because I'm sure."*

⤬

Wednesday, August 9, 4:00 p.m.

Allie didn't look up when her office door clicked open. "I know, Ruby, but it's only a category one right now. And the strike zone is from Miami to Daytona. Can't you. . .right, I understand. Sure, you, too." She dropped the phone's receiver onto the cradle and propped her forehead in her hand.

"Something wrong?" Eva asked.

Allie peeked from behind her hand. "My wedding coordinator is bugging out."

"Oh, Allie, I'm sorry."

"Her son still has nightmares from the last year's storms and her husband wants to leave before traffic gets too bad." Allie got up and walked over to the window. "The sun is shining and everyone's running around like Chicken Little."

"You know that hurricane could shift our way at any moment," Eva said.

Allie whirled around to face her. "Yes, but it won't."

"Let's pray it won't," Eva said, hovering over Allie's desk, picking through the stacks of papers.

"Can I help you?" Allie asked, folding her arms, raising one eyebrow.

Eva stepped back and waved her arm over the piles. "Where in this haystack is the Lombardy materials quote?"

"Let the master," Allie said. With precision, she shifted one stack here, another there, and produced the Lombardy information.

"Amazing. Like finding a needle in the haystack." Eva shook her head and grinned.

Allie moved the piles back into place. "My haystack. My needle."

"Eva?" Julie Peres, the firm's administrative assistant, peered into Allie's office. "Do you want me to call Richard?"

Allie glanced between Julie and Eva. "Richard? The handyman?"

"We need to board up," Julie said with wide eyes. "The hurricane shifted about an hour ago and the strike probably is Vero Beach sometime tomorrow."

"What?" Panic pelted Allie as she ran out of her office to view the tiny TV behind Julie's desk.

"Well, folks, looks like Hurricane Allie is heading our way. If the eye doesn't come over us, we're going to get the worst of the northeast rain bands. . . ."

"No!" Allie popped the top of the television with the palm of her hand. The screen showed Vero Beach residents already in line for supplies at Publix and Wal-Mart. "Battery and water supplies are running low," said a reporter's voice-over.

Allie shouted at the TV. "We can*not* have a hurricane. We cannot! I'm getting married Saturday. Kyle's still in New York." She sat back on Julie's desk.

Eva touched her shoulder and Allie dropped her chin to her chest, feeling every bit like Charlie Brown when Lucy pulled the football out from under him. "It's happening, isn't it?" she muttered.

"Yes." Eva stroked her hand over Allie's hair.

"They're predicting a Thursday evening landfall," Julie said.

"I guess it could still swing south," Eva said. "They've been wrong before."

Allie headed for her office. "Wrong? When? Nineteen fifty?"

Eva trailed after her. "We could always walk out to the beach, face southeast, and blow real hard."

Allie made a wry face. "Very funny. My wedding day is ruined and you're joking."

Julie called from her desk, "Richard's on his way. He said we should unplug the computers and move them away from the windows."

"Good idea," Eva said, meeting Julie just outside Allie's door. The two walked away discussing how to handle business if they were shut down for a week or so.

Allie sank into her chair, tears in her eyes. *This is not happening*, she thought.

Julie called from her desk. "Make sure you backed up, Allie."

"Right, Jules," she muttered, trying to focus on her computer screen. She'd have to organize and file the "haystack" on her desk and. . .

But how do I back up my wedding plans? How do I recover from this?

Reaching for a tissue, Allie shut her office door and sat quietly in a chair by the southern window.

"Oh, Lord, this isn't the wedding we planned, remember? I gave up dating to wait for the right guy and this is my reward?"

A light knock interrupted her petition. "Come in," Allie called, dabbing the water from under her eyes.

"These just came for you."

Allie sniffled and smiled as Julie set a gorgeous vase of roses on her desk.

⤟⤞

Wednesday evening, 10:00 p.m.

Kyle unbuttoned his collar and leaned against the hotel's wide window, wishing he shared the night view with Allie.

Instead, he spent the entire evening listening to Art's partners suggest alternate design ideas. In the end, they clapped him on the shoulder and said, "Well, you're the expert, do what you think is best."

Kyle exhaled his frustration. He wanted to talk to Allie, not ponder Eventide dealings. He unclipped his cell from his belt and autodialed her cell. When she answered, his shoulders relaxed and the tightness in his middle vanished.

"I miss you," he said.

"The roses are beautiful, Kyle."

"I meant what I wrote on the card," he said, opening the mini fridge. Where were those almonds?

"I know you're sure," she replied.

"And you?" He hated this dance.

"Have you seen the news, Kyle?"

He noticed a slight tremor in her voice. "No, what's the latest?" Why was she avoiding his questions lately? He grabbed the remote and clicked over to the Weather Station.

Meteorologist Tammy Chen announced: "As you can see, Hurricane Allie is a solid category two storm and moving toward the central Florida coast."

Kyle sank down to the edge of the bed. "Babe, this isn't good."

"Our wedding is ruined."

Kyle tossed the remote onto the bedside table. "Allie, honey, we can still get married, it just may not be the one we planned."

"Kyle, I don't want to say I love you with sweat running into my eyes while the icing melts off the cake. If there is a cake. There won't be electricity, maybe no guests. And I don't have my dress."

He bristled a little. "Okay, Allie, I hear you. It's not ideal. What are our options? Wait? Until when? Didn't you say the Vandercliff Mansion is booked until next spring?"

"Maybe we should just rethink this whole thing."

Kyle clinched and opened his fist. "Rethink what whole thing?"

"I don't know," Allie said with an exhale. "I hate hurricanes."

"Join the club." He wondered if he should ask his nagging question tonight.

"I-95 is already backed up and two-thirds of the grocery store shelves are empty," Allie said.

"Did you get a stash of M&Ms?" He grinned.

"Yes," she snorted. "You think you know me so well, don't you?"

Kyle laughed. "Yes, I do."

"I'm sticking my tongue out at you right now." There was a lilt in her tone.

"I wish I was there with you, babe," he said with tenderness.

"Me, too," she said. "Our first hurricane as a couple and you're missing the party."

"Allie," Kyle said, deciding to wade into the deep waters. "When I asked you the other day if you wanted to marry me, you said, 'Yes, I want to get married.'"

"Right," she said low, as if wondering where he was going with the conversation.

"Every girl wants to *get* married, Allie, but do you want to marry *me*?" Kyle's pulse thumped so loud he couldn't hear.

"What a thing to ask, Kyle." Her tone was hard and weighty.

"I want to know, Allie. Are you in love with me, or in love with love and getting married?"

"I can't believe this. Just because a girl wants a beautiful wedding—"

Kyle interrupted. "Don't you know, Allie? You are the one that makes the wedding beautiful."

⊷⊷

Thursday, August 10, 2:00 p.m.

Allie met her father on Kyle's back porch as wind gusts

whistled under the eaves.

"Getting blustery," Dad said, tipping his head toward the choppy Indian River. "Kyle's shutters are lowered."

Allie glanced toward the covered windows. "Thanks, Daddy. I can't believe the storm is actually heading for us."

Dad walked to the French doors. "I know you're disappointed, but the Lord will bring good from all of this, you'll see. You'll have your wedding."

Allie watched the wind turn the leaves of the scrub oaks upside down. She glanced over at her father. "Do you think I'm getting married just to get married? Am I in love with love?"

He paused with his hand on the doorknob. "I don't know, Allie. Only you can answer that question. I know you've been planning this wedding since you where twelve—"

"No, not twelve." She fell against the deck railing and crossed her arms, trying to smother her smile. "Thirteen, maybe, but not twelve."

"I stand corrected," he said, laughing. His thinning brown hair lifted in the breeze. "I guess you have to ask yourself if Kyle is the man God has for you. Do you have things in common? The same life goals? I know you both love Jesus. . . ."

"Yes," Allie said, the turmoil in her heart gusting and fading like the wind.

"Why are you asking me this?"

Allie sighed and recounted her conversation with Kyle. When she finished, Woodward rubbed his chin. "That's a fine line, but a good one to examine."

"I suppose so," Allie said. Of course she wanted to marry

Kyle. She loved him. But, she also wanted *her* wedding with all the pomp and trimmings.

"Allie, consider all the angles, but ultimately you have to answer this question. Is Kyle the one you want to be with at the end of each day? More than your friends, more than your family? Do you trust him? Do you feel safe with him? Does he make you uneasy when he challenges your weaknesses?"

Allie laughed. "Yes, to all the above. He definitely makes me aware of my weaknesses, challenges my comfort zones. But, because of that, I'm stronger," she said.

She moved across Kyle's deck to his assortment of dying plants and picked up one in each hand. "You've given me a lot to think about."

Woodward kissed her forehead. "The Lord will give you wisdom. I'm going to head out, run some errands, get some cash before the storm hits. Are you set for money?"

"Yes," Allie said. "Bye, Daddy."

When she'd finished moving the plants inside and watering them, Allie walked through Kyle's house. Brown boxes lined the walls where he had started packing, preparing to move to her beach bungalow. While his condo was larger and newer than Allie's place, they both loved the bungalow's charm and history. Living there after they were married didn't require discussion. They both just knew.

With that thought in her mind, Allie settled on the leather couch and cradled a thick throw pillow. She'd never connected with anyone like she connected with Kyle. He was her best friend, her comfort, her soul mate. He was the one she wanted to be with at the end of the day.

Was she so shallow that one hurricane challenged her love and commitment? "Lord," she whispered, "this is right, isn't it? Marrying Kyle?"

Allie prayed awhile longer, listening and thinking. But when a strong wind knocked against the north corner of the condo, she decided to head home.

She stood and tossed the pillow to the corner of the couch and knocked a book from the end table. She stooped to pick it up, reading the spine. *The Courtship of Robert Browning and Elizabeth Barrett.*

Kyle! Reading love letters and poetry. She flipped through the pages, smiling, and found a piece of paper bearing Kyle's block lettering.

Allie, how do I love thee?

She laughed. "Oh, Kyle, stealing from Elizabeth Barrett Browning?"

Chapter 5

Thursday, August 10, 6:00 p.m.

Meteorologist Michelle Burg's voice declared from the TV: "I'm here in Vero Beach and we're just now getting the first rain bands with winds gusting up to sixty miles per hour. But this is just the beginning of this category two hurricane moving about ten miles an hour, toward shore."

Allie looked out the slight gap between the sheet metal and the edge of her parents' sliding glass door. The treetops twisted and bent in the wind.

"Have a sandwich, Allie." Her dad lifted a triple-decker Dagwood in salute. "What's the fun in a hurricane party if you're sulking by the window?"

"I'm not hungry, Dad, but thanks," Allie said as she fell into the club chair, dangling her long legs over one of its broad arms. "It's going to be a long night, isn't it?"

She hated the eerie feeling of being in a boarded-up house.

And the constant updates from the weather station added to her anxiety.

"Sure you're not hungry?" Dad asked.

Allie glanced at his sandwich. Maybe she was a little hungry. She'd half decided to get up and make a Dagwood when the phone rang. She bolted from her chair. *Please let it be Kyle.*

Mom held the phone out with a smile. "It's Kendall."

Allie hurried over to the breakfast counter. "How are you?" She perched on a tall stool.

"Fine, except my flight's canceled."

"Oh, Kendall. . ."

"I'm driving down," Kendall said. "As soon as possible."

"Well, call me before you do—just in case there's no wedding."

"What?"

"We don't know what the storm will do and besides, Kyle's stuck in New York."

"Oh, Allie, did you ever imagine this would happen to *your* day?" Kendall's voice rose at the end of each word.

"Not in a million years."

Suddenly the lights flickered, the phone clicked off, and the house faded to black.

"Now," her dad said, "the party's getting started."

⟡

Thursday, 8:00 p.m.

Kyle sat with Jamis at John F. Kennedy's Gate 15, two among hundreds of stranded travelers. "Jamis, do you think they're violating New York City fire codes?" Kyle asked, wrenching around to find an emergency exit, just in case.

Jamis chuckled. "Always the architect?"

"Yes," Kyle answered as his gaze roamed over the weary people, many sleeping in chairs and in huddled clumps on the floor. This was insane.

Jamis popped open the *Wall Street Journal* and settled back. "Can you believe one storm in Florida affected travel from New York City?"

Kyle slipped forward in his seat, clasping his hands behind his head. "What time is our flight, again?"

"Nine a.m. flight to Atlanta. But we're on standby along with a hundred other people."

"Great. Just great." Kyle fought frustration. He wanted to be on a flight home, now. A hurricane was ripping through his hometown and he was trapped in New York. He fidgeted and sat forward. *So many people.* He felt suffocated.

"Hopefully, we'll get on. I flirted with the ticket agent."

Kyle made a face. "Then we're sunk for sure. We'll never get home. We may never be allowed to fly again."

"Keep it up. I'll leave you here."

Kyle laughed and pulled a piece of paper from his pocket and found a pen in his laptop case.

Allie, how do I love thee? he wrote, then grimaced and scratched out the words. The famous line was stuck in his head. He'd warned Allie that he wasn't good with the mushy stuff, but plagiarizing a great American poet for his wedding vows seemed void of all romantic sincerity.

He wasn't sorry they'd agreed to write their vows; he just wished he could do it without sounding like a third grader. If he could express his emotions by designing a building, it would look something like the Taj Mahal. But, no, he was stuck in the world of words.

Kyle heard the rustle of news pages. "What are you doing?" Jamis asked.

"Trying to write my vows," Kyle said without looking up.

Jamis leaned over Kyle's shoulder. "Nothing like waiting until the last minute. Allie, how do I—"

Kyle snatched the paper away from Jamis's gaze. "Excuse me, these are personal."

"Personal? Aren't vows the things you say out loud during a wedding ceremony?" Jamis smirked.

"Go back to your paper."

Jamis popped open the *Wall Street Journal*. "Okay, but just so you know, I think that line has been used before." His laugh billowed behind the newsprint.

"You should go on the road. You're so funny."

"My Edgar Bergen to your Charlie McCarthy."

Kyle laughed and just shook his head. Jamis had a way of making the worst situation a little brighter. He set his paper aside and reached for his cell phone. "Do you think the phones are working?"

"Hard to say," Jamis said.

Kyle autodialed Allie's cell, then her house, then her parents'. "No answer. They must have lost power already."

Jamis folded the paper. "There'll be a lot of cleanup to do when we get home," he said, glancing at his watch. "I got a hold of Forrest to board up the office, but I'm sure we'll have debris everywhere."

Kyle grinned. "While you clean up downed limbs and frayed roof shingles, I'll be on my honeymoon."

"*If* you get married. You know most of the city will still be recovering and without power on Saturday."

"I'm getting married if I have to get married in the dark and in a foot of water."

"To Allie? The queen of weddings? Do you think she'll go for no church, no food, no photographer, and no air conditioning? Most of your guests are probably on the road home if they're not busy just surviving."

Kyle regarded Jamis. "You make her sound shallow."

"Sorry, man. I know she's not, but her dream of the big fancy wedding is being blown away like Dorothy and Toto over the rainbow."

"Yeah, I know." *Are you in love with me, or in love with love. . . ?*

Kyle picked up his vow scratch sheet and wrote down his next thought. *Allie, you are the sunshine of my life.* He read it over a few times, then grimaced. *Can't steal from Stevie Wonder, either.*

"Are you getting hungry?" Jamis asked. "It's late and if we want to eat, we'd better do it now."

Kyle stood and stretched, slipping the paper into his pocket. "Sitting around a crowded airport does work up a guy's appetite. You got the tickets, I'll hunt for food."

"Get Chinese."

Kyle patted his stomach. "Sounds good." He looked down the terminal thoroughfare. "I think I'll find the duty-free shop first. Pick up a gift for Allie."

"Spending some of the Eventide money?" Jamis asked with a chuckle.

"Yeah, why not."

Duty-free was farther away than Kyle remembered. Yet, on his journey over, he visualized Allie wearing a diamond tennis bracelet or diamond pendant and he refused to give up his quest.

Allie, when a man falls in love like I have fallen for you. . . He shook his head. No, no, no.

Duty Free had a lot to choose from. Kyle examined every jewelry piece under the glass before deciding on a diamond tennis bracelet. Then he sniffed several bottles of perfume trying to match her scent.

The saleswoman suggested purchasing Allie a new perfume, but Kyle declined, quite sure he didn't want to tamper with perfection. Allie's sage and rose aura had scented the recesses of his mind for so long it felt like a part of him.

"I'll just take the bracelet," he said. It was after nine p.m. when he left the shop and he hurried to find a Chinese place. He groaned when he saw the line to the restaurant.

"Long line," the guy in front of him said.

Kyle looked into his tired eyes. "Lots of hungry people."

"Are you holed up here because of the hurricane?"

"Yes. You?"

The man nodded. "I'm trying to get to Florida for a friend's wedding."

Kyle chuckled. "Me, too."

⁂

Vero Beach, Friday, August 11, 7:00 a.m.

Allie drove around town with her father, viewing the aftermath of Hurricane Allie. The scream of last night's hurricane winds still echoed in her ears. She jiggled her finger against her eardrum trying to squelch the howl.

"This is about what I expected," Dad said, maneuvering carefully through the flooded streets and under traffic lights dangling from thin power lines. "We're blessed the hurricane didn't go to a cat three or higher."

"Yes," Allie murmured. Along the streets, trees were broken in two like after-meal toothpicks. Power poles straddled streets, driveways, and parking lots.

"Can we go by the church?" Allie asked, biting the tip of her thumbnail.

"Good idea," Dad said, turning right on the next street. Allie gazed out the passenger side window. They could still hold the wedding without electricity if the church wasn't flooded or damaged.

Dad slowed the car. Two power poles lay crisscrossed over New Life's entrance.

"We're blocked out," Allie said, motioning with her hand.

Dad nodded. "There won't be a wedding here on Saturday, Allie." He glanced at her and smoothed his hand over hers. "Sorry."

Allie blinked away her tears. "It's okay."

"Don't worry, maybe the Vandercliff will be available." Dad drove on, heading toward the historic mansion. But the road to the Vandercliff was flooded and impassable.

Allie exhaled, battling discouragement, fighting the drab images being inked onto her heart.

What kind of couple starts out their married life in the midst of disaster? Wasn't marriage difficult enough? Did they want to look back on their wedding and remember a hurricane?

She longed to talk to Kyle, but she had no cell service and the wireless house phone was useless without power.

"We'll think of something, Allie. Don't worry." Dad patted her knee once. "Let's see if we can get over to the beach and check out your place."

My place, Allie thought. After Saturday, it was supposed to be *their* place. As they neared the causeway, Allie spotted the flashing lights of patrol cars.

"The beaches are closed until further notice," the sheriff's deputy told her, leaning into her window.

"Thank you," Allie said with a faint smile.

Dad pressed on the gas and headed north on U.S. 1. "I'm sure your bungalow is fine. It's weathered many storms."

"I know," Allie replied softly, picturing her home with the sloping eaves and wide front window.

                  ❧

Throughout the morning, Allie worked with her parents in their yard, picking up debris while her dad used the chain saw on downed limbs.

Already, the balmy winds trailing the hurricane were dying down and the sun made the day feel like a sauna.

After dragging the last of the sawed tree limbs to the curb, Allie went inside for a cold drink. She scooped ice cubes from the cooler in the kitchen and pressed them along the back of her neck.

"This feels good," she said, sitting at the kitchen counter, hooking her forefinger over a stray strand of hair that clung to her sweaty cheeks.

Mom looked up from where she plugged an oscillating fan into a power strip. "Dad is starting the generator. Hopefully, we can cool things off here in a minute." Mom fanned her face with a stack of napkins.

Allie laughed. "Right, circulating the hot air will cool things off."

Mom made a face. "It will help. . .a little."

Just then, Jewel walked in and dropped a box and a clipboard on the kitchen table. "All right, let's get planning." She smiled at her mother and sister then flipped open the cooler for a bottle of water.

Allie leaned over the breakfast counter. "Plan what?"

"Your wedding, of course." Jewel propped her elbows on the edge of the sink.

Allie laughed a hearty, fake laugh. "The one with no electricity, no caterer, no wedding dress, and here's the kicker, Jewel, no groom."

Jewel looked into her eyes. "Still haven't heard from Kyle?"

"No. My cell doesn't work. Neither does Dad and Mom's phone."

Jewel reached inside the box. "Here, plug this in." She handed Allie a corded telephone with a dangling hookup.

"Hmm, what's this, Watson?" Allie reached for the phone, examining the thin, clear wire. "Something from 1901?"

"Plug that into a phone jack and ta-da, you have communication with the outside world." Jewel tipped her water bottle for a long swig.

"Very old-fashioned of you," Allie said. She plugged the

phone in and lifted the receiver to hear the beautiful buzz of the dial tone.

"I'm calling Kyle," she said, punching in his cell number and listening with anticipation to each ring.

But he never answered.

Chapter 6

JFK, Friday, 8:00 a.m.

Kyle woke with a start. He glanced at his watch and rose from the narrow airport chair, squeezing the back of his neck with his hand. His shoulders and back ached from being wadded into the seat all night, but he didn't care. He was going home today. Next to him, Jamis slept curled in a ball, snoring.

The smell of coffee wafted down the thoroughfare and Kyle decided to forage for food before their flight. Hopefully, he and Jamis were high enough on the standby list to get a seat.

"Going for breakfast," he said, shaking Jamis's shoulder.

Seems everyone else had the same idea. The restaurant lines were long and the workers slow. Fifty minutes later, when Kyle returned to his seat at gate 15 balancing breakfast bagels and two tall coffees, he stopped short. "What?"

He turned in a circle, glancing around. "Jamis? Am I at the wrong. . ."

He stepped back, checking his gate number. Gate 15. Did Jamis move? Kyle walked the perimeter of the gate, looking for his partner, but he was gone, along with all their gear. Kyle surveyed the waiting area. Seats were available and many of the waiting passengers were gone.

"Excuse me," Kyle asked the agent at the ticket counter. Her name tag read Mary. "What happened? People are missing. Including my friend."

"We were able to get some of the standbys on the eight forty."

"Eight forty? What about the nine o'clock?"

Mary shook her head. "No nine o'clock. Are you Kyle Landon?"

"Yes, I am," Kyle said, feeling heat rise from the core of his chest. It was just like Jamis to think an eight forty flight was a nine o'clock flight.

"Your friend had you paged," Mary said. "The nine o'clock flight was moved to eight forty."

"What?" Kyle whipped around to see behind him as if the motion would reverse the truth. "The flight was changed?"

Kyle fumed. How could Jamis leave without him? "Then what flight am I on?" He fumbled with the coffee caddie and reached in his back pocket for his folded ticket. But it wasn't there. It was in his laptop case, which was now winging its way home with Jamis.

Kyle pleaded with his eyes. "I need a flight to Florida today. Please. I'm getting married tomorrow."

While Mary clicked over the keyboard, Kyle padded his pockets for his cell phone. Nope. Jamis had that, too.

"I can get you on flight 109 to Atlanta, this afternoon at three, routing through Dallas."

"Dallas?" Kyle pressed his fingers against his eyes. How was this happening? He was the one getting married, yet Jamis was the one with a seat and a bag of peanuts.

"Is that all you have? What about Miami or Jacksonville?"

"All the flights are full," she answered, peering up at him from under her brow, "with long standby lists."

"Naturally. When does the Dallas flight get in?"

"Arriving in Atlanta at nine p.m."

"I'll take it."

❦

"Woohoo, knock, knock."

Allie looked up as a singsong, high-pitched voice rolled from the front door.

"Come in, Gracie," Jewel hollered with a wave of her hand. "We've got a lot of work to do."

Gracie Gunter entered, her plump face red and moist. "Can you believe this heat? And barely a breeze to help one breathe!"

"Sit here, Gracie," Jewel said, offering the older woman a chair. "Right in front of the fan."

Gracie sat with an *oomph*. "Maybe I can sweat off a few pounds, uh?"

Allie pinched her lips to keep from laughing out loud.

"That's what I'm hoping for," Jewel said without flinching.

"Well, Allie, this presents a challenge, doesn't it? A hurricane," Gracie said, wiping her forehead with a handkerchief.

"Yes, it does," Allie said, sitting in the chair next to Gracie. She propped her chin in her hand. She wondered where Kyle was and why he hadn't called. She longed for the reassurance of his voice.

"You can always postpone," Gracie said.

"Gracie! That's not what you're here to do," Jewel said.

Gracie patted Allie's arm. "I just don't want you to have any regrets."

Regrets. The word slammed into Allie's heart and rattled her bones. Maybe that was her hidden anxiety, regret. Sure she wanted to marry Kyle, but without denying herself the perfect wedding and reception. Should she hold out for another day? One that wasn't shadowed by disaster? Or should she marry Kyle on the day they chose together, August 12?

Allie glanced at Gracie. In that instant, she knew she didn't need to ponder this any longer. "Besides meeting Jesus when I was six, Kyle is the best thing that's happened to me."

"Then marry him," Jewel said, angling over the kitchen table, squeezing Allie's arm.

"I think I will." Allie smiled and scrunched her shoulders.

Jewel clapped. "The wedding is on!"

Frannie James rounded the corner and fell against the door frame. "I made it." She drew a deep breath. "The roads are terrible, just terrible. Now, where's the bride-to-be? We've got some work to do."

Allie waved at Frannie.

"There she is. Is it hot in here or just me?"

A chorus of "it's hot" pealed throughout the large kitchen.

❧

Jewel commanded the "Get Allie Married" crew and doled out assignments. "We have twenty-four hours to pull this together, so no slacking." She pointed her pencil at each one of them. "We're about to hit Vero Beach with a second Hurricane Allie."

"Gotcha."

"We hear you, Jewel."

"We can do this, don't worry, Allie."

"Thank you all so much," Allie said. "But, please pray for Kyle to make it home. If he doesn't, all of this is for nothing." She looked at the glistening faces around the Seton kitchen table.

There were Frannie and Gracie, fanning themselves with folded pieces of paper, Grandma Alice, who had one of those little battery-operated hand fans, Aunt Rebekah, holding her hair off her neck with her hands, and Allie's best friends Reneé, Laura, and Eva.

Dad stood off in the corner, pretending not to listen. Allie wiggled her fingers hello at him when he peeked over.

"Mom, you and Aunt Rebekah are in charge of food," Jewel said.

Mom nodded and jotted a note. "Allie, we'll do the best we can. There's not going to be any meat, probably, but we'll get some nice gourmet cookies and crackers. Peanuts and mints."

"M&Ms," Allie muttered.

Mom smiled. "Naturally."

Gracie suggested using Mamie Lovett's home to bake a cake. "She has a huge kitchen and for some reason, never loses power in a storm."

Eva volunteered to find a place to hold the event, but when she did, Dad stepped from the shadows. "If you don't mind, Eva, I'd like to handle that part."

Allie's eyes misted. "Pop, really?"

He cleared his throat and nodded.

"Okay, then what can I do?" Eva asked, glancing around.

"What you do best. Decorate," Frannie suggested. "Who better than the great Eva Drysdale. My sister still envies my kitchen. You and Allie did a wonderful job."

Eva grinned. "All right, I'll handle decorations."

Laura took responsibility for the music. "I have more CDs than Best Buy. And I have enough batteries for the boom box to last three hurricanes."

The ladies laughed and Allie asked, "Do you have Pachelbel's Canon for my processional?"

Laura looked at Allie wide-eyed. "Of course."

Eva jumped up from the table. "Do you have a phone? I have an idea."

"It's on the wall," Mom said, pointing over her head.

Frannie offered to round up volunteers for setup and cleanup. "Just let me know when and where." She started a list of names. "Allie, do you have your guest lists? We should call people. . . ."

Allie sighed. "Ruby has it and she's left."

"I think I have our original list, Allie," Mom said.

"All right," Frannie said. "Louise, let's go through your list and the church directory. We'll call who we can, though most of the phones will be out."

Mom hopped up and headed to her bedroom. "Allie, you should call Kyle's parents."

"Yes, I will." Allie sat back and watched the motion around the table. How could she doubt marrying Kyle? How could she question the Lord's favor when nine women sat in a stifling-hot room working to make her wedding-day dreams come true?

"Thank you, all," she said, her voice warbling. "Thank you."

The ladies stopped mid motion, mid sentence. Gracie wiped perspiration from her upper lip and Frannie wiped her eyes. Jewel said, "You're more than welcome, Allie."

"Can we keep the wedding time the same?" Allie pointed to Jewel's clipboard. "Five o'clock. Kyle might make it by then."

"We'll try. Let's see what Dad turns up," Jewel said.

"What about our rings?" Allie asked.

Reneé's hand shot up. "Did you get them at Martin's Jewelers?"

"Yeah, we did."

Reneé slapped her hand on the table. "Percy Martin kissed me on the school playground when I was six. I think he owes me one."

The women hooted with laughter and the subject of a playground kiss got them talking about their first loves.

In the midst of the "first love" conversation, Grandma asked the million-dollar question. "What about Allie's dress?"

"Good question, Grandma," Allie replied. "I guess we'll have to wear our Sunday clothes. Or jeans, depending on what Dad comes up with."

"No!" the table chorused.

"Then what?"

Jewel looked at Frannie. "Did you bring it?"

Frannie bobbed her head. She pushed away from the table and came back with a large garment box. She handed it to Allie with glistening eyes.

"When I married Duke in '48, we had dreams of having

a large family. I hoped one of my daughters would wear my dress."

Jewel interrupted, "Allie, it's vintage 1948."

"It's no secret Duke and I never had children. Just three miscarriages and a lot of heartache." Frannie opened the box. "I'd be honored if you would wear my gown for your wedding dress."

Allie fingered the rayon slipper satin and silk crepe. "Frannie, it's beautiful." The dress had aged to a lovely candlelight color, but it was nonetheless beautiful.

"I purchased it at Neiman-Marcus." Frannie looked at the women, smiling. "It's a princess design with a flared skirt." Frannie lift the dress up to Allie.

Allie cried, "Frannie, it's lovely. I'd be honored to wear this dress for my wedding." She kissed the older woman's cheek.

The room was silent except for the sniffles of tender hearts. Louise passed a box of tissues.

"Duke and I were married one very hot July and I kept cool in this dress."

Gracie and Grandma moved past Allie for an inspection. "It's in fine shape, Frannie."

"Let's air it out on the line," Grandma suggested. "We can press it out with a cool iron."

Grandma held Allie's arms and gazed into her face. "You're going to be beautiful."

"I'm going to try it on." With a tiny squeal, Allie hurried to her room.

Chapter 7

JFK, Friday, August 11, 2:00 p.m.

The day crept by. Kyle jiggled his leg and tapped his heel against the floor. In an hour, he'd be winging his way to Dallas, then Atlanta, then driving home. He had a long journey ahead and he was anxious to get started.

Earlier, he'd purchased a phone card at a newsstand and hunted down a pay phone. But when he dialed the Setons', the phone buzzed with a busy signal.

How was he supposed to tell Allie he'd be home as soon as possible? How was he supposed to tell her that what-a-friend Jamis had abandoned him?

Kyle exhaled and settled his nervous leg. *Work on your vows.* He slipped his hand in his pocket for the paper.

Allie, you mean more to me than life itself. He made a face as he reread the words. Corny. Stilted. Why couldn't he just say what he felt—pure and simple?

He thought for a moment and stared at nothing. *Forget*

prose and poetry; just write from your heart.

Allie, I'm sitting in JFK, alone, abandoned by Jamis. He has my laptop, my hanging bag, and my cell phone, but all I can do is miss you. All I want is to make it home in time for our wedding, which I hope we are still having.

I miss you, babe, and I'm so sorry you had to endure a hurricane without me holding you. But know that I want to weather all of life's storms with you. I will always be by your side.

I fell in love with you the moment I saw you. Not the day we met for the Hayes complex, but a sunny fall day in '99. Remember the FSU–Miami game and the crazy guy who climbed over everyone to kiss you? That was me, Allie. The guy who followed you out of the stadium, begging for a date. The guy who stood on a car hood and hollered, "Beautiful, will you marry me?"

Shocking, isn't it? I'm sorry I haven't confessed before now, but I want you to know how much a part of my heart you really are. I used to look for you when I was in Tallahassee for football games. I didn't even know your name, but I wanted to see you again.

But I wasn't the right guy for you. It took a few years of hanging out with Jesus before I was ready to meet you.

Time passed. I started the business with Jamis and gave up the idea of you. Then, you walked into DeLeo & Landon's conference room and I knew my heart had found its home.

Now, by God's amazing mercy and goodness, you're

going to be my wife. I'm blessed beyond measure. The Bible is right. He who finds a wife finds a good thing.

I promise to love and cherish you. Respect and encourage you. I will pray for you and be faithful to you. I promise to lead and listen, and to teach our children to love Jesus.

I promise walks on the beach. I promise to take out the garbage. I won't drop my clothes on the floor. I'll cook, sometimes, and help with the dishes.

I'll hold your hand when you're sick and kiss you for no reason. I won't forget birthdays or anniversaries, or that you're lovely. I promise to help decorate the Christmas tree, but can't make the same vow when taking it down. Especially if it's New Year's Day. Football, you know.

Allie, I love you. Forgive me for being a boorish oaf seven years ago, but now you know the length of our connection, and the depth of my affection and devotion to you.

I am forever yours, Kyle.

❦

The ladies rose from their chairs and Frannie covered her mouth with her trembling hand when Allie walked into the kitchen.

"Oh, dear girl, you look so beautiful."

"It's absolutely perfect," Jewel said, clutching the clipboard to her chest.

Gracie and Grandma walked around her, inspecting the

dress. "I think we could let the arms out some. Allie, does it feel a little tight?"

"Yes, a little, but I don't want to alter Frannie's dress."

"My dress?" Frannie held Allie and peered into her eyes. "This dress is yours now. And one day, hopefully, your daughter's."

"Oh, Frannie," Allie said, barely above a whisper. "You are too generous."

"Veil," Jewel said with a quick glance at the ladies' faces. "What about a veil?"

Frannie and Gracie waved her off. "We have plenty of tulle and lace left from the church's Christmas program."

So, Allie had a dress and a veil. She waited patiently in the afternoon heat while Grandma and Gracie measured the dress for alterations.

As she went back to her room to change, Allie sensed the Lord's pleasure. The notion gave her peace. As she stepped out of her dress, she whispered, *I love You, Lord. Thank You for Kyle.*

She heard the phone jingle from the kitchen wall and hurried into her shorts and T-shirt. "Please be Kyle."

"Jamis is on the phone," Jewel called.

When Allie rounded the kitchen corner, Jewel held the receiver out to her, stretching the cord as far as it would go.

"Jamis? Where are you guys?"

"I'm in Atlanta," Jamis said. "I'm not sure about Kyle."

"What?" Allie fanned her face with her hand. Did the room just get hotter? "How can you not know where Kyle is?"

"We were on standby for a Friday morning flight to Atlanta.

Every flight is booked and overbooked. But we got on the passenger list and—"

"We? Jamis, is Kyle with you or not?"

"Our flight was at nine, but we left twenty minutes early."

"I don't believe this."

"I was sleeping, but I think I remember him saying something about going for breakfast."

Allie gasped. "So, you left him?"

"I had him paged, grabbed our stuff, and got on the plane. How long does it take to get breakfast anyway? I was in the back, so when we took off, I figured he was up front and I'd connect with him in Atlanta."

"But he wasn't." Allie propped her shoulder against the wall. This twist was like something out of a B movie.

"Nope, he wasn't."

"And he doesn't have his cell phone?"

"I have it."

Allie rubbed her forehead with the palm of her hand and laughed.

❧

Dallas, Friday, 9:00 p.m.

Kyle sat on the crowded airliner, agitated. They'd boarded an hour and half ago and taxied out to the runway only to sit, waiting for clearance to take off.

"Lots of air traffic tonight, folks," the captain said in a deep, calm voice, "so we just have to wait our turn. The hurricane has backed us up, so we apologize for any inconvenience. We'll do the best we can to make it up in the air."

Kyle sighed and slipped down into his seat. He was supposed to be landing in Atlanta now instead of sitting on a runway in Dallas with two hundred other people who obviously needed a shower as much as he did.

He'd paid ten bucks at a newsstand for what amounted to an ounce of deodorant and squirt of toothpaste, but it didn't do much to remove his grunge feeling.

He wondered how Allie was doing. At the moment, he had a tangible awareness of his love for her, as if the journey home had shaken all his subtle and hidden emotions to the surface. He didn't want to postpone the wedding. August 12 was their day. No hurricane or plane delays could take that away.

Kyle leaned forward and cupped his hands around his face. "Oh, Lord, I need a miracle. Please, get me home."

⊰⊱

The squeak of the front door echoed down the hall to the family room. "Problem solved," Dad called as he walked in, a big smile on his face.

Allie jumped to her feet. "You found a place for the wedding?"

"I did."

Allie attacked him with a hug. "Really? Where? The Carrington Bed & Breakfast?"

"No," Dad said, his expression falling.

"Oh, okay, that's fine. Where then?"

"How about the old Pinewood Chapel for a wedding? I drove over there and caught Reverend Markinson out front chainsawing tree limbs. I offered to help in exchange for using the chapel tomorrow evening."

"The old Pinewood Chapel?" Allie pictured the old, run-down church, long on charm, short on paint. "Daddy, it's out in the boonies!"

"I know, but it's perfect, Al. The Pinewood isn't missing so much as a shingle. And the reverend offered us the use of his generator. We'll haul ours out and have all the fans and lights we need."

Jewel tugged on Allie's arm. "The chapel is really beautiful inside, especially with candlelight."

Dad jumped on Jewel's bandwagon. "Looks like he's had the interior painted recently, Allie. The wood floors are polished and there's new carpet on the altar."

Allie chewed on her bottom lip. The *old* Pinewood. Didn't Kyle once say he loved the place? She glanced at her father's expectant expression. His hazel eyes were wide and waiting. "Daddy, it sounds perfect," Allie said.

Woodward clapped his hands together. "Good." He started toward his bedroom. "I'd better get back to help the reverend. He's got to be in his late seventies if he's a day. He'll do the ceremony, too, Allie, if we can't find Pastor Tim."

Watching her father made Allie tear up. He'd been excluded from so much of the wedding planning. Now, in the aftermath of a storm, she could clearly see his heart. He'd wanted to help all along. "Thank you, Daddy."

He grinned so that his eyes twinkled. "Oh, one more thing. The reverend says we can use the old horse barn for a reception. It has new wood flooring and no horses." Dad winked. "This is going to be fun, Allie."

Allie walked over to her father and pressed her face to his chest, her arms around his neck. "You're the best. I love you."

He coughed and patted her shoulder. "Love you, too, kiddo."

❧

Atlanta, Saturday, August 12, 12:30 a.m.

Kyle ran through the airport hoping to get to the rental car counters before they closed. Deep down, he knew he was too late, but he'd been praying. *Need a miracle.*

When he arrived at the Ground Transportation Center, all the car rental stations were dark and closed.

With a heavy sigh, Kyle sank into one of the waiting area chairs and exhaled. He was exhausted and hungry, but aching to see Allie.

He'd tried the Setons' phone again from a Dallas pay phone, but the busy signal buzzed again in his ear. Now, at one in the morning, it was too late to call.

Kyle set the alarm on his watch. He'd nap until the car rentals opened. Stretching out across a row of chairs, he closed his eyes. It felt good to lie down, even for a few hours.

"Kyle!"

He bolted upright.

"I've been looking for you."

Kyle squinted in the dim lights. Jamis? He grinned. "Man, you are a sight for sore eyes."

Jamis slapped his hand into Kyle's. "You don't know what I went through to find out what flight you were on."

"Tell me you didn't break the law."

Jamis looked him in the eye. "I didn't break the law." He tugged on Kyle's arm. "Let's go. I have a car waiting."

Kyle laughed. Now this was the miracle he'd been expecting. "So, Jamis, tell me why you abandoned me in New York."

Chapter 8

Allie couldn't sleep. Hot, heavy air hovered over her bed as she tossed and turned, wondering where Kyle might be. Would he make it home in time for the wedding? Why didn't he call? Surely airports still had pay phones.

She clicked on her flashlight and plumped her pillows behind her back, reaching for her journal.

At the top of a blank page, she wrote: *My updated vows to Kyle*. She thought for a long time, praying and picturing him, shoving aside her memories of the past week and letting her heart dwell on the man she loved.

You color my world. My once unpredictable, watercolored days are now splashed with a boldness that is you. You ground me, Kyle, and make my crazy world sane.

I've been waiting and wondering when you'd come into my life. Praying for God to send me a husband like you. Perhaps it's cliché to simply say I love you, but I do. You're not here now and I have no idea where you are, but I long to lose myself in your embrace. I'm sorry I made you doubt my love for you. I commit to marry you, not just get married. I want to marry you, Kyle Landon.

I promise to love you. Honor you and respect you. I will be faithful. Always. I promise a home filled with laughter and love, and peace. I promise clean sheets and towels, and a full-course, home-cooked meal twice, no, once a week. I won't iron or sew on buttons, but I will make regular trips to the dry cleaner's. I'll laugh at your jokes, cry when you cry, and try to understand football.

I give myself to you, Kyle. I know our life will be beautiful. I'm scared and nervous, in all the good ways, but I trust you with my heart and soul. I am yours, as you are mine.

❧

Kyle woke when the car jerked forward. He sat up and caught the time on the dash clock, 6:00 a.m. He'd been sleeping in the backseat ever since Atlanta.

Peering forward out the dash window, he caught a glimpse of the beautiful sunrise as it painted pink hues and gold streamers across a twilit sky. It was as if dark swirling storms never existed.

"Where are we?" His mouth was dry and his teeth felt like they were covered with wool.

"Just past the Georgia-Florida line," Jamis said, reaching for his coffee. "The traffic is brutal."

Kyle fell back against the seat, his body tired and sore. "Looks like everyone who ran from the hurricane is going home."

"It's going to be hard to find gas," Jamis said.

"Oh, dude, you're right," Kyle answered, suddenly aware

that arriving home was not the end of his worries, but the beginning. *Lord, help us find gas when we need it.*

He wanted to sleep more but thought he should offer Jamis a reprieve. "Do you need me to drive?"

"I'm okay for now."

"I could use a stop for water. My mouth is dryer than the Mojave."

"I'll get off at the next exit," Jamis said. "Why don't you call Allie?" He passed back Kyle's cell phone.

Kyle took the phone, laughing. "I almost forgot I could."

She answered on the first ring. "Hello?"

"Babe, it's me."

❧

Allie's heart danced. "Where are you?"

"I-10, heading toward Jacksonville with Jamis."

"You'll be home before five, then." Her stomach contracted with excitement. Now that she heard his voice, she knew beyond a shadow of a doubt that marrying him was the right thing. All her old wedding plans faded with the excitement of the new ones.

"By five?" Kyle echoed.

Allie heard the smile in his voice. "Yes, by five. We're getting married at the old Pinewood Chapel."

"No way. Really? I love that place."

"I know and it's going to be fabulous. You wouldn't believe all the little miracles God has done for us. My dress, the rings, the food, the photographer—"

Kyle laughed. "Yes, I would."

"Kyle," she said in a whisper, twirling a strand of her

ponytail between her fingers, "I don't want to get married."

"Wha—" He stopped. "Allie, you're not making sense."

"Kyle, I don't want to just get married, I want to marry *you*. I'm so sorry for being a ditz about the whole thing—"

He chuckled. "That's okay. You're entitled to one freak-out before the biggest commitment of your life. Especially if a hurricane drops by for a visit."

"I have no doubts, Kyle. I actually felt the Lord's joy when I tried on Frannie's dress."

"Frannie's dress?" Kyle echoed.

Allie told him the story of Frannie's wedding dress, locked away in a cedar chest, waiting for such a time as this.

"God has taken care of us, Allie."

"He has. I love you, Kyle," she said.

"Love you more."

"So, how'd you catch up with Jamis?"

"He found out what flight I was on and waited for me in Atlanta."

Allie wrapped the phone cord around her fingers. "Tell him thanks."

"I will."

"Hurry home, okay?"

"Jamis," Kyle bellowed, "get me to the church on time."

❧

Ormond Beach, Saturday, August 12, Noon

Kyle drove south down I-95 while Jamis slept in the passenger seat, his head pillowed against the door with his suit coat. They'd been fortunate and found a gas station just south of

Jacksonville. The line of cars waiting to fuel up wrapped around the tiny station and back toward the exit ramp.

"Better get it now while we can," Jamis had said. Kyle agreed. He wanted to know they had enough gas to take them home.

By his calculations, Kyle figured they were about four hours away from Vero Beach. Traffic moved at a steady pace, and if it didn't slow down, he would make it home in time to shower and change before the wedding.

He really didn't want to marry Allie looking and smelling like he'd been camping for a week. *Allie. . .*

Kyle propped his arm on the windowsill and pictured the piquant brunette. Was it only six days ago that he'd kissed her good-bye at the Melbourne airport?

"Where are we?" Jamis asked, jerking upright, suddenly awake.

"Ormond Beach."

Jamis rubbed his face with his hands. "You'll get to the church in plenty of time."

"Yep," Kyle said, leaning forward, catching sight of something ahead. Flashing blue lights. "Uh-oh, this isn't going to be good."

⸎

Vero Beach, Saturday, August 12, 2:00 p.m.

Allie followed Eva down the center aisle of Pinewood's quaint, small sanctuary, her arm linked with Kendall's. Her old friend had arrived tired but safe an hour ago.

The room was suffocating and hot, but Eva had propped

open the back windows and was cooling the room with six oscillating fans.

Kendall took a deep breath. "I love the smell in here. It reminds me of the North Carolina cabin we went to when I was a kid."

Allie breathed in deep, too. "I smell cinnamon."

Eva motioned to the front of the church. "I lit a few scented candles." She looked at Allie and Kendall. "Well, what do you think?"

Allie turned in a slow circle, stopping when she faced the north wall and the hundred-year-old stained glass windows. "I love the windows. They give the room so much character and history."

Eva smirked. "Okay, great, but I didn't *do* those. What about the wedding decorations?"

Allie laughed. "Right." She continued turning. Hooked to each windowsill was a cluster of white bows and bright-colored flowers. The same bows and flowers topped the aisle side of each pew. Twelve candle stands holding a column candle under glass lined both sides of the aisle.

"Eva, it's wonderful. So perfect."

Kendall bobbed her head. "I love it."

Eva ran her hands through her wild red hair. She looked tired, but happy. "Well, wait." She ran over to the wall, stooped, and suddenly a thousand white lights lit the sanctuary. Eva popped up again. "Reverend Markinson helped me hang the lights."

Allie gasped. *Eva, Eva. . .* "This is absolutely amazing. Where did you get everything?"

"Remember the phone call I made yesterday?"

"Yeah, I think," Allie said, anchoring her arm on Kendall's shoulder.

"A friend of mine owns the Party Place." Eva sighed with a shrug and anchored her hands on her hips. "I was able to track her down and she let me have whatever I wanted."

Allie walked slowly down the aisle. *How incredible.* The altar was decorated with tiered brass candelabras holding tall, tapered candles, and white wooden chairs formed a semicircle along the back of the polished wood stage. Eva had set vibrant-colored floral arrangements in each one. Allie loved the simple elegance of Eva's design.

Eva stood next to her. "I know you wanted real flowers, but—"

Allie turned to her. "Eva, please, no apologies. This is what I wanted and more."

Eva dabbed the sweat from her upper lip. "If we get tired of interior design, we can go into the wedding business."

Behind them the doors creaked open. Allie looked back with a flicker of hope. *Let it be Kyle.* But it was Laura and Reneé.

"Eva, I love it," Laura said, turning in a circle, taking in the room. "When I get married, you're doing my decorations."

Reneé tugged on Allie's arm. "Let's go. We got hair and makeup to do. Your mom said the photographer would be here at three."

Allie glanced at her friends. "I can't believe it's happening." She let out a muffled squeal. "I'm getting married."

Laura shook her head. "When the photographer tracked

down your mom and said he'd be here, I knew God wanted this wedding to take place."

Reneé linked her arm with Allie's. "The reverend has a surprise waiting for you outside."

Allie glanced at her friend. "Really?"

∽∾

4:00 p.m.

The Florida Troopers had routed all southbound I-95 traffic over to U.S. 1. Downed trees blocked the highway and now Kyle and Jamis crept along slower than ever.

Every traffic light on U.S. 1 south of Titusville was out, turning every intersection into a four-way stop. Kyle wanted to jump out of his skin.

"I could walk home faster than this," he said, motioning out the window at the long lines of traffic. He glanced at the dash clock. It read 3:33. "We're not going to make it."

Shaking his head, he picked up his cell phone to dial Allie, his heart heavy. He'd disappointed her so much already. Leaving town the week of their wedding, knowing a hurricane could hit. And now he couldn't get home in time for the ceremony everyone worked so hard to put together.

Father, please. He looked at his phone, then over at Jamis, who took over driving just after they entered Brevard County. "No cell service."

"Let's just keep driving south," Jamis said. "We'll get there sooner or later."

Kyle slumped down in his seat, closed his eyes, and meditated on Psalm 131:2, the Bible verse he'd read in New York.

Surely I have calmed and quieted my soul; like a weaned child with his mother, like a weaned child is my soul within me.

He muttered the words over and over as Jamis inched the car southward.

Chapter 9

Vero Beach, Saturday, August 12, 4:30 p.m.

Allie peered out the window of Reverend Markinson's living room. Three more cars turned into the pine-needle-covered parking lot.

"There must be fifty or sixty guests already," she said, twisting her grandmother's handkerchief in her hand. "How many can the chapel hold?"

"About seventy," Jewel said, patting the cushion next to her on the couch. "Come, sit down. You're making me nervous."

Allie exhaled as she sat. Around her, Laura, Reneé, Eva, and Jewel waited patiently in bridesmaid's gowns they'd worn for other weddings. The colors and styles were completely different and Allie wondered if the eclectic dresses would work. But like everything else that came together for this hurricane wedding weekend, so did the dresses.

"Still no word from Kyle?" Mom asked, coming out of the bathroom, smoothing her navy A-line skirt.

"No," Allie said. "I tried to call from the reverend's phone, but he didn't answer."

"He'll be here," Jewel said, squeezing Allie's hand.

Allie glanced at her sister and a sensation of gratitude quieted her anxiety. "I know the Lord didn't bring us this far for nothing, but we really have no idea where Kyle is."

"Did you like Reverend Markinson's surprise?" Kendall asked from across the room. Her bangs fluttered as she fanned herself with an old bulletin. "A horse-drawn carriage?"

"I can't believe he went to all the trouble." Allie smiled softly at the image of the old brown mare hitched to the shiny black carriage. "I tried to hire a horse and carriage for this weekend, but never could find anyone who could do it."

Allie looked over her shoulder out the window. The mare stood quietly in the shade. The reverend's voice sounded across her mind.

"I borrowed the horse from the neighbor down the way," he'd explained when Allie and the girls exited the chapel. "And the carriage has been in the horse barn for fifty years. I just gave it a little spit and polish."

"Oh, Reverend, how wonderful," Allie had said, smoothing her hand along the mare's bare back. "What a lovely surprise."

He'd beamed. "You can leave the church after the ceremony. Take a ride around the grounds before the reception." He winked. "Get a little time alone."

Allie's eyes misted. "Thank you for making our day so special, Reverend."

"You look beautiful," Eva said, bringing Allie's thoughts back into the room.

"So do you," Allie said, then drew an anxious breath. "Come on, Kyle."

"He'll be here," Reneé said.

Allie wandered over to the picture window as the girls chatted about past weddings they'd attended. She listened with half an ear, glancing every few minutes at the clock.

It was becoming the eleventh hour. What if Kyle didn't show? What if he was in an accident? What if he changed his mind? She bit her bottom lip and wound Grandma's handkerchief tighter around her fingers.

The front door swung open and Frannie and Gracie breezed into the reverend's living room. "The horse-barn-reception-hall is perfect," Frannie said, her eyes bright in her flushed face. "Eva has outdone herself."

"Yes, she has," Allie agreed absently.

Frannie came over and slipped her arm around Allie's shoulders. "You know he's doing all he can to be here."

Allie sighed. Seems to be all anyone can say. She gripped Frannie's hand. "I know. Thank you."

"You look absolutely stunning in your dress." Frannie swiped her fingers under her eyes. "I'm so proud to have you wear it."

"Enough of this," Gracie said, shoving in next to Allie. "Let's get down to business. What do you know about the birds and the bees?"

"Miss Gracie," Allie shouted with laughter.

❧

5:00 p.m.

As Jamis passed the Melbourne city limits sign, Kyle motioned with his left hand. "Pull over, Jamis. Pull over."

"What for?" Jamis asked, pulling onto the berm and stopping the car behind a Florida State Trooper.

"I have an idea." Kyle hopped out and jogged over to the trooper's vehicle. The officer's window slid down as Kyle approached.

"Good evening, Officer," Kyle said, smiling. He didn't want to imagine how he looked with a three-day-old beard, unwashed hair, and bloodshot eyes, but he was desperate.

"What can I do for you?" The officer removed his reflective sunglasses from his thin face.

"Well, I need a favor."

"What kind of favor?" The officer's eyes narrowed.

"Well, sir, I'm suppose to get married in a few minutes down in Vero Beach, but it doesn't look like I'm going to make it."

The officer grinned. "No, it sure doesn't."

"That's where you come in," Kyle said.

❧

"Allie?" Kyle's dad knocked on the reverend's front door and peered inside. He stopped short as Allie walked over to greet him. "You look beautiful."

"Thank you, Judge Landon." Allie kissed him lightly on the cheek.

"Call me Ellis or Dad, but not Judge or Mr. Landon."

Allie laughed. "All right. . .Dad." She liked Kyle's father, a top Miami judge with a reputation for fairness.

"Oh, Allie." Mrs. Landon stepped around her husband with her slender hand resting on the string of pearls about her neck. "You look stunning. Oh, if that boy of mine doesn't get here soon. . ." Her brown eyes snapped.

"Don't worry," Allie said more for herself than Kyle's mom. "He'll make it if he can."

"If he knows what's good for him, he will." Mom Landon embraced Allie, then stepped back, surveying her dress. "Your gown is beautiful. Where did you find it?"

Allie glanced down at the candlelight dress. "A dear friend kept it waiting for me." Allie smiled at Frannie with her eyes.

Despite the circumstances, she felt like a princess in Frannie's dress. The tiara veil fit perfectly when Laura and Reneé swept her hair on top of her head and crowned her Princess Allie.

Dad Landon touched her shoulder with his fingertips. "Kyle's friends Eric and Max just arrived."

"Really?" Allie pulled the curtain aside. Two handsome men stood on the parsonage carport, hands in their suit pockets, talking to Joshua and Wade. They looked like the kind of men Kyle would be friends with and it made her miss him even more.

She turned to her father-in-law. "Did they come with you?" She glanced at them again. How odd. They looked familiar.

"Yes, they followed us up from Miami."

Eric and Max caught her watching. Wide smiles spread across their faces.

Allie went to the door. "I suppose I should say hello." She stepped outside just as a Florida Trooper pulled into the parking lot.

◦⊱∞⊰◦

Allie felt all the blood drain from her face. "Something's happened to Kyle." She stumbled down the porch steps, tripping

255

over the fragile hem of her dress.

All the wedding guests stopped and stared. A hush settled over the Pinewood yard.

A round-bellied trooper stepped out of his car. "Are you Allie Seton?"

"Yes." Allie stopped, unable to move another step. Dad Landon steadied her with his hand around her waist and she leaned into him.

The trooper smiled, making his flabby cheeks jiggle. "I got radioed that your husband-to-be is on his way. He's stuck in traffic on U.S. 1. He thinks he can be here, cleaned up, by eight." He grinned wide.

Allie exhaled then gripped the officer in a hug. "Thank you. Thank you so much."

The guests cheered, then started moving and talking again as if God had called "Action."

"Might as well eat while we're waiting," Allie's dad called from the horse barn's open door. "The reception hall is open."

Allie walked over to Eric and Max. "I'm Allie," she said, offering her hand. "Thank you for coming."

"We know," the tall blond said, shaking her hand. "I'm Eric."

"You know?" Allie asked, peering into his blue eyes, unsure why his confession carried an intimate tone.

"And I'm Max." He pumped Allie's hand. Slightly shorter than Eric, Max had dark brown hair and laughing brown eyes.

"Thank you for coming." Allie grinned. She liked them both. Max reminded her of Kyle, smiling as if he knew something the rest of the world didn't. And Eric reminded her of Jewel's husband, Tony—confidence covered by tenderness.

Eric glanced at Max, then at Allie. "You don't remember, do you?"

Allie squinted and tipped her head to one side. "Am I supposed to remember something?"

Max held up his hands. "I can't believe he hasn't told her. No way am I getting my man in trouble on his wedding night."

Eric clasped his hands behind his back and bent slightly to look Allie in the eyes. "FSU-Miami game, fall of '99. Kyle's the crazy guy who kissed you and followed you out of the stadium. We were with him."

Allie's jaw dropped. "No, he's not. You're kidding."

"No, we're not kidding." Eric glanced at Max like back-me-up-here.

"That was Kyle? Really?"

Max tugged on Eric's arm. "Didn't I hear something about food?"

"Wait," Allie said, her hand on Eric's shoulder. "If that was Kyle, why did he do that?"

Eric leaned close. "He fell in love with you the moment he saw you and has been ever since."

Max added. "He believes in miracles, or so he says."

Allie stood still, stunned. "That's unbelievable. Why didn't he tell me?"

Eric and Max shook their heads. "That, you have to ask him."

Allie smiled, feeling as if a silent question had been asked and answered. She looked at Max. "I'll ask him. And by the way, God does do miracles."

Max studied her for a moment. "I'll have to consider that, then."

"Yes, you should."

Eric slapped his hand on Max's shoulder. "Didn't I hear you mention food?"

Allie pointed toward the horse barn. "This way, gentlemen."

❧

8:10 p.m.

"Allie, it's getting late, but we just can't leave," Mr. Noble said, scooping the last of the peanuts from Aunt Rebekah's crystal bowl. "Anna Marie is dying to see how this day ends."

That makes two of us. Allie forced a smile. "Thank you for waiting, Mr. Noble."

Mr. Noble tossed a few peanuts into his mouth. "Interesting mix of food."

"Best we could do in the aftermath," Allie said, the weight of the emotional day bearing down on her. She felt weary. And, though she hadn't looked in the mirror lately, she just knew her makeup had melted and her hair had gone flat.

Kyle, come, please.

"Guess ole Hurricane Allie messed things up for you, but you showed her," Mr. Noble said, reaching for a napkin.

"Yes, I suppose I did." Allie lifted her chin. Mr. Noble's attitude strengthened her.

"It's lovely what you all have done here." He motioned with his hand toward the candles and lights. Outside the barn doors, the generator hummed.

"My partner at DESA Designs, Eva, gets all the credit,"

Allie said, then excused herself and wandered toward the chapel. The windows were beacons of soft, white lights and the little church stood out in the darkness.

Kyle, please, come! Allie squeezed her fists together and prayed with faith. She entered the sanctuary and walked down the aisle, her skirt swishing about her ankles. When she arrived at the front, she sat on the red cushioned pew and closed her eyes to pray. *Please, Lord.*

⌘

8:20 p.m.

Kyle burst through the chapel doors expecting to see a room full of waiting-weary guests. But instead, he found his beautiful bride alone in the quiet, warm room.

He stopped, his heavy heartbeat stealing his breath. Allie's chestnut hair cascaded down her back in a tumble of shiny curls.

"Waiting for me?" he asked as he approached her.

Allie shot to her feet and whirled around. "Kyle. You're here!" She ran into his arms.

The smell of sage and roses drifted under his nose and for the first time in days, Kyle felt like himself. "Babe, I'm so sorry." He buried his face in her neck.

"You're here. You're here." She slipped her arms around his neck and kissed his face over and over. "I've been waiting and praying."

"I—" His lips touched hers and satisfied every yearning in him.

When he released her, he pressed his forehead to hers and

muttered, "Are you ready to get married?"

Allie murmured. "Oh, yes." She fell against him and breathed deep. After a moment, she said, "It was you."

He brushed her cheek with the back of his hand. "What was me?"

"You're the one who kissed me at the FSU-Miami game."

Kyle's eyes grew wide. "Eric or Max?"

Allie laughed. "Eric."

Kyle wrapped her in his arms. "Yeah, it was me."

"I can't believe it! Why didn't you tell me?" Allie looked into his eyes.

Kyle shrugged. "I don't know; I was such a jerk that day." He pulled his vows from his suit pocket and with a sheepish grin said, "I planned to tell you today."

Allie put her hands on his face and kissed him. "Maybe later tonight you can tell me all about how you kissed me one day and seven years later managed to marry me."

Kyle laughed and kissed her forehead. "Oh, I will. It's quite a tale."

"But right now, can we just get married?" She tugged on his lapels.

"Absolutely."

Allie patted his chest. "I'll call the guests."

"No," Kyle said, stepping away from her, his hands sliding down her silky arms. "I'm the groom. I'll call the guests to the chapel."

He strode down the aisle with purpose and flung open the heavy chapel doors. "Hello, everyone, the groom has arrived! It's time for the wedding."

Loud cheering erupted from the churchyard. The guests scurried inside and filled the chapel's pews.

Several of the women tried to push Allie out one side door and Kyle out the other.

"You can't see each other."

"Allie has to come in from the back. Walk down the aisle."

Kyle stopped the commotion with a flash of his hands. "Please, everyone. Sit down." He looked around the room. "I appreciate everything you all have done to give Allie and me this beautiful wedding. I'm sorry I took so long to get here. But, I've already seen my beautiful bride and if you all don't mind, I'd like to forgo tradition and have Reverend Markinson perform the ceremony right now."

A few guests shouted their consent.

Allie took his hand, her misty gaze on his face. "I love you," she said.

Suddenly, Pachelbel's Canon in D filled the sanctuary. Jewel, Eva, Laura, and Reneé hurried to take their places beside Allie. Josh, Wade, Max, and Eric stood alongside Kyle.

Woodward Seton stepped forward. "If you don't mind, son, there's one tradition I'd like to keep." He cleared his throat with a guttural cough and took Allie's arm. "I *am* giving her away."

Kyle grinned. "Yes, sir."

Reverend Markinson stood behind Kyle, and Allie stepped into the aisle with her father.

"Well, welcome everyone," the reverend said. "Especially you, Kyle." The reverend gave Kyle a sideways grin. "It's always good when the groom arrives."

A soft laugh rippled through the twinkling sanctuary.

"Woodward, do you give this woman to this man?" Reverend Markinson motioned between Allie and Kyle.

"I. . . ," Dad faltered, clearing his throat. "I do." He placed Allie's hand in Kyle's, kissed her lightly on the cheek, and stepped away.

"Kyle, face your bride," Reverend Markinson said.

"With pleasure." He winked at Allie and gripped her hands.

The reverend opened with prayer, then turned to Kyle. "Do you, Kyle Montgomery Landon, take Allie Jane Seton to be your wife, in good times and bad. . ."

And so, Allie Seton got married.

RACHEL HAUCK

Rachel Hauck lives in Palm Bay, Florida, with her husband, Tony, their two dogs, and one cat. She endured life before, during, and after 2004's hurricanes Frances and Jeanne. She never wants to do that again.

Rachel works with Tony, an associate pastor, in training young people to have a passion for Jesus. She is a prayer and worship leader and a speaker. She also holds a BA in journalism from The Ohio State University and is a huge Buckeyes football fan. She loves to read and play sports.

Rachel is a multi-published author and the past president of American Christian Fiction Writers. Visit her web site at www.rachelhauck.com for more information on her books and blog.

Heart's Refuge

Lynette Sowell

Dedication

To my mom, who gave me a love of story by reading to me before I was born, and Dad, who traveled with me to Narnia and taught me to dream big.

My fellow authors and friends in American Christian Fiction Writers—I'm in your debt. You have mentored, encouraged, prayed for, and given to me in so many ways. If I tried to list everyone who's impacted my writing, I'd run out of room and still leave someone out.

Rachel Hauck, Lena Nelson Dooley, and Pamela Griffin—I've had a ball being on your team. Thanks! Also thanks to Christine Lynxwiler for the critique; and to Pat Loomis who lives in California wildfire country, for checking my story. Also thanks to Jenny Peery, Amber Miller, Melody Lee, and Jennifer Vihel for your assistance in my research.

CJ, my hero. For loving me, cheering me on, and not letting me quit. Zach and Hannah, thanks for putting up with leftovers some nights. If all teenagers came like you, I'd order a few more.

Prologue

It is with great joy that we
Krista Marie Schmidt
and
Luke Michael Hansen
Invite you to witness our exchange of vows
Saturday, the Seventeenth of June
Four o'clock in the afternoon
Settler Lake Chapel
Settler Lake, California

Chapter 1

N ana, it's me! Sorry I'm late!" Krista Schmidt let the screen door bang behind her just in case Nana didn't hear, although skidding her Jeep to a stop in front of the sprawling ranch home could hardly be considered arriving quietly. She would have been on time if she hadn't needed someone to jump-start her battery at the college.

"I'm in the sewing room, dear." Nana's voice filtered toward the entryway.

Krista moved down the front hall to Nana's haven. The snowy-haired woman was kneeling before a dress form covered with a gown of feathery cream lace.

"Oh, it's beautiful." Pre-wedding jitters fluttered in Krista's stomach like butterflies.

Nana used the edge of her sewing table to help herself up, then smoothed an invisible wrinkle on her tailored pants. "The cleaner cared for the dress as if it had belonged to the First Lady."

"I can't wait to try it on."

Nana unfastened the buttons of the gown's neck and bodice

and removed the dress from the body form. "Here, you get into this, and I'll be right back. I want to show you something." A frown crossed her face. "Is Luke coming by? Can't let him see you in your wedding gown."

"Well, he's on his way back from the airport in Sacramento with Jeff. They should be in town soon. I imagine he might stop by." Krista's hands shook as she held the dress, but she stilled them.

"Jeff, huh?"

Krista hoped her shrug appeared as though she didn't care. "I'm just glad Luke and I are getting married. Finally." Saturday she would walk down the aisle at the Settler's chapel and become Mrs. Luke Hansen. If only he hadn't asked Jeff, of all people, to be his best man. Krista thought she had forgiven Jeff for the past, but her throat caught.

"Keep looking forward, Krista. Don't look back." Nana squeezed her arm before she left the room.

Krista slipped from her shorts and T-shirt and slid the gown over her head. The fabric settled around her. She swished the skirt a little so the length would fall to the floor. Nana would do the hooks. Krista fingered the material and turned to the full-length mirror.

Her great-great-grandmother Elfi had worn this dress as a mail-order bride to Settler Lake just after the turn of the last century. How did it feel to marry a man she'd barely met after a harrowing journey west?

Krista stared at her reflection. A crinkle appeared between her eyebrows. She rubbed the skin and the crinkle went away. Too much time in the sun. She tried to pile her hair on her head—she still couldn't decide between an updo or long.

"You dressed?"

"Yes."

Nana came in, carrying the tooled leather album Krista spent hours poring through when she was a little girl. "Here. You look as beautiful as Elfi in the gown."

Krista reached for the book while Nana moved behind her to fasten the bodice. "She must have been an amazing woman."

"I'm told she was. And now it's time for another amazing woman to wear this dress."

"Ha. I don't feel amazing. But thank you." Krista smiled at Nana, then found the daguerreotype taken of Elfriede von Braun on the day she became Elfriede Meyer. "She looks scared."

Nana looked over her shoulder. "I think all brides are a little scared. Did I ever tell you how she knew she'd chosen the right man from the sea of eligible bachelors waiting for an Eastern bride?"

"Tell me again. I need the reassurance." Krista studied the hem, which barely skimmed the floor. Nana had altered the gown to fit Krista's height and modern figure. Carefully tea-stained lace matched the dress perfectly. Krista turned to the side and viewed the simple train. If she took careful steps on the big day, she might not snag a toe through the now-lengthened hem. Shoes! She needed shoes, yet another detail she'd forgotten in the hubbub of wedding preparations. *Calm down. Listen to Nana.*

"When my grandmother stepped off the wagon and stood

with the other women who had come west to meet their husbands, she prayed that God would direct her to the right man, and him to her. She saw a tall, thin man with a mustache and a threadbare suit. When he asked if anyone spoke German, she smiled."

"And she replied in German," Krista finished, "and told him she made the best schnitzel he would ever eat—besides his mother's."

"Elfi's prayer was answered. They found companionship and love, which weren't guaranteed in those days. And here we are, generations later where marriage is never easy."

"Oh, Nana, I love Luke so much."

The front door banged. "Hey, is there a bride-to-be in the house?"

"Luke Hansen, don't you dare come in here!" Krista tried to spring for the sewing room door, but Nana beat her to it before she ripped a seam. Nana entered the hall and closed the door behind her.

Krista listened through the door. "Young man, if you cross the threshold to this room, I'll see to it you never eat an Elfi's schnitzel again!" She imagined Nana standing as tall as her five-foot-three height would let her in front of Luke's six-foot-plus frame.

"No problem, Nana." The timbre of Luke's voice made Krista want to rush to his arms. Maybe Jeff hadn't come after all.

"This is my best man, Jeff Worley. We were at UCLA together. Jeff, meet Nana Schmidt."

Krista frowned and looked down at the dress. She couldn't escape seeing the man who had split up her and Luke once before. *Give me strength, Lord, not to give Jeff a piece of my mind I can't spare. Why didn't I tell Luke this was a bad idea?*

"Welcome to Settler Lake."

"Thanks, Mrs. Schmidt."

Now Luke spoke. "We'll wait in the living room, Nana. Are you about done with Krista? I promised her dinner tonight."

"I must help her take off the dress first. Go on, we'll be out soon."

"You got it. C'mon, Jeff." The men's voices grew quieter as they moved to the front room.

Krista itched inside the gown. The weather was too hot for June in northern California. Too dry. She preferred a quick swim in Nana's pool before dinner instead of facing Jeff in the front room. She had forgiven him a thousand times in the past four years, but still—

Nana wore a satisfied smile when she opened the door. "Let's get you out of that dress and hang it in the closet until Saturday morning." Nana put her hands on Krista's shoulders and studied her in the mirror. "You look so much like Elfi. She was strong like you, too."

Krista compared her image to that of her ancestor on the page. "I see her in my eyes, nose, and chin. But I don't feel very strong." She closed the album and placed it on the sewing table.

Nana worked at undoing the hooks on the bodice. "Strength doesn't come from the inside. Remember that. 'God is our refuge and strength, a very present help in trouble.' Along with this wedding, a time of joy, I should think you'll have plenty of strength."

"I hope so." Krista worried her lower lip, then stopped. She didn't need chapped lips. It was hard enough to keep from fidgeting. "I've enjoyed planning the wedding with Luke. It's what comes after that I'm scared about. I know God intended us to marry 'till death do us part,' but I'm scared. It's so. . .permanent."

"That it is."

"Not that I want to get out of marriage or even think of life without Luke." Krista paused. "How many years were you and Grandpa Schmidt married?"

"Forty-five. We had our share of troubles, within and without. We just learned to run to each other—and to God, rather than run somewhere else."

Krista nodded. "I plan to do that. After all, Luke is my best friend." She wanted to share more of her uneasy thoughts but stopped. Why voice her fears and give them a life of their own? She let the gown fall softly to the floor and stepped carefully over the pile of cloth. Nana hung the dress back on the hanger and placed it inside a zippered bag while Krista dressed. Now, to face Luke—and Jeff—in the living room.

"Thank you." Krista hugged her grandmother.

"Your parents arrive Friday?"

"That's right. Mom's been begging for something to do. I told her just to buy a pretty dress and show up and not worry about a thing."

Nana laughed. "As if your mother would listen to that request."

They left the sewing room, which Nana securely locked behind them, and headed for the living room. Pictures lined the front hallway, and Krista felt as if the Schmidts who'd gone on before nodded at the newest family bride.

"So I told them we needed to get serious about clearing brush before the full heat of summer." Luke's voice rang out with that I'm-on-my-soapbox tone again. "Settler Lake hasn't been affected by fires like some of the other towns—like French Gulch—but we should learn from their planning."

Jeff asked, "It's that serious?"

Krista rounded the corner to see Jeff shaking his head. His focus snapped to her, and she nodded. "Hey, Jeff." She wouldn't lie and say she was glad to see him again.

"What about me?" Luke sidestepped the coffee table and enveloped Krista in a hug followed by a quick kiss. Her stomach turned over from butterflies of a different kind.

"Hi to you, too." His nearness reminded her of one reason she looked forward to being married.

Nana cleared her throat. "I'll get us a pitcher of lemonade. If you have your swimming trunks, you're welcome to a dip in the pool. But I'll stick to the hot tub. My hip's been hurting me lately."

Krista turned at Nana's words. "You never said anything about your hip. And you let me drag you along on those errands the other day—"

"Shush, it's nothing." Nana waved off Krista's concern and headed for the kitchen.

Krista and Luke sat down on the embroidered settee and she smiled. Jeff might be Luke's buddy from the old days, but he was on her home turf and they could wait before gallivanting off for the evening after dinner.

"Did you have a good trip, then?" She laced her fingers

through Luke's and gave a squeeze.

"It wasn't bad. Jeff wanted to stop and eat, but I wanted to get back to you." He raised her hand to his lips and kissed it.

"Wow, Kris-Kris, you've already got him tethered with the old ball and chain, and you haven't even gotten him to the church yet." Jeff snickered.

Krista wanted to smack him, but she reminded herself she didn't hit *boys*. Instead she managed a smile without clenching her teeth. Amazing what an actress she could be if she tried. She would definitely pray and do an extra ten laps in the pool tonight. *You brought this on yourself. You assured Luke you were just fine with Jeff as best man.*

"Don't listen to him. He's just jealous. I'm planning to grow old with you and hang family pictures on the walls of our house, just like Nana's got here." Luke shot Jeff a look that satisfied Krista more than any slap on the face. She might have an independent streak, but she liked having Luke be her champion.

"Oh, yes, the house you two had built." Jeff shifted his tall form in the wingback chair. "Can't wait to see it."

"I'll show you after dinner. I'm all moved in so you can bunk with me. There's plenty of room."

Krista gaped at Luke. How could she get the rest of her things moved into their home with that—that—*Jeff* lurking around? Already she could hear him wisecracking about Luke losing his freedom. She might as well go by the bowling alley and see if Uncle Al could attach a length of chain to a twenty-pound ball, and give it to Luke as a wedding gift. *Ball and chain—right!*

Chapter 2

K rista sat beside Luke at Jody's Pizza Palace, listening to Jeff's resonating voice go on and on about life in LA. They had one of the locally coveted outdoor tables with a spectacular view of the mountains to the west. A special table would have meant more if it was just her and Luke sharing it. She frowned when another diner flicked a cigarette onto the patio stones. *Tourist.* Thunder echoed off the mountains in the distance. Krista much preferred the sound of thunder to Jeff's voice. Thunder meant rain. Jeff's voice meant only aggravation.

"Kris-Kris, you haven't heard a word I just said, have you?"

She would *not* roll her eyes at the unwanted nickname Jeff had given her years ago. "I wish that guy hadn't tossed that cigarette. What if it had rolled into the bushes?" Krista shook her head. Luke stood. She reached for his arm. "Wait—don't say anything. Let it go."

"I'm just going to put it out and throw it away." Luke moved across the patio to where the discarded cigarette glowed. He extinguished it with a sneakered foot, picked it up, and headed for the nearest trash can after pointedly staring at the FIRE HAZARD sign in the restaurant window.

Jeff shook his head. "We used to really tear it up on the beach volleyball circuit. Now look at him."

"That life is years and miles away from here. He's not the same guy—I mean, he's still Luke, but he's different, too." How much had Luke told Jeff about the changes in his life? She glanced in Luke's direction. Good. He was on his way back.

"You can take the boy out of the party, but you can't take the party out of the boy."

Krista shrugged and grabbed another slice of extra-cheese pepperoni. Better to stuff her mouth with pizza than say something she'd regret. Luke slid onto the seat next to her.

"I hope those clouds have rain." He studied the western sky.

"Me, too," she mumbled around her pizza.

"Not much nightlife here, is there?" Jeff looked at the other diners. "What do they do with the sidewalks at night?"

"We tuck them in every night, nice and snug." Luke grinned. "After dinner, I'll—or we'll—give you the grand tour of the house."

Krista was glad Luke found a comeback. She couldn't think of anything clever to say all night, but then she hadn't counted on dinner with Jeff. What she'd planned on—or hoped for, rather—was a romantic dinner at Mountaintop complete with candles, soft music, and sharing plans for the future. Instead she found herself pasting on a smile and making light conversation.

She grabbed the chance to call it an early evening. "Luke,

I'll let you show Jeff around. I know you guys will want some talk time. I need to call Sami to make sure she's confirmed her flight for tomorrow. Plus, I'm worried about Nana. Her back's bothering her." The excuses tumbled out, sounding feeble to her ears. But she wanted—no, needed—a break from Jeff's comments. She hoped Luke would set him straight on lots of things.

Jeff paid the check, a gesture that surprised yet pleased Krista.

She caught Luke studying her face as they headed to his car. He glanced at his friend. "Jeff, can you give us a minute?"

Jeff nodded and moved under a parking lot light that had just flickered on. He flipped open his cell phone and dialed.

Krista stopped at the front passenger door and turned to face Luke.

He rubbed her arm. "Hey, are you okay? You don't seem yourself tonight."

She sighed. "It's Jeff. I don't like his comments. I know he was your roommate, your buddy, your teammate, but. . ." She gestured as if waving her hand might summon the right words.

"But you're my best friend, and after Saturday we'll start the rest of our lives together." Luke surrounded her with his arms and she leaned on him for a moment. "In the last few hours, I've realized how much Jeff and I don't have in common anymore. Deep down he's a good guy who's searching for something. Or Someone. And I always promised him he could be my best man. I stood up for him at his first wedding, so I can't expect him not to return the favor."

She moved back so she wouldn't mumble into his shirt. "You've known him a long time."

Luke nodded. "That's why I hope I can reach out to him this week. Communicating by phone or e-mail isn't the same as in person. I feel pretty bad that I moved home and never shared my faith with him. But back then I also did some stupid things."

"We promised never to bring any of that up again." Krista smiled at him. "I love you now, more than then, and we've come through so much. When I told you back in October that I was okay with Jeff coming, I meant it. I really did."

"I know." He touched his forehead to hers. "That's why I'll talk to Jeff later and tell him to cool it. Then Saturday we'll marry and begin our life together. Isn't that something to look forward to? How long have we been planning this wedding?"

"Forever, it seems. Thanks for bearing with me. I've been cranky lately and—"

He kissed her into silence, and Krista relished the closeness. *Please, let it always be like this.*

"Oh, lovebirds, I think the storm is getting closer." Jeff again.

Krista and Luke moved apart as a flash lit the twilight. A few seconds later, a boom echoed across the parking lot.

"Time to go, Kris." Luke unlocked the car and opened her door.

She slid onto the passenger seat. The stuffy air inside the car made it hard to breathe, and she inhaled fresh air with relief when Luke lowered the windows and they headed into the evening. Heat of the day radiated from the pavement. Even with the approaching storm, none of the cool air they'd hoped for had come from the mountains.

Luke pointed out a few local spots to Jeff, including the road to the ranger station where he worked for the local logging company, and Krista tried not to picture Jeff's expression of disdain behind them in the dark. Instead, her heart longed for home, but she wasn't sure what home was just yet. Her apartment near the college was already vacant. She almost wanted to keep her old bedroom at Nana's that she used to stay in when she was a child. This weekend she was marrying the man of her dreams. No specters from the past would ruin their time of joy. Nothing would change her mind.

But what about Luke's mind? Krista pushed the thought away.

⁕

"Man, you're really taking the plunge." Jeff popped the top to his can. "You left all we had in Southern Cal and came back to this." Lightning flickered in the kitchen windows, but still no rain fell.

Luke grinned while hunting in the fridge for the jar of microwavable cheese. "Yeah, I sure am." And he could hardly wait. Already touches of Krista's presence filled the home he'd worked on for the past year. Then Saturday night, he would carry her across the threshold and they'd spend the night here before flying to Hawaii the next morning.

"I've done it twice, and I'm a much wiser and poorer man." Jeff ambled to the den, a few steps down from the sprawling kitchen. "Marriage is highly overrated, and there are plenty of desperate women in the world who just want a date and a good time. No strings attached."

Luke shook his head. *How do I tell him I know Krista and I will make it?* He put the cheese in a bowl and popped it into the microwave. "Those nachos will be ready in a few." He found a half-eaten bag of tortilla chips. Its companion bag, unopened, was behind it in the pantry.

Jeff clicked on the TV and changed the channel to ESPN. "Hey, Keefer and Cranfill are playing. Remember them? They were just starting out when we were winding down."

Luke looked across the breakfast bar toward the den. Two teams of two men were battling out a volleyball game in the sand. "I remember. My shoulder and ankle remind me every time, just before it rains."

The microwave's beep drowned out the cheering crowd as one of the players—Cranfill—leaped with the agility of a cat and spiked the ball into the sand on the other side of the court. Luke shook his head and went to the microwave. Once he took out the cheese and grabbed the chips, he headed to the den. He settled next to Jeff on the couch, which still smelled new.

Jeff reached for a handful of nacho chips. "Do you regret we missed out on the Olympics?"

"Sometimes." Luke touched the scar on his right shoulder from rotator cuff surgery. "If my shoulder hadn't blown, we might have made it to Athens. I'm sorry."

"We said back then we wouldn't ever talk like this—no regrets. You got me to graduate and dragged me into our crazy career. I'll always be in your debt." Jeff plunged a hand into the chip bag as soon as Luke put it on the coffee table. "Do I guess correctly that you built this house with those sunglasses and sunblock endorsements you did? I figure working for a logging company and a part-time firefighter doesn't pay the big bucks."

"That's right. I figured one day my body wouldn't cooperate like it did in those 'glory days,' and I'd be just a regular guy." Luke felt the wave of loss break over him, just as it had when the orthopedic surgeon told him he'd never play pro volleyball again. "I invested some of the money and gave Krista this house. What did you do with yours?"

Jeff shrugged. "I invested a little, bought a couple fast cars and a few fast women."

Luke stared at the game on TV. *God, was I like that? Not all of the other guys on the circuit were.*

"You game for a run in the morning after this pig-out event tonight?" Jeff's outward bravado masked the hurt Luke knew lurked below the surface.

"Probably. Not far, though." Luke opened his soda. "I'm sorry it didn't work out with Misti. Are you sure there's no chance you can get back together?"

"Not unless the guy she left me for drops off the face of the earth." Jeff glared at the television. A muscled, tan player dove to the sand.

"Do you want her back?"

Jeff nodded and blinked. "I do. She had me fooled, and I thought I'd fooled her. She beat me at my own game of not getting tied down. The strange thing is, I still love her. I—I know why she did what she did, running off with Emilio." His face assumed a blank expression as he stared at the screen.

"What are you looking for, Jeff?" *Tell him—you know what he wants so desperately.*

"I have no idea." Jeff's shoulders sank.

"You won't find it in cars, women, or anything else."

Jeff sat up straight again. "But I can have fun trying." Then he stood.

The smart-aleck approach used to crack Luke up. They used to carry on like a couple of wiseacres for hours. Now it just seemed sad. *Oh, Krista, I wouldn't trade our life together for any of that. Not anymore.*

Chapter 3

The sun peered through the pines and slanted across the weight bench and into Luke's eyes. Another hot one on the way. Luke finished his bench press and let the bar onto the rack. He sat up on the bench and then moved across the room to close the blind. What he wouldn't give for a good, soaking rainstorm to sweep down from the west. After the lightning show last night—nothing.

Luke shrugged his shoulders in small circles. The weights on the bar looked like something a 98-pound weakling might bench press. He would have pushed himself with something a bit heavier, but that would mean Jeff needed to spot him. When he passed by the guest room this morning on the way downstairs, Jeff was still sprawled out snoring, and Luke wasn't surprised.

A figure with tousled hair and wearing shorts appeared in the doorway. "Man, what time is it?"

"Going on eight thirty. Sleep good?"

"Once I slept. It's quiet here. Nice, but quiet." Jeff trudged into the room, cast a glance at the weight bench, and headed to the window instead.

"We're due at Nana's in an hour for breakfast."

"I was going to get a few more minutes of sleep."

"Right." Luke chuckled.

"You need a spot?" Jeff moved to the weight stand.

"Sure." Luke added another twenty-five pounds to each end of the bar. "You want to do a few reps after I'm through?"

"Nah, I'm pretty out of it this morning."

"Up late, huh?" Luke lay back on the bench and grasped the bar. Jeff stood ready.

"Yeah. Misti and I were talking. You heard?"

Luke grinned and exhaled as he pushed the weight up. "Yup."

"I was kinda loud."

"Yup." Luke lowered the weight then pushed up again. He felt the burn of his pecs flexing at the weights.

"Sorry. She really hacked me off."

Luke gave up. He let the weight settle onto the stand, ducked under the bar, and sat up. He couldn't count, bench press, and respond to Jeff at the same time. "So what's going on?"

"I—I told her once and for all that I want her in my life. I don't want to share her with anyone."

"Really. Do you think she wants to share you?"

Jeff hung his head. "No. I know what you're going to say. I'm getting what I deserve. Last night all that stuff about buying women? I'm tired. It just doesn't work anymore. Misti's the one for me."

Luke grabbed Jeff's shoulder. "I think you're growing up."

Jeff blinked and rubbed his eyes with his forearm. "You've

sure changed. This place has got you back on the straight and narrow."

"It's not the place."

"Well, you've got a good woman."

"It's not just her, either. It's the power of forgiveness."

"Getting her to take you back must have taken a long time."

"I was talking about God's forgiveness."

"Well, you came home and got religion. Good for you. I think I'm going to patch things up with Misti, send her flowers, or even order a bracelet online and have it shipped to her. You got DSL or dial-up in that office down the hall?"

"DSL." Luke grabbed his towel. "But she needs to see your heart. Gifts alone don't work. I tried that after I got back here and spent six months feeling sorry for myself. Once I realized I needed God's forgiveness, I needed to get Krista's, too."

"Uh-huh." He didn't sound convinced.

"It took awhile to build that bridge, and it took time for her to trust me as a friend, but eventually we knew we needed more—we were meant for more." Luke's heart pounded at remembering when he'd proposed. "One night last summer, we were hiking, and I popped the question. Can't believe I did it. Then I had to wait a week for an answer 'cause I got called out on a fire."

"So like they say, the rest is history."

"You could say that." He'd blown it as a witness in the past. How could he share his faith with Jeff now? Luke slung the towel over his shoulder. "I'm ready for some coffee." Here Jeff had shared his pain, and all Luke could offer was talk about forgiveness and morning coffee. He wanted to share more than positive thoughts and caffeine. Forgiveness, though—now that was a start.

They moved into the hall and headed downstairs to the kitchen. The coffeepot gurgled, signaling the end of the brewing cycle, so Luke found two mugs.

"I don't deserve to be your best man." Jeff accepted the mug and filled it from the pot. "You've probably got a friend here who would be a better choice. I made you crash and burn with Krista before."

"A promise is a promise, and I believe in second chances."

Jeff's brown eyes moistened, but his gaze remained fixed out the kitchen window. "Thanks. I'm—I'm happy for you. You've made a good life here, and I want you and Krista to be happy."

"I've got to warn you, though. Krista's really skeptical about your intentions. She didn't appreciate your comments last night."

"Huh? What'd I say?"

"Something about having me on a ball and chain."

Jeff turned red. "I—er, had a couple drinks on the plane and was feeling kinda loose."

"Well, don't let loose. Not around here."

"Gotcha."

∞

Krista stretched under the covers and caught a whiff of Nana's coffee drifting down the hallway. Four more days, and she'd be waking up as Luke's wife. She'd better start learning how to make coffee. She still couldn't brew it without grounds ending up swirling in the pot. Krista smiled to herself and rolled over to face the opposite wall, its rose wallpaper partially obscured by a long sheet of white butcher paper labeled "Wedding Flow Chart." So far she'd accomplished everything on her timeline on schedule, sort of.

Today's agenda included wedding shoes. Plus, she needed to call her mother and double-check the confirmed head count for the reception food. Belonging to the family who owned the regionally renowned "Elfi's Schnitzel" restaurant chain had its perks. The list also reminded her she needed to remind Luke that they needed to pick up their marriage license.

Another must-do included clearing the last of the brush from the wooded area at the back and sides of Nana's house. Seeing to the brush around Nana's property wasn't a wedding duty, but she had to fit it in her plans, especially this time of year.

She flopped onto her back and gave a huff at the ceiling. Hacking at brush would help burn off some of the aggravation that had flared up about Jeff. Maybe part of the aggravation was with herself.

"You shouldn't have agreed to have that kind of guy be best man at your wedding," Krista said aloud. "What *were* you thinking?"

Thinking? She was in love with the only man who had ever claimed her heart, and at long last they were set to walk down the aisle together. Her stomach trembled as she sat up. Luke might have claimed her heart, but once upon a time he had tossed it away like a banana peel.

Krista stuffed her feet into her fluffy slippers, then reconsidered and kicked them off. The tiles would feel good on her toes this morning, and hopefully cool her jets and calm her nerves.

She followed the aroma of breakfast to the kitchen where she found Nana making fried potatoes, eggs, bacon, and toast all at once.

Nana turned from the stove. "Morning, dear. How many eggs?"

"Just one, over medium, and pop the yolk, please." Krista went for the coffeepot. "Nana, how much do you think we're going to eat?"

"This isn't just for you and me. I invited Luke and his friend to join us, plus I thought when your friend gets here from the airport, she'll be hungry."

"Sami won't arrive until maybe lunchtime." Krista glanced at the clock on the microwave. "It's nine fifteen already? When are the guys getting here?"

"In about fifteen minutes."

"Nana! Why didn't you wake me up earlier?"

"I did, shortly after eight. You mumbled something about getting up in a few minutes. I assumed you'd been getting ready this whole time."

"Really, I've never needed much time to get ready. But I do have a fuzzy memory of someone calling my name earlier. Guess I thought I was dreaming." Krista grabbed a slice of bacon and crunched on it for a moment. "Keep cooking like this, and I'll need to have Sami hunt me down another dress. I'd better jump in the shower and throw myself together."

She'd also give herself a pep talk before Jeff arrived with Luke. Now look at her, she was thinking about Jeff before Luke. This would never do.

"Nana, I have to say I wish we didn't have to invite Jeff to breakfast, too."

"It simply wouldn't be good manners to exclude him. Plus, Luke mentioned to me one evening that Jeff was coming a few days early. He's had some personal troubles and wanted to get away for some thinking time."

"Great. So he decides to use *my* town and the week before *my* wedding to *my* fiancé to get his head on straight." Krista jammed the coffeepot back onto the hot pad, sloshing its contents. The words cut through the air like a knife's jab, but Krista didn't care just then.

Nana turned from the stove. "I know your wedding is important to you, but so far Jeff hasn't demanded anything of you. Some things are eternal and more important than preparations for one day."

The sound of sizzling breakfast filled the kitchen.

"I know, Nana, I know." Krista swallowed a sip of coffee. Her shoulders slumped a bit. "This is just harder than I imagined. I was so busy teaching the spring semester and taking care of wedding details, I didn't think about how it would feel to see Jeff again. This is my fault. I'm an idiot."

"Don't berate yourself." Nana moved to get some plates from the glass-doored cabinet above the dish drainer. "Forgiveness doesn't always happen instantly."

"I wish it did in this case." Krista frowned. "Well, I should get ready. They'll be here any minute, and I'm still kicking my bad attitude around the kitchen. Be right back!" She whirled and left the way she came, wishing she could retract her words.

Yet thinking the words and saying them weren't much different. She couldn't count the times she'd bitten back retorts, only to scream them in her mind. Krista found her robe in the bedroom and put her coffee cup on the bureau. Maybe she could wash away some of the feelings. She needed to look forward to Sami arriving and catching up with her old college roomie, not waste her emotions on Jeff.

While hot water rushed over her in the shower, Krista realized she hadn't prayed that morning but instead focused on her wedding first thing. Listen to her—*her* wedding. It was Luke's wedding, too.

Luke certainly wasn't the same person he was four years ago. Krista could still see the closed-off look in his blue eyes as she faced him on the beach volleyball court. She had impulsively run onto the sand when he and Jeff had changed sides after a game. She couldn't feel the sand burning her feet. In her desperation, she practically begged him to come home.

"I'm staying here. With Jennifer." If he had punched her outright, Krista didn't think it could have hurt more.

"You're not coming back to Settler Lake?" The words hissed from her mouth like a deflating balloon.

"There's nothing there for me. My life is here now." The crowd cheered in the background. Some girls in bathing suits stood near the edge of the stands and cheered at the players during the intermission. Krista glanced at them. No wonder Luke was treating her like a stranger.

Sweat stung Krista's eyes, or was it tears? "You're turning your back on it all—your faith—me?" She could feel Jeff's dark expression boring into her from across the court. "Because of him—"

"Not because of Jeff, because I grew up, Krista. This is real life for me. Go on back to your own."

A referee wearing red swim trunks strode in their direction. Sand flew up from his heels. "Are you two through? We have a match to continue."

Krista nodded. "I guess we are." Then she fled. She never wanted to see that blank expression in Luke's eyes again.

Cold water jerked her back from her nightmare—no, day-mare. Krista opened her eyes to see the blue ceramic tiles in Nana's bathroom. Her eyes burned now as they did then. She let the water pelt her face. If she had showered long enough to use all the hot water, Luke and Jeff had probably arrived.

She should have prayed this morning before getting up. *Lord, help me let go. Once and for all.*

By the time she headed to the kitchen ten minutes later, she had managed to throw on some shorts and a T-shirt. A quick blow-dry without the styling brush left her hair skimming her shoulders.

"Hi, guys."

Luke rose from his seat at the table and Krista went to his arms. With Luke's kiss, the memory that had assaulted her in the shower skulked back to wherever such things lived. Krista inhaled the scent of his cologne and tears tried to prick her eyes once more. She staved them off and returned his kiss.

"Whoa, you two, I can feel that from over here."

Krista pulled back and glanced over at Jeff. "We're practicing for Saturday." Then she snapped her attention back to Luke.

His eyes were lit with a bright blue flame. "I'd say that was more like practice for Sunday morning."

Heat swept down her face and into her neck. "We'll have lots of years to get it right."

He leaned down and whispered in her ear. "That we will. Sit by me, so we can do that again if we want to?"

"Sure." Krista squeezed Luke's hand then went to get another coffee cup since she'd left the other one in the bedroom. "Do you still plan to clear some brush this morning?"

"I do." A smile teased at the corner of Luke's mouth.

"Well, then, I do, too."

Nana smiled at their exchange and then at Jeff. "I'm glad you two could make it. Now, we just need the maid of honor to arrive to make the immediate bridal party complete."

The phone warbled as if on cue. Krista yanked the receiver from the wall and noted the caller ID on the way to the coffee mugs. She leaned against the counter and watched Luke pile his plate with breakfast.

"Sami! Where are you?"

"I just left the airport. Tell me again how I get to Settler Lake."

Jeff let out a guffaw at something Luke said. Krista shot him a look and put a finger in her free ear. "Hang on a second." She moved to the hall. It was going to be a long day.

Chapter 4

Luke watched Krista swing the ax. She had the grace of a dancer. Good thing she hadn't applied to train for the fire lines. He would probably spend his time watching her work instead of fighting fires. He turned his attention back to the stubborn bush at his feet and hacked at it with his Pulaski. The blade caught hold, and he tugged the roots to the surface.

"Am I doing this right?" Jeff called across the space between them. He was wrestling a young pine to the edge of the clearing near Nana's house.

"You're doing fine. We need to clear at least a hundred feet from the edge of the house."

"All in one day?"

"No, Krista and I have actually been working on clearing the land since early spring. We should have finished already, but. . ." Luke heaved the stump across to the pile of brush destined to go into the wood chipper. "We've been a little busy."

He stopped to watch Krista again. She leaned over and picked up a bush she'd just cut down. "Hey, beautiful, you doing okay?" Just as he'd hoped, Krista turned in his direction and a smile lit her face along with the glow of perspiration.

"Just great." She tugged the bush alongside her and joined him at the brush pile.

"C'mere." He reached for her with gloved hands and she moved into the circle of his arms.

She sniffed. "You stink."

"Oh, now that's romantic." He glanced over his shoulder at Jeff. "See? She just killed the moment!"

Jeff dragged the young pine to the other brush. "Like spending the morning hacking through the woods is romantic. Maybe having a private picnic in the woods—"

"Be quiet, Jeff." The last thing Luke needed was Jeff shooting off his mouth. He was thanking God for the truce between Krista and his old friend. Luke focused on Krista again. "We should try to sneak in a date before the frenzy sets in."

"I'd like that." She gave him a quick kiss. He would never tire of the feeling of her lips. Their softness covered her strength like a satin glove. All too soon the kiss was over. Well, come Saturday. . .

Jeff's voice intruded. "Why are you doing this the week of your wedding?"

Krista spoke up. "It's been so dry, we don't know when a fire will pop up. Anytime between now and September is fair game. The bigger tree pines are pretty hardy, but the newer underbrush goes up like that." She snapped her fingers.

"I've got to work tomorrow," Luke offered, "and today's the best day for me to clear Nana's brush. So, here we are." He gave Jeff credit for helping out at all, but he wondered if Jeff pictured a certain brunette in his mind as he tore up the spring's growth.

"All I can say is I'm glad I live in a gated community. We don't worry about stuff like this."

Luke's pager started beeping, and Krista frowned at it as he took it from his belt. He glanced at the number. "Great. They need me at the station."

"Don't worry about it." Krista formed a smile on her face, but Luke saw through her bravery. "I need to get out of here and go shopping anyway. I don't think I'll have to twist Sami's arm very hard to have her take me."

"Jeff, do you mind hanging out here?" Luke took off his gloves and laced his fingers through Krista's as the three of them walked to the house. "Al should be along later with the wood chipper, so he can get rid of all this brush."

"Not a problem. Say, I need to throw you a party. You got a list of names?"

"For what?"

Jeff punched him in the arm. "A bachelor party, of course."

Luke felt Krista's hand stiffen. "I don't want one."

"You don't want one? No last hurrah as a single guy?"

"I wouldn't mind a relaxing evening hanging out with my friends, but not the kind of bachelor party you're used to." From the corner of his eye, Luke saw Krista's face assuming a range of emotions. "Besides, I don't think we can fit it in the schedule this week."

Jeff shrugged. "Well, I tried. You want pizza and soda pop, that's fine." He beat them to the patio.

"Go ahead inside. We'll catch up." Luke paused and pulled

Krista's hand to his lips. "You handled that well."

Krista pulled her hand free. "What did he want to do? Have a girl jump out of a cake or something?"

"Or something." Luke put his arms around her. "Hey, I stood my ground and I hope I didn't offend him, either. But I *am* proud of you. I know how hard it is for you to keep your temper under control."

"Thanks. I'm glad you can't read my mind right now." She gave a sheepish grin.

"I love you anyway." He hated to leave her, especially now. "I need to go, though."

"What do you think they wanted? You're not scheduled to work until tomorrow."

Luke shrugged, hoping to appear nonchalant. The logging company hadn't called from the emergency line reserved for urgent matters such as a fire, but there was that possibility, with the lightning storm last night. He glanced at the clearing behind them. They'd done the best they could, but he still felt as though they were in an open dry field holding a lit torch. The whole thing could go up in a flash. But he wouldn't worry Krista, not with the wedding only days away.

⤞⤝

"I can't believe you forgot to buy shoes," Sami, Krista's maid of honor and former partner in crime, hollered over the noise of the open convertible she'd driven from the airport.

"Don't you remember? I always left style to you."

"I should have guessed. I would've brought some shoes, accessories—something!" Which is why Sami insisted on going shopping right away. Krista could have sent Sami to buy her something white in a size eleven with a low heel while she stayed behind and finished clearing brush with Luke, but she didn't trust Sami to pick the right style. Sami was well intentioned, but her taste didn't usually match Krista's.

"Don't worry about it."

"Where am I driving?"

"Seconds Please. It's a neat little consignment store in town."

Sami shook her head. "You sure about that?"

Krista held up her hand. She still loved the sunlight sparkling off her diamond. "Hey, I'm only a volleyball coach, not a department store buyer. Plus I don't care to drive to Sacramento just for shoes."

"I didn't say anything. But you might find something great if we took a quick trip. Um, where do I turn?"

"Take a right at the first stoplight at the bottom of the hill."

Sami downshifted and grinned at Krista. The wind teased at Sami's dark hair held in place by a scarf. If Krista tried tying a scarf like that over her head, everyone would wonder if she was getting ready to start housecleaning. If she had possessed Sami's exotic dark elegance, would Luke have strayed?

The unbidden question popped into her head. Honestly, she'd been on this emotional roller coaster before and hadn't recalled buying a ticket to ride again. She still couldn't believe the crack Jeff had made earlier about a bachelor party. Sami hung a right at the light.

"Okay, Seconds is up on the left. There should be parking on the side street," Krista said. Oh, why couldn't she be the kind of woman who could lose herself in her shopping?

Sami found the side street and slowed the car to a crawl. "Ooh, I hate parallel parking. Is there a lot somewhere?"

"A block over." Krista imagined Sami's ears perking up like a hound picking up a scent.

Sami whipped the convertible into a narrow space in the side lot. Krista let Sami's enthusiasm carry her along. She clutched her bag tightly to her side as they left the car.

"Wow, what a view." Sami studied the mountains rising to the north and west above the pines. "And the breeze!"

"Yes, it's gorgeous" She followed Sami's gaze. The sharp green of the pines contrasted with the pale blue sky. A few wispy clouds drifted overhead. "The wind carries the scent of pine from the mountains after the rain—which we sure could use more of."

"You should have asked. I would have packed some in my carry-on from Seattle!" Sami grinned. "So do you get many fires down here?"

"It depends. The season usually starts about now through October. I'm counting on a quiet June." Krista paused. "That sounds bad. I don't want fire or loss for any of us, at all. I—"

"You want a perfect wedding."

They continued down the sidewalk, their backs to the mountains.

"I don't think it has to be perfect. Crazy things always happen at weddings. I just want Luke and me to be together—always. I don't want anyone to come between us."

"Jeff?"

Krista paused in front of the consignment shop. "Hold that

thought—we'll pick it up later." Vangie, her uncle Al's second wife, waved from the display window. She was wrestling a blouse onto a mannequin. Krista liked the woman her uncle had wed after Aunt Beth passed away, but she still wasn't used to Vangie's flamboyance when compared to Aunt Beth's quiet demeanor.

"Here comes the bride!" Aunt Vangie sang out as they entered the store.

"I'm a barefoot bride at the moment. I need shoes." Krista grinned. "Aunt Vangie, this is my maid of honor, Sami Chen."

"Nice to meet you." Sami extended her hand, and Vangie hugged her instead. "You've got a cute store here." Sami's eyes widened over Vangie's shoulder.

Krista scanned the shelves. "Like I said, I'm looking for some shoes. I'll only wear them once, but—"

Vangie released Sami and whirled in Krista's direction. "Why don't you take a seat at the bench and I'll be right back." She moved on high heels behind the counter and into a back room. "I know just the ones—I went on a buying trip last weekend and found some adorable shoes in larger sizes—got them for next to nothing." Vangie's voice competed with the blare of a radio on her desk.

"Wow, she's enthusiastic." Sami smiled. They moved to a bench covered with a pink chintz cushion.

"Yes, that she is. She and my mom take turns doing circles around the rest of us when we're all together."

The local announcer at KSET broke in at the close of the song. "A beautiful sunny day today in Settler Lake. We'll see highs in the upper eighties to near ninety and dry, dry, dry conditions through the weekend with highs near the century mark. Chance of rain slim to none, folks. So be sure to clear out that underbrush from your wooded areas and watch those sparks from barbecues. No open burning. If you need the wood chipper to come by, schedule an appointment with the Code Compliance office at City Hall." Then came a commercial for Seconds Please.

Vangie clattered out from the back room. Shoe boxes rose in a stack above her head. Krista tried not to groan. New Balance, Nike, K-Swiss—those, she knew. The names she read on the shoe boxes read like another language.

"Here we are. Did you like the new ad? Al said it was a good idea." Vangie placed the boxes on the floor. Without waiting for a response, she continued. "You're an eleven, right?"

"Don't remind me." The boxes all had different brands. "All I want is something white, pretty, comfortable, and a low heel."

"Luke's tall enough for you to wear a higher heel than normal." Sami reached for a box that said *Stuart Weitzman*. "Oh wow! Krista!"

A customer entered the store, and Vangie seemed to sigh reluctantly as she moved to greet them. Good. Krista didn't want an audience.

"I refuse to sacrifice comfort for shoes that nobody's really going to see."

Sami removed a medium-heeled elegant strappy sandal. "These will look gorgeous. You'll find them more comfortable than you think."

Krista took the shoe. "Well, even for elevens they might not make my feet look like flotation devices."

"I thought it didn't matter how they looked." Sami leaned closer. "After all, no one sees them."

Her singsong tone made Krista chuckle. "Ouch—you got me on that one." Krista slipped her comfy flip-flops from her feet. The shoe slid onto her foot with the familiarity of a long-lost pal. Krista slipped its mate on the opposite foot and stood. Her ankles didn't wobble. She didn't feel like the Jolly Green Giant, either.

Her phone warbled from inside her purse, and she managed to reach down and retrieve it without hurting herself. "Sami, don't flip when I say this, but so far these are perfect." She checked the number—Luke! She punched the button. "Hey!"

❧

"Where are you?" Luke tilted his head back and looked up the length of a pine.

"I'm at Vangie's shop trying on some shoes with Sami. Where are *you*?"

"I'm out on West Range Road. There's been a few fires sparked by that lightning storm a few nights ago." The wind whipped his words around and carried them away.

"Oh no!"

"They're under control and dying as I speak, but it's dry as a bone up here."

"What did you need?"

He braced himself for what he had to tell Krista. "I heard from Uncle Al. He said the mayor's called a town meeting for this week."

"Oh, that's just great," Krista said as if it were anything *but* a great idea. "I'll let Nana know so we can call our precinct list. When is it?"

He hesitated. "Thursday night."

"But our rehearsal—"

"I know, I know. I already thought about that. We can have the rehearsal Wednesday. Al can stand in for your dad—"

"Oh. I'm not sure about that."

"Meet me for a late lunch and we can talk about it?"

"I can't." Disappointment radiated from the phone. "Sami and I are going for her dress fitting."

"Well, we should talk about these changes to the schedule. Maybe we can squeeze in a rehearsal Friday before your parents throw that dinner party. How's that list of yours coming along?" He grinned at the thought of her organized chaos.

"I forgot it at Nana's. But I do know you and the guys need to get the tuxes on Thursday. Did Jeff bring shoes? Because Vangie's got a ton here at the store."

"I don't know. I'll have to ask him later. I think Nana put him to work."

Krista's throaty chuckle did his heart good. "I'm glad. A little hard work never hurt anyone."

"Listen, baby, I've got to go. Come by the house later. Bring Sami and we can all hang out. Plus we can iron out some of the last-minute details. I was thinking of having Todd come over and meet Sami and Jeff."

"Okay, it'll almost be like a party for the wedding party. Except Jana won't be here until Friday." Krista sounded a bit more cheerful.

"See you later then. I love you!"

"I love you, too."

Luke closed the phone. That had gone well. He knew Krista wanted things a certain way, and this town meeting, while necessary, was throwing a kink into her plans. He put his Jeep into drive and squinted up the hill. Was that a wisp of smoking curling up from the ridge? Uneasiness traveled into the pit of his stomach.

Chapter 5

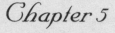

L uke's throat caught when he saw Krista on her uncle's arm. Music swelled from the organ. Krista wore her usual summer uniform of T-shirt and shorts, but he tried to imagine her white gown.

White, the symbol of purity. His sweet, faithful, funny Krista had kept herself for him. He had a few major regrets in his life. The biggest was realizing the woman he loved stood before him with a heart that had taken a long time to heal. Jeff, who stood at his elbow, was a reminder of the damaged witness Luke's life had been. His weak faith had been a sputtering candle that he alone had snuffed out, with Jeff watching. When would he forget?

"Hey, don't look so somber." Luke felt Pastor Mike nudge him. "This is supposed to be fun, remember?"

Luke nodded and kept his gazed fixed on Krista.

Pastor Mike raised a hand. Al and Krista paused a few steps away. "Now, Al—or Tom, as you're supposed to be today—"

A few in the open-air chapel chuckled.

"I'll say, 'Who gives this woman to be married?' and you'll say—"

"My kid brother, who's footing the bill for all this."

More laughter. Luke's mouth went dry. He liked the fact that someone had opened the lakeside walls of the chapel to expose the sanctuary to the lake view. Wisps of Krista's hair had freed themselves from her ponytail and floated in the lake breeze. She caught her lower lip in her teeth for an instant, then glanced Luke's way. He winked. Krista's smile spread across her face, and Luke wanted to tell Pastor to make this ceremony the real thing.

Now he was holding her hand, and he squeezed her strong, capable fingers. Pastor reminded them to face him.

Luke barely heard the words, but snapped to attention when Pastor got to a particular section of the ceremony.

"If anyone knows why these two may not lawfully wed, speak now or forever hold his peace."

I know a good reason; I don't deserve her. He must have increased his grip on her hand, for Krista looked sideways at him sharply. He didn't deserve her, but he'd sure spend the rest of his life being the kind of man she did deserve.

⊗

Krista watched Sami move to the upper corner of the platform. She practically glided up the steps, and Krista prepared herself to hear Sami's voice. The music began, and Sami glanced her direction before launching into the song.

Fire or no fire, scrambled schedule or not, she was going to marry Luke Hansen. Krista grinned in triumph. The only damper on the evening's fun was that her parents weren't here, nor her sister Jana.

Luke's lips moved silently and she leaned forward to catch his words.

"What's that?" Krista whispered.

"I love you, and this song speaks my heart." His blue eyes reflected the light outside and for a moment she saw nothing else.

"I love you, too. So much." Krista wanted to kiss him just then, but they hadn't arrived at that part of the ceremony yet.

Sami's voice soared up the scale as she sang about faithful love that cherishes through laughter and pain, through sun and rain.

Please, Lord, let us make it.

A movement behind Luke caught her attention. Jeff. How did such so-called ancient history get to raise its ugly head now, only days before the wedding? Oh, Krista had been fine once at the idea of allowing Jeff to be best man. Their love was strong. It could endure, they had told each other. But now she couldn't let Luke out of her sight without the old doubts and fears returning like uninvited guests.

⌘

After they had finished rehearsal, Luke didn't release Krista's hand.

Her aunt Vangie clapped, bangle bracelets clanging on her wrists. "Okay, everyone. We've got some sandwiches in the fellowship hall so we can all take a breather."

He glanced at Krista. "Do you want to stay?" Jeff was

chatting with Sami at the moment, who kept darting looks at both him and Krista.

"I was hoping we could get away, but I ought to rescue Sami."

"Hey." Luke reached for her other hand. "Just a few more days."

"I know." Her thumbs rubbed the back of his hand. "But I do want to get away with you for a bit before the craziness really sets in."

Luke pulled her close, not caring who saw them. "I know. I'm keeping Jeff entertained plus checking in at the station. How about tomorrow night after the town meeting?"

"It'll have to be tomorrow. Mom and Dad arrive Friday and they planned dinner for out-of-town guests, don't forget."

"Of course not." She must think he'd forgotten everything this week. "I'll call Mountaintop to see if we can get a good table."

"I'd love that, although if it meant being with you I'd settle for Burger Barn."

"I can arrange that."

"No, no, Mountaintop is just fine." She slid her arms around his waist, stood on her tiptoes, and kissed him quickly. "I've missed our time together." A crease appeared between her eyes.

"What's wrong?"

"I—I can't explain it." She glanced toward the few people left in the sanctuary. "I feel like something's going to go wrong."

He kissed his worrywart fiancée on her nose. "Don't you

worry about a thing. We've had to rearrange our plans, but other than that, we're going full-steam ahead."

❧

A breeze from the lake cooled Krista's cheeks as she and Luke left the chapel. "One more thing done."

Luke hugged her with one arm. "Are you disappointed your parents couldn't make it?"

"Yes, I am. But this couldn't be helped. Everything's going to work out." The feeling that had assaulted her earlier fizzled out after time spent with Luke and their friends.

Luke paused, and so did she. He caught both of her hands in his. "I was a fool."

"Don't—" She pulled one hand free and placed a finger on his lips. "The past is best left dead and buried. I'm trying to only focus on our future."

Why did he look as if guilt were still eating him alive? They'd been through that already.

He held her close under the trees. "I don't ever want to make you cry again unless you're happy."

"I know. So don't be gloomy. I didn't want my nerves from earlier to rub off on you. Oops—left my sunglasses in the chapel. I'll be right back!" She gave him a quick kiss and jogged across the parking lot.

Sami was heading to her convertible. "I guess you'll get a ride from Luke?"

Krista nodded. "I'll catch up with you when I get back to Nana's."

"No problem. I'm going to hit the pool." Sami hugged her.

"You did good tonight."

"Thanks. I'm glad this part's over now. If only we remember what to do on Saturday."

"I just hope I don't forget when to take your bouquet and all that."

"Who's reassuring whom here?" Krista gave Sami a wave. "Go on. I'll see you at the house."

Krista entered the chapel and felt peace wrap around her. The past few days—no, months—had been a roller coaster of highs and lows, mania and quiet. Now she knew why marriage was only supposed to happen once. She couldn't remember on which pew she'd laid her glasses.

The door that led to the reception hall opened, and Jeff entered. Her stomach lurched as if she'd just hit the downhill slope of the roller coaster.

"Kris-Kris."

"Hi, Jeff." She regarded him carefully. "Um, thanks for supporting us. I guess you know I really wasn't happy about Luke inviting you."

"That goes without saying." He clutched the edge of a pew.

"But I respect Luke's loyalty to you as a friend—"

"I told you I felt lousy about what I did back then."

"And I—I've forgiven you." The words sounded feeble to her ears.

A spark ignited in Jeff's expression. "You ought to know I didn't make Luke's choices for him. He was a big boy who knew exactly what he was doing."

The words hit her like a punch, but she forced herself to

recover and hold his gaze. "That's right, he did. But you *knew* he and I were a couple. It's taken us *years* to rebuild what was destroyed between us." Krista's chest tightened as if a vise were pressing on her rib cage. *Stop, stop.* She struggled to breathe.

"He really does love you." Jeff glanced at the altar as he spoke.

"I know."

"No, I mean, he's changed. And—I envy him. Just don't put him on some kind of a pedestal. That's a lot of pressure for a guy."

"You're in no position to give me advice." She spotted her sunglasses and swooped down on them with one hand, then jammed them onto her forehead.

"He's still human. And cheaters cheat."

"But he's not the same guy you knew."

"Forget I said anything. It seems once you get religion, you can do no wrong."

"I've got to catch my ride." *Please, Sami, be there.* She remembered she'd have to ride with Luke *and* Jeff if she went in Luke's car. Krista pushed the door to the parking lot open just in time to see Sami's convertible zip onto the road.

She trudged to Luke's car and opened the passenger door.

"Find them?" he asked as she slid onto the front seat.

"Oh, yeah." She'd blown it, and big-time.

"What's wrong?"

"I—"

The rear passenger door clicked open. "Here I am." Jeff entered the vehicle.

Silence hung in the air like a wet blanket dragging down a clothesline. Krista faced the window. Jitters, just jitters. And now she smarted from Jeff's words, and worse, her reaction to them. Jeff couldn't be right. What did he know about choices except to make wrong ones? She felt Luke's hand squeeze hers in the darkened car. *Hurry, Saturday, hurry!*

Chapter 6

Settler Lake Lodge brimmed with people, but it wasn't for Krista and Luke's wedding reception. Krista turned from the view out the window. No one else seemed interested in the sunlight bouncing off the surface of the lake or the fan of water that arced behind a skier. Krista glanced across the crowd. Few in town chose to miss the meeting, and those who were required to miss would no doubt get the information from friends or family.

Mayor Stefanie Woods went to the podium. "Thanks, everyone, for coming tonight. I realize many of you have had to rearrange schedules to be here." Stefanie turned to Uncle Al, who stood with a stack of papers. "Al here is going to start passing out these property safety guides. I know this is probably something most of you have heard before, but it bears repeating."

Uncle Al stepped from the platform and headed in Krista's direction. "Give me a hand with these?"

Krista reached out for the fliers. "Sure." She smiled at Luke. "I'll be right back." She did not offer a smile to Jeff, who sat on the other side of Luke. His presence would only haunt them the rest of the week. She quit thinking about Jeff and instead concentrated on passing out the leaflets, but once she found herself empty-handed, there was nothing left to do except return to her seat. Luke put his arm around her and she leaned into his strength.

"Don't they make a wonderful couple?" an elderly voice whispered behind them.

"Oh, yes, they've come so far, too."

Krista had to agree with them on that one. A few years ago, she would have thought running a marathon more attainable than a future with Luke Hansen. But now, a certain carefully folded piece of paper was in his pocket. Their quick trip to Redding at the courthouse had secured their license. *Hallelujah, nothing's going to stop us now!*

❦

The sun still hung in the west as if it were waiting just for Krista and Luke to watch it sink. The canvas of the evening sky had been painted a rich pink that blended into purple then a deep indigo. Krista moved a little closer to Luke in the driver's seat as they sped up the mountain road to their favorite local bit of class, Mountaintop. Luke kissed her hand.

"Did I ever tell you how smart you are, Mr. Hansen?"

"No, not really." He grinned at her and winked.

"Well, stealing me away for a breather was a brilliant idea."

"I've missed our 'us' time." He released her hand to turn the car into the parking lot.

"I have, too."

"We have the rest of our lives to look forward to moments like this."

They were shown to a table with a sunset view. Krista wanted to seal this moment into her box of treasured memories. The look in Luke's eyes. The twilight glinting off his sand-and-caramel hair. The way his hand covered hers across the table. She would enjoy the feeling of being loved and cherished by him always.

"Quite frankly," Krista admitted over her steak soup, "I'm glad to have a break from Jeff. Although I think he's starting to get the idea and tone it down a bit."

"I have to admit since Jeff's been in town he's really made me do some thinking."

Krista's stomach lurched. "About what?"

"I was so wrong, Krista. I made a bad choice."

"You could always ask Todd to stand up for you." *At last, he's realizing what he should have months ago.*

"What are you talking about?" Luke shook his head.

"You've decided not to have Jeff be your best man."

"That's not what I meant. He's shown me how I deceived myself into believing that everything I have right now was disposable."

"And now?"

He looked at her with an intensity that sent a shiver down her spine. "I wouldn't give any of this up—or you—for the world."

Krista circled back around to her earlier request. "Which is why I think Jeff represents everything you left behind."

The muscles clenched in Luke's jaw. "You told me it was all right to have him be best man."

"Months ago it was. Only now, hearing his comments and

seeing him again—I honestly hadn't thought much about what it would be like to see him again. I mean, love is supposed to cover a multitude of sins, but. . ." She clamped her lips together. Everything was coming out wrong. Her gaze shifted to the mountains. Her throat caught at the sight of a plume of gray smoke rising miles away to the southwest. *Please, not now.*

"I won't change my mind. I'm trying to reach out to him and keep a connection—"

"I think you could probably have chosen a different mode of outreach than having him as your best man." There. She'd said it. Stress—memories—whatever. Her eyes stung.

"Like I said before, you should have told me how you really felt months ago when we were deciding this." Luke's phone buzzed. He unclipped it from his belt. "Hang on—"

Krista wanted to grab the phone and stuff it in his ice water. She'd blown it. The way she'd talked to Jeff the other night, the way she'd sniped at Luke now. . .

"I have to go. They need me right now. The ridge is starting to light up like the Fourth of July." He slapped his phone shut.

The lump in her throat kept the words from coming out, and even if she could talk, she didn't know if the words would be the right ones.

Luke stood. "All this aside, I love you, Krista Schmidt. I'm going to marry you, no matter what." He gestured for the check and apologized to the waiter, who had just enough time to cancel their order. She slunk from the restaurant with Luke, who already looked as if he'd forgotten about her.

What a hypocrite. She had been raised to show the love

of God, and she wasn't doing a very good job of it. Okay, she probably could have told Luke months ago that she wasn't truly comfortable with Jeff being best man. Luke would have chosen Todd if she'd insisted.

Communication was key to a good marriage. And now look at them. He wordlessly unlocked her door for her, and she slid onto the passenger seat without breaking the silence. A fire raged somewhere, and his other "job" of firefighting was calling him away from her.

This was not her—their—dream wedding. Not at all.

When he dropped her off at Nana's, he gave her an extra kiss good-bye.

"Don't leave without saying anything, Krista." Luke caressed her cheek and a tear splashed on his fingers.

"This wasn't how I planned to say good night. There's so much to say. . ."

"I love you, and I know you love me. I'll be praying while we're apart, and I know you will, too. If we can get through this—"

"We can get through anything." Krista gave him one last look, searching for the words that still escaped her. Instead she only found her purse and left the car. He sped off, leaving her on the curb.

❧

Luke jammed the accelerator to get to the house. He had ten minutes to grab his gear, make sure Jeff had a house key, and meet the guys at the station.

"Lord, I hadn't planned on any of this. What happened to Krista and me getting married without a hitch?" He still stung from her words. Where was the forgiveness she had supposedly offered? If she still harbored such feelings toward Jeff, then what about him?

He parked in front of the house and jogged up the walk, then let himself in. Jeff had ESPN up at full volume. A six-pack carton lay on its side on the coffee table. His friend lay prostrate on the couch, snoring.

"Jeff!" Luke shook his shoulder. "Wake up."

He blinked and rolled onto his side. "Man, what's going on? Sorry about the bottles—"

"Just have it cleaned up. I've gotta go fight a fire. Feel free to use the car. I left the spare keys for it and the house on the break-fast bar. If you need anything, call. . ." Luke knew he couldn't say "Krista." He fumbled for a name. "You can call Pastor Mike. The phone list is on the fridge."

He moved to the front hall closet and pulled out his gear, already double-checked for such a time as this.

"How long are you going to be gone?"

"I—I really don't know. It depends on this fire."

"But your wedding—"

"I know."

"How's Krista taking this?"

"She knew this was a possibility. We'll figure something out." Luke shouldered his pack. "I'll call you when I get a chance."

"Stay safe, man." Then Jeff surprised him by clapping him on the back in an awkward hug.

"I will." Luke headed out to his work truck. To his relief he realized he hadn't been tempted by the sight of the bottles in the house. Old things had become new. The past was just—past—through the grace of God poured over him.

He needed to go. Luke opened the hatch and slung his pack into the back of his truck.

When he arrived at the station, the rest of the team was assembling.

"All right, Luke's here! Thought you were getting married."

"I'm planning on it." But he could only guess at what the fire had in store.

∽∾

Krista cried more than she wanted to while rummaging through the bureau for her swimsuit. After finding it on the clothes dryer in the laundry room, she changed into her swimsuit and joined Nana and Sami at the pool. Being with them ought to cheer her up.

"There she is! Are you doing better, dear?" Nana waved at her from her spot in the hot tub.

"A little. I don't want to look to those mountains." She left her towel on the patio table and sunk into the hot water. Yet her gaze wandered to the southwest. She couldn't see a finger of smoke streaming across the sky, but she knew it was somewhere miles away in the darkness.

"Hey, are you going to do some laps?" Sami called from the main pool.

"Maybe in a few." She smiled at Nana, not wanting to worry her. "The water feels great. Every muscle in my shoulders, back, legs—you name it—it's tight." The lump in her throat threatened to lodge itself there again.

"What's got you tied up in knots?" Nana's soothing voice

and the hot water were making Krista relax.

"It's the wedding, the fire, everything at once." Krista tilted her head back and watched steam from the bubbling water drift into the sky and disappear. "Mom and Dad get here tomorrow, and Jana. I've got the caterer all set, plus the musicians, the cake, the. . ." She swallowed hard, and like a big baby, here came her tears again. "I really don't know what to do. What if we have to cancel?"

"But there's something else, something more than Luke fighting the fire, isn't there?"

Krista nodded. "Luke and I—we had a fight right before he left. There we were, trying to take a moment just for us—"

The story rushed out like a fire sweeping across a dry field, from Krista's own struggle about Jeff, to the fire in the mountains, to the fight at dinner.

Krista ended with, "I know I can trust Luke, that he won't let me down again, yet I'm still scared."

"We don't have guarantees."

"But what if something happens?"

"Krista, things will always happen. I know in some aspects you've had wedding bells ringing in your ears and stars in your eyes, but days will come when Luke will *not* be your favorite person."

"I know." A movement from the direction of the pool caught Krista's attention.

Sami left the pool and used the handrail to slide into the hot tub. "I hope you don't mind me joining."

"Not at all." Nana moved over a little.

Krista shifted in front of one of the water jets and let it pound her back. "Nana's been giving me a pep talk about marriage."

"Is it getting through?" Nana smiled at her.

"I think so." Krista returned the grin, though her heart still quavered a bit.

"I ought to take notes." Sami flicked her wet ponytail over her shoulder. "I'm not even seeing anyone. It's been ages. I got burned once, figured the right guy will pursue me long enough if he's the one. So what does Nana say?"

"Nana says you need to pray lots, not just about the heart of the man you'll marry, but about the state of your own heart." Nana stood and moved for the railing. "Girls, I should prepare for bed. We've got a big day tomorrow. Don't stay up too late." She carefully stepped out of the hot tub, fetched her towel, and headed across the patio to the rear of the house.

"She's in great shape for her age." Sami gestured with her head.

"That she is. Every morning, without fail, she does twenty minutes of stretches." Krista extended her legs in front of her and let the bubbling water massage them. "Would you believe she can still do the splits?"

"Honest?"

"Yup." Krista closed her eyes and leaned her head back. She grinned, but the expression felt like a tied-on mask.

"What's eating you now?"

"I made an idiot out of myself with Jeff. In spite of myself, I do care. And I can't take back what I said. But he had the nerve to suggest Luke went wholeheartedly into his party life headfirst."

"Jeff *is* right, you know." Sami held up one hand. "Don't get mad at me for agreeing with him. Luke's a red-blooded adult male who's capable of making his own decisions. God gave him free will just like He did to you. To all of us."

"I know that, too. Here I've been blaming Jeff one hundred percent for influencing Luke to leave his faith and leave me." Krista swallowed hard. "But now—the idea that there's a possibility that one day Luke could let me down like that again—like I told Nana, that terrifies me."

"Love is risk. Which is why I'm steering clear until I know I've found a man I can trust with my heart."

"You're a smart girl not to settle. I've seen people do just that." Krista lifted her left hand out of the bubbling froth and looked at her sparkling ring. He had placed that ring on her finger under the shadow of pines. Was he there now, among the pines?

"Krista, you should see your face. Two days before your wedding, and you look mopey. The whole idea of having a wedding is speaking your vows before God, your friends, your family. We're all behind you two lasting for the rest of your lives." Sami's grin spread across her face. "Now that's a cause for celebration. You could spend time worrying about what could go wrong. Just think about everything the two of you have gone through and all that can go *right*."

Krista tried to smile, but her thoughts lay miles away with the fire and not her wedding.

Chapter 7

Smoke rose above the forest floor and mocked the line of firefighters on the hillside. Luke gritted his teeth and swung his Pulaski, removing some low-lying scrub from the earth. The fire would not win, even if his group had to work through the night when humidity was on their side.

He paused to snatch his water bottle from his pack and surveyed the progress. The Fire Breathers had cut a swath of defensible space twenty feet wide from the edge of the fire. His fellow workers in their yellow Nomex jackets showed up against the ground and among the pines.

"Okay, boys!" Greer, the crew chief, approached the line. "We got a report that the southwest ridge is contained, but that don't help us much. The winds are supposed to pick up toward dawn. We've got to get this western section under control before we join the gang on the northwest side."

Northwest? Settler Lake lay in the northwestern foothills. "Greer?"

"Yeah?"

"How close is the fire to Settler Lake?"

Greer's toothy grin flashed in the glare of their working lights. "Far enough away to be under control by your wedding." He socked Luke on the arm. "Now gebacktawork!"

Luke put the cap back on his water bottle and stuffed it inside his pack, then slung the pack onto his back. He wouldn't let the fact he was getting married in less than forty-eight hours distract him. He'd put in his time and see if Greer would have mercy on him and let him out for a while Saturday.

He prayed for help against this fire.

"Look out, we got a flare-up!" someone called out in a hoarse voice.

Luke's gaze darted to a sudden flash to his right. A small pine about the size of a Christmas tree succumbed to the encroaching fire. Another young tree close to the seven-foot torch was next in line.

"Let's get it!" Bud, the guy next to him in the line, grabbed his ax.

Luke did likewise. They ran to the tree and began swinging at the trunk. Sweat stung Luke's eyes. He could barely remember anything except the urgency to get this fire line held back. Krista. He ached to hold her, to tell her how much he loved her, how sorry he was they had fought at dinner. A million little things swept through his mind.

He chopped harder at the tree. Bud gave it a push, and the pine fell. "We won, Hansen!"

"Not yet, we haven't."

"Don't worry, Romeo. We'll get it done so you can get back to your bride!"

They joined the rest of the line and Luke picked up the

pace. Luke's shoulder started to hurt, so he backed off a bit. He wouldn't be any good to them if his shoulder blew again.

"You feelin' lonely, Hansen?" one of the guys hollered.

"What, with all of you around? No way!" Luke grinned and kicked at a bit of earth.

"Aw, leave him alone. It stinks having this happen right before his wedding." The sounds of more chopping punctuated the air.

"It's okay, guys." Luke straightened and then flexed his back. "You do me the favor of helping me make it to my wedding, and you're all invited!"

He couldn't believe his words. He'd just added eleven men, one woman, and their spouses or significant others to the guest list. Their list had been trimmed and cut repeatedly. The fellow seasonal firefighters he rarely saw during the rest of the year had been axed from the too-long list at some point during the Guest List Massacre, as Krista called it.

Sometime around two that morning, they conquered their section of the blaze. Luke and his crew clapped backs and shook hands. The air crew had helped earlier, and the Fire Breathers finished it off.

They piled back into their van and headed for the make-shift command center on the northwest ridge. Luke knew these woods like he knew the layout of his home. How many times had he made the rounds as range inspector for the logging company?

The air felt thick in the extended van until someone up front turned on the air conditioning. Yet the closer the van wound uphill, the more it looked like fog curling across the road.

"Where there's smoke, there's fire," said Bud.

"We'll tackle it." Luke glared outside at the night. Nothing would keep him from marrying Krista as planned.

❧

"Mom, you shouldn't have!" Krista clamped a hand over her mouth. A refrigerated truck was backing up to the kitchen entrance at Settler Lake lodge.

"You're my daughter, and your dad and I wanted to do something special." Her mother squinted at the truck.

"When you said dinner, I figured we'd be eating out or something—not Elfi's schnitzel being trucked in." Krista glanced at Sami, who wore a bemused expression.

"Your father got Al to recruit a couple of servers for tonight—"

"Servers? It's just us and the bridal party. And I should have my groom here." She glanced toward the hills. The ridge looked as if it were spewing a stream of smoke that was sweeping down toward Settler Lake.

"I think there might be close to thirty of us." Her mother straightened the collar of her tailored jacket.

"Thirty?" Krista gaped at Sami. "The way things are going, I'll be glad to have any kind of a wedding tomorrow."

"Which is why your father phoned everyone to keep their orders on hold—if we have to cancel, we're out for the flowers and the rental clothes. Since Elfi's is doing the food, anything we don't eat tomorrow will be donated to the Shepherd's Shelter." Her mother motioned to the deliveryman to unload the food into the kitchen. "In that main walk-in fridge to the left. Thanks!"

326

Krista's throat constricted. She wanted Luke here, with his strong reassurance that everything would be all right. Here came his car, with Jeff at the wheel.

"Did you hear from him today?" Sami touched her elbow.

Krista nodded and found her voice. "Luke called this morning. He sounded tired. He hoped he might get a break tonight, but it didn't look too good. He said he'd call by two if he could make it." Krista looked at her watch. It was now four thirty. A wave of disappointment rolled over her.

"Chin up." Sami gave her a hug, and Krista fought back tears.

"I am. Did you know, some people are evacuating just as a precautionary measure?" Krista had been up early for a change and had caught the morning fire report. "As long as this wind holds the fire back, the crews can beat the fire, too."

Sami's forehead wrinkled. "Should—should we leave?"

Krista shrugged. "I think we'll be okay. Dad and Al are the long-timers here. If they hear a report that we should go, we will."

Krista looked up at Jeff crunching across the gravel parking lot toward them. She hadn't seen him since the town meeting the night before.

"Hi. You're here early."

Jeff looked sheepish. "I—I thought I'd see if they need any help in there. Plus, Luke wanted me to drop off the cake knife and the server."

"Oh, thanks." Krista could scarcely believe it—Jeff, doing something to help? "Have you heard from him?"

"Not since this morning when he called to see if I could

bring these by this afternoon." Jeff held up two slim white rectangular boxes.

Sami reached for them. "I'll take those to the cake table." She disappeared inside the door to the hall before Krista could grab the cake server set and escape.

Silence hung between them for a moment before Krista spoke. "This is why I love Luke so much. He's risking his life, but he still remembered a silly cake knife!" She blinked hard. No way would she turn into a blubbering bride and ruin her mascara.

Jeff swallowed hard and shifted from one foot to the other. "I really owe you an apology. I messed up your week; I was a bad influence on Luke years ago. I—"

Krista held up her hand. "Wait, it's my turn. I need to apologize to you." How could she explain? "You know, I'm, well—I'm a Christian, and I should behave better than I have."

"But you didn't treat me any worse than anyone else would have. Besides, we're only human."

"I know. I get reminded of that every day. But as a Christian, if I'm supposed to treat people like Jesus would, then I've really messed up."

"Don't be so hard on yourself. Don't worry about it." Jeff waved off her words. She couldn't gauge his expression.

He didn't get it, not exactly, but Krista had tried. "Well, thanks. Please forgive me?" She extended her hand.

"Sure, why not?" They shook hands. Jeff glanced toward the side door to the lodge. "So, do you need any help?"

Krista shrugged. "I have no earthly idea. Since my parents got here, Mom's kinda steamrolled along."

"Just to let you know, I got the tuxes—Luke's buddy Todd has his. I forgot shoes, so your aunt Vangie set me up." Jeff cracked his knuckles and shifted on his feet again.

"That's great." Krista smiled. Once she let herself see Jeff as he was—a needy, fallible man—it was easier to quit holding so tightly to her feelings. "I should have talked to you about these wedding details earlier." Another thought struck her. "The rings! What did Luke do with them?"

"Got it covered."

Krista racked her brain. "I should have brought my list."

"Relax." Jeff patted her arm awkwardly. Was he afraid she'd bite and have him draw back a bloody stump? She didn't blame him for being wary of her. "I think that's what Luke would say."

"You're right, he would." Krista looked to the smoke rising miles to the west. "I'm glad you reminded me, but I wish he were here right now."

❧

A night and a day into the fight, and they weren't winning. Luke sat down at the portable table and placed his hard hat on the ground between his feet. Without a word he grabbed a plate and dug into the food set out for them. Someone in town had sent up meals for the entire crew. He inhaled the scent of burgers and thick steak fries. The tossed salad even looked good.

"Oh yeah, come to Papa." Bud piled two burgers on one bun.

"I'm so hungry I could devour that salad, too." Luke squirted mustard onto his burger.

"My back is killing me." Bud flexed, and Luke thought he heard a crack.

"Mine, too."

Bud pressed the top bun onto the top of his stacked burgers. "Aw, c'mon, you're a young pup. I got twenty years on you at least."

Luke grinned. "This pup played too much when he was younger."

One of the guys asked to say the blessing just then, so once that was done, they tore into the food. Luke wanted to find a quiet spot and lie down under a pine and dream of his Krista. Better yet, to nap with her in his arms. He kept quiet about his shoulder and the ankle that now complained to him.

He looked down at his clothes. The normally screaming-yellow Nomex fire shirt was now a shade of dark mustard, covered with dust and soot. His green fire pants hadn't fared much better. He didn't want to see his face. In twenty-four hours, he was supposed to watch Krista walk down the aisle toward him. Smoke choked the air, and the light orange sky made it hard to guess where the sun lay beyond the haze. Wedding white seemed light years from the Fire Breathers' command center, not a dozen miles or so away.

"Missing her, huh?" Bud interrupted his thoughts.

"I am. But she wants me to be here."

"You're getting yanked all over the place, aren't ya?"

Luke took a swallow of burger. "Yeah. I know usually weddings are all about the bride, but it's important to this groom, too. We went through a lot to get to this day. It almost didn't happen at all." His gut tightened, and it wasn't from the burger and fries. Luke hoped he hadn't said too much.

"I know. We've all got lives we put on hold for a few days."

Yet what a few days for him to put life on hold. He found his phone in his pack and tried to call Krista's cell.

"Hi, this is Krista. I'm not available right now, so leave a message." His pulse pounded at the sound of her voice. Not knowing if they could walk down the aisle tomorrow was sheer torture.

"It's me. I'm at a break right now. I wanted to say I love you, and I miss you. I'll let you know as soon as I'm free—"

"Listen up!" Greer put his fingers to his lips and whistled.

"I have to go. I'll call again when I can." Luke turned off his phone and looked in Greer's direction.

"Okay, we need to make a final push here." Greer gestured to another worker, who set up an easel and propped up a large display board.

The map on the board showed the topography of the area northwest of Settler Lake. Luke's throat tightened when he saw the border for the town on the map. His throat nearly closed off when he saw how much closer the fire had burned.

"This is what we've got." Greer used a pointer to indicate several lines of fire burning downhill. "Instead of in a nice, even wave of fire, we've got fingers of flame reaching down the hill." Luke looked at the shaded-in areas, which stretched toward Settler Lake.

"Normally we'd try to contain each area, but with these winds"—a gust whipped Greer's words away from him—"with these winds, it'll take too long and the fire moves too fast. What we're going to do is set up three teams—us, the Heat Seekers, and the Flame Kickers, and fight it in one big line."

Luke frowned. They'd have to clear more land that way, and

more would burn. He didn't like the alternative: Settler Lake in flames.

"So chow down, step it up." Greer motioned again. "We've got a pile of energy bars and more water if any of you need to reload."

Luke grabbed his burger and started eating, but his appetite had left him.

After loading his pack and checking his gear, he joined the crew on the line. Again, the grunt work of hacking down to soil to create a line continued. The sun must have moved lower in the horizon, Luke judged, by the lengthening shadows and harsh light filtering through the cloud of smoke in the sky. Another long night stretched ahead of them.

Thunder rolled across the air. Not lightning. They didn't need anything else to keep this fire going.

"Snag!" Greer ran to the edge of the line where a half-burned tree was crumpling to the ground. "Get back—get back!"

Chunks of burning wood flew up into the air and sprayed the crew. Was anyone hurt? Luke shrugged off the pelting wood and ran for Greer.

"Help us here." They started beating back the glowing wood. "Any fires start on this line are gonna be backfires, and we're not ready for that. Not yet."

Luke intensified the chopping. With the fire flaring up at this hot spot, their work just became a lot harder. A flash of lightning illuminated the dusk. Rain. What they really needed was rain. His shoulder felt as if he'd been ramming it with flaming sticks. He shrugged and rotated it. Being sent home would not be a bad thing, but he didn't want to let the group down.

Luke paused, grabbed some anti-inflammatory out of his pack, gulped the tablet down, and kept working.

The fire burned and they inched along the line to the north.

Krista, I'm doing this for you. For all of us.

Chapter 8

Krista left the lodge just as a flash of lightning lit up the parking lot. A boom of thunder echoed in response. Sami and Jana, both of them giggling, followed her. Krista had enjoyed the dinner, seeing her family, and having her friends around her. But Luke absent from her side? She had never pictured that. Jeff paused on the way to Luke's car.

"He's going to be okay."

"I know. I'm just missing him. Thanks." She offered him a smile.

Her father chose that moment to make an announcement to the group milling outside the lodge. "Listen up, everyone. We're grateful for all of you coming tonight. It's been great seeing you again. I didn't realize how much we missed Settler Lake after moving Elfi's corporate offices to Sacramento. All that aside, we've decided to have a wedding tomorrow on two conditions. First, if we can get a groom off the mountain by noon tomorrow. Second, if we don't have to evacuate. I trust you'll use good judgment and do just that if you don't feel safe. Maggie and I have our bags packed and in our car at the Lakeside Inn, and we're ready to leave at a moment's notice."

That was Dad, the take-charge and reassuring man. In some ways Luke reminded her of him.

"Hey—woo-hoo, Krista?"

Krista snapped to attention when she saw Jana's hand moving up and down in front of her face.

"Come to my room? We'll sit up and talk—Sami's coming, too. We'll take my car."

Krista glanced around. "What about Nana?"

"I'm going home to walk Rufus, steam my dress, and go to bed," Nana's wizened voice spoke behind her. "Go—have fun!"

Krista turned and smiled at Nana, then hugged her. "I will!"

✖

Dawn came, and they were winning for a change. Luke woke from where he'd dozed a couple of hours. When he moved his right shoulder, it burst into flames of pain inside the joint. He tried to pick up his pack, but his arm was useless as a spaghetti noodle.

"You're done for now." Greer spoke up. "Go on, take a break."

"When do you want me back?"

"See your doctor, then come see us."

"You mean?"

"Get outta here, go get married."

If it wasn't for his shoulder. . .Luke's heart soared as he caught a ride back to the station where his truck waited.

When he turned his cell phone on, he saw he had a message. He dialed the number for his voice mail.

"It's me—Nana. Krista's at the house, but she's not answering the phone." Why would Nana call him? Luke started dialing.

❧

Krista smiled at the wedding gown on the dress form that caught the morning light. Rufus barked impatiently somewhere. She'd have slept longer if it weren't for him. Today's agenda read, "Lunch with wedding party girls, hair at one. MARRY LUKE at four."

"Hang on, Rufus! Don't get your tail in a knot!" Krista left the room and closed the door behind her. Rufus did a pinwheel dance on the tiles in the front entry. She opened the door.

"Go." Rufus scampered out.

Where was everyone? The clock in the kitchen said it was nearly nine. The scent of burnt toast hung in the air. When she looked at the grease-covered stove, she knew something was wrong. Charred bacon soaked in the cast-iron skillet. Nana never left the stove cluttered or messy.

Krista searched for the phone and found it in the laundry room. She remembered she'd left it there last night after getting home late. Now the phone was dead and needed recharging. A first aid kit's contents were spread across the top of the washer.

Someone had been hurt. Why didn't they wake her? The light filtering through the curtains grew a bit dimmer, as if a cloud had drifted across the morning sky. Was rain in the forecast?

The stillness inside the house made her wonder at a rushing noise outside. Krista went to the back door. Her heart crumbled inside her. The hills beyond the house to the west were ablaze.

Flames soared above the pines and a dark cloud squeezed the light from the sky. Krista wanted to move, but her legs seemed bolted to the floor.

❧

"Calm down, Nana." Luke sat in his truck while he tried to track people down. "Explain again."

"I burned my arm this morning while cooking breakfast, so Sami drove me to the weekend emergency clinic. We tried to call her from the doctor's office, but Krista wouldn't answer. Tom and Eileen don't know where she is, either."

"Why are you so worried? Just go home."

"I—I can't. Lightning started a fire not far from our cul-de-sac, and they didn't discover it until this morning after we left. They're not letting anyone back into the development."

"Didn't they send anyone door to door to make sure everyone was out?"

"I don't know, but if they did, Krista's a heavy sleeper."

"Where are you, Nana?"

"Sami and I are at the lodge."

He gritted his teeth and ignored the firebrand of pain in his shoulder as he turned the ignition. "I'm on my way." Luke floored the accelerator. His truck shot past the city limits sign for Settler Lake. He'd be there in five minutes. He just hoped Krista had five minutes.

❧

The sky glowed an eerie shade of burnished copper. Wind blew ashes through the air.

Krista ran for her keys and purse. Her dress—the family pictures. She stopped herself and grabbed a tote bag from the front hall closet. In went the dress, the pictures, the packet of vital records Nana kept in quick access for times like this. What else to bring—how could someone fit keepsakes into one bag? Her breath caught in her throat at all the things she saw. *Move!*

Times like this. . . "Jesus, please, help me get out of here."

Krista let the front door bang behind her and ran for her Jeep. Nana's vehicle was gone, and Sami's was still at the lodge where she'd left it after the party the night before. The Jeep's engine wouldn't turn over. *Stupid battery!*

"C'mon, c'mon!" Priceless minutes slipped through her fingers. She tried again, but nothing. The wind yanked her hair.

Her cell phone rang and she flipped it open. "Luke—"

"I'm coming—"

"The Jeep won't start, and I don't think I can outrun this."

"Turn on the lawn sprinklers." A plane passed overhead, nearly drowning out his voice.

"Okay." Krista craned her neck to see the plane head over the treetops. She couldn't see flames yet, but. . .

"I'm coming for you. Get Rufus and stay put. Crack some windows open. Worst case scenario, get in the pool."

"Okay." She grabbed the duffel and ran, holding the phone clamped to her ear. "Don't put yourself in danger."

"I'm not. If I can't get down the street, I'll park and come up the south side of the hill."

"I'll be waiting."

"I love you."

"And I love you." Then the phone went dead and she ran into the house, with Rufus on her heels.

The sprinklers! Krista ran to the outdoor timer, slipped on the back patio, and nearly wrenched her ankle. She gave the handle on the main water control a twist. Water sprang up in a feeble arc from the watering system. She turned the handle on full blast. Nothing more. What had happened to the water pressure?

She dialed Nana's cell phone. "Nana, where are you?"

"Don't worry about us! Get out of there."

"I—I can't. The Jeep won't start." Her throat hurt. "But Luke's coming."

"Lord, please keep my granddaughter safe, and surround her with Your protection—"

The phone went dead.

"Thanks, Nana. Amen," Krista whispered. Her hands shook.

☙

Luke didn't bother to bypass the roadblock prohibiting vehicles on Northern Hills. He parked on a side street and secured his truck. He slung his pack onto his back, checked to be sure he had his flare blanket just in case.

He gasped from the pain, feeling like a wimp. If he could make the sensation of a hot knife gliding through butter go away, he would.

Krista's face came to mind. She'd sounded scared, but not panicked. He knew his future wife had a good dose of common sense in her head, but when cornered, some people's senses vanished. Luke started jogging. The smell of burning filled the air—of old leaves, of new wood. The heat of the day was intensifying already and the evening's humidity was burning off faster than he hoped. Run. He ran through a backyard at the edge of the cul-de-sac and found a crew working at beating back a finger of flames that threatened to enter this edge of the development.

Their crew chief raised his head. "What you doin' here?"

"Luke Hansen, off duty. I'm part of the Fire Breathers, Greer Johns' crew."

"I know Greer."

"My fiancée is stranded at 10 Valley View Circle. What's the containment up there?" Precious seconds ticked away. He pictured the blaze inching closer to Nana's street, but he had to know what he was running into.

"We got some boys attacking that edge. The latest report came at the top of the hour. They've held the line. 'Course if the wind changes—"

"Got it. I'll keep going." Luke resumed his jog, which turned into a sprint when he heard shouting behind him. *I'm coming for you, Krista.*

The smoke in the air grew thicker the closer he got to the south end of the development. Just a sprint uphill to Valley View and Nana's. *Just* a sprint. What irony.

He used to run in the sand. He should have taped his knee. Sweat soaked his cotton shirt under the Nomex shirt, which he'd kept on.

The smoke intensified suddenly, and Luke pulled up short. One more block and he'd hit Valley View.

The wind had changed and now the heat of an open fire rushed to meet him, faster than anyone could sprint.

❧

Krista sat on the front steps. Logic told her to run. Her gut told her to sit tight and wait for Luke. She had no equipment, no vehicle. A dead phone—the cordless at Nana's had been off the hook too long. People died running from fires. People probably died sitting on the step, just as she was now.

A figure running uphill caught her eye.

Luke!

She stood, feeling for the first time this morning that she stood a chance of getting out of here alive. He was shouting.

"What?" A roaring from behind the house obscured the sound of his voice.

"The pool! Run to the pool!"

"It's in the backyard, closer to the fire!"

"Go, it's our only chance! The wind's changed direction—"

Her legs wouldn't move. "Luke—"

He grabbed her arm so hard she thought he would snap it from the socket, but the shock was covered up by a kiss as he dragged her into the front hall.

She found her feet worked and ran. "Rufus!" A blond shadow was on her other side, his ears flopping.

They hit the patio running. She almost skidded to a stop when she saw the forest behind the house in flames. The pool beckoned from a few yards away. Krista clutched Luke's hand as they raced across the patio, and they jumped.

Chapter 9

Tepid water splashed up around them. Krista clung to Luke's jacket. He smelled like two days of no shower and of campfire. She didn't care. Now the tears came.

He rubbed in circles on her back. "It's going to be all right," he said, then began to pray. "Lord, we know that You are with us right now, even in the fire. Be our refuge. Deliver us. Give us a new beginning from this day forward." She could not look at what caused the roar that flared past the house.

Krista forced her eyes open and peered over his shoulder, beyond Rufus who splashed around and barked in the pool. Another beloved piñon pine went up in a flash of flame. But so far the clearing she and Luke had worked on all spring held the fire back from the house.

She shifted and looked into Luke's eyes. "From this day forward? This was supposed to be our wedding day." A sob caught in her throat. "I feel so selfish. I'm crying over our wedding, and I'm worried about the house."

"Shh. . .as long as we're together, I'm happy. We'll tackle

all that later. Because I wouldn't want to be anywhere else right now."

"Me, either," she whispered, "except maybe on a beach in Hawaii with you." She smiled.

"Listen, I want to do something today. God is here, as our witness." Luke took her hands.

"What?"

"I, Luke Hansen, before God our Father, take you, Krista Schmidt, as my wife."

Oh no, he wasn't. Now the tears came faster. She tried not to tremble as she tore her gaze from the flames around them and looked into Luke's eyes.

"For richer, for poorer, through laughter and pain, through fire and rain." He grinned, his teeth showing white in his grimy face. "For the rest of my days on earth, I pledge myself to you and you alone, as God is our witness and guide. I make my heart your refuge."

"You can't possibly be so calm." Krista managed a smile in spite of herself.

"We did well on Nana's space around her house. No fuel, no fire. The planes are doing their work, too. We just need to wait for this heat to die down. Now it's your turn. C'mon."

He was crazy, and she loved him all the more for it. She should be terrified out of her wits, but now, all she wanted was to be right here in the circle of his arms. "I, Krista Schmidt, take you, Luke Hansen, as my husband."

She'd spoken them to him in all seriousness, the words she had rehearsed in front of a mirror countless times. "For richer, for poorer, through joy and through pain, through fire and rain.

For the rest of my days on earth, I pledge myself to you alone as God is our witness and guide. I make my heart—"

She couldn't say it and turned from him.

"What? What is it?" With callused hands, he cupped her face.

"I mean these vows with all my heart, but I'm terrified, Luke." She didn't want her frailty to hurt or anger him.

"That I'm going to disappoint you again?" Luke let her hands go and winced. "I'm human, Krista, and I guarantee you I will let you down. But I'm not the man I was years ago. I willingly walked away from the best things God gave me—my walk with Him, and you. I won't do that again."

"I know you won't."

"I know I won't because I'm going to build us a defensible space. Just like we did around Nana's house."

"So when the fire comes it will burn around us?"

The sound of a plane overhead made Krista look to the sky. The hold of the plane opened up beyond the canopy of flames and dumped a reddish rain on the fire.

"Yes, it will. But inside, we'll be safe."

The roaring around them intensified. Krista's head swam. She blinked and looked at Luke again. His face, while dirty, had turned an ashen color. The water was too warm. She felt like she had in the sauna last night at Jana's hotel.

"We need to get out of this pool," Krista said.

"I'm beat. That last charge up the hill got me." Now it was Luke's turn to lean on her, and she held him in her arms, not wanting to let go.

"I know you're tired." Another plane roared overhead. Did

she hear shouts? Krista looked toward the front of the house and saw nothing but smoke. She coughed.

"I was stupid to lead you here." Krista had to lean to catch his words. "Water raises humidity. Steam. . .makes it harder to breathe. Dry heat. . .better."

"Don't worry about us being in the pool." She was soaked, frightened, still unsure of how they were going to get out of the firestorm that raged around three sides of Nana's property. "I think help's on the way."

"I passed a crew when I ran up the hill." His teeth glowed white in his soot-covered face. Krista kissed his dry lips. "They'll get us out of here when they get this flash fire under control."

"Well, for now, I'm safe right here with you."

"Think we'll eventually make it to the church on time and make this marriage official on paper?"

"I do."

Epilogue

Was is it just two Saturdays ago that she and Luke had been caught in the fire? Krista smoothed the gown that fell to her feet where the cute shoes Sami had helped her pick out winked at her. Cute shoes? The firestorm must have done something to her brain. Krista shook her head and smiled at her dad, who tucked her hand under his arm.

"Are you ready?" Nana poked her head outside the chapel doors.

"Nana! You're supposed to be seated already—go!" Krista waved her away with her silk bouquet. The beautiful arrangement of roses had been donated by a friend who was handy with flowers, and they'd reproduced the wilted fresh bouquet that never made it down the aisle. Nana pulled her head inside the chapel like a turtle going back in its shell.

"Now, the question is: Are you ready?" Dad's eyes twinkled.

"I'm past ready." She couldn't stop smiling, which was a good thing. At the strains of the wedding march on the organ, they entered the chapel together.

And there he was, standing next to Jeff, who had returned with a spunky brunette. Sami stood opposite Luke and Jeff. *Thank You, Lord, for a good friend to come twice for my wedding.* And Jana, and Mom.

Uncle Al beamed from his seat and nearly blinded her with a flash from his digital camera. He'd better make good on his promise to get great shots, since the photographer they'd originally hired couldn't make it this weekend. Aunt Vangie's mascara was already running.

The sea of faces blurred the farther she moved down the aisle. Among the congregation were two families who had lost their homes. Only two homes lost in the fire that had raged for nearly a week. But still, what a loss. *I have so much to be thankful for—our house, Nana's house, most everyone else's were spared.* Krista hoped people had brought food and clothes for the drive she and Luke sponsored today.

Then everything else drifted away when she saw Luke. Dear, sweet Luke who had come through the fire just to be with her. And in more ways than one, she had come through the fire to be with him. Dad pulled back her veil, kissed her on the cheek, and released her to Luke's care.

Pastor Mike began, "Dearly beloved, we are gathered here today, to witness the covenant of marriage between this man and woman. Because God is our refuge and strength. . . ."

LYNETTE SOWELL

Lynette works as a medical transcriptionist for a large HMO. But that's her day job. In her spare time, she loves to spin adventures for the characters who emerge from story ideas in her head. She hopes to spread the truth of God's love and Person while taking readers on an entertaining journey. She has contributed to several nonfiction books and published various magazine articles. Lynette has been an active member of American Christian Fiction Writers for years. Lynette's a Massachusetts transplant who makes her home in central Texas with her husband, two kids by love and marriage (what's a stepkid?), and five cats who have their humans well trained. She loves to read, travel, and spend time with her family and friends. You can visit her web site at www.lynettesowell.com.

A Letter to Our Readers

Dear Readers:

In order that we might better contribute to your reading enjoyment, we would appreciate your taking a few minutes to respond to the following questions. When completed, please return to the following: Fiction Editor, Barbour Publishing, Inc., P.O. Box 719, Uhrichsville, OH 44683.

1. Did you enjoy reading *Windswept Weddings*?
   ❑ Very much—I would like to see more books like this.
   ❑ Moderately—I would have enjoyed it more if _____

   _____

   _____

2. What influenced your decision to purchase this book?
   (Check those that apply.)
   ❑ Cover   ❑ Back cover copy   ❑ Title   ❑ Price
   ❑ Friends   ❑ Publicity   ❑ Other

3. Which story was your favorite?
   ❑ *Move a Mountain*   ❑ *Hurricane Allie*
   ❑ *Blown Away by Love*   ❑ *Heart's Refuge*

4. Please check your age range:
   ❑ Under 18   ❑ 18–24   ❑ 25–34
   ❑ 35–45   ❑ 46–55   ❑ Over 55

5. How many hours per week do you read? _____

Name _____

Occupation _____

Address _____

City_____ State_____ Zip_____

E-mail_____